The Lies that Blind Us

A Romance Thriller
Amora Sway

CONTENT WARNING This book contains scenes of violence, including mentions of family violence between spouses. While these scenes are not highly graphic, they may still be distressing for some readers. Reader discretion is advised. There is also strong language.

AUTHOR NOTE Regarding the spelling: Since the manuscript includes both an American first-person POV and a UK first-person POV, it uses a mix of American and British spelling. The manuscript has been thoroughly edited and proofread, so the variations are intentional and NOT grammatical mistakes or typos.

PROLOGUE

"YOU'RE A bore. I should never have married you!" my mother yells, not caring that my bedroom is there at the top of the stairs.

"Shh, you'll wake Mallory," my dad whispers loudly.

It's the same every night. She gets drunk then heaps abuse at him.

I hear everything. She's always taunting him with that booming voice of hers. My mother tells everyone he hits her, but my dad's a lamb. She's the bully and the abuser, not him.

She also hates me. According to her, I messed up her body.

I wonder what I was supposed to say to that. "Sorry for being born, Mom."

"You've ruined my life!" she screams at my dad.

She hates him because he doesn't have a lot of money. My father is the hardest-working, kindest man on this planet, but that's not enough for her.

To block the sounds of her abuse, I stick my head under the pillow, something I do most nights. I had even asked if I could move into the garage to escape these cringey fights.

Dad never raises his voice. He's so patient, unlike me. I give as good as I get. I never used to, but two years ago, as soon as I turned thirteen, I changed. I'd had enough of hearing my father being subjected to my mom's drunken tirades.

When she's at his throat, he says things like "Now calm down, Alicia. You've had too much to drink."

"You don't even touch me anymore!" she yells.

"That's because you're with *him*," he says in a loud whisper.

My heart sinks. Who's *him*?

From what I gather, and that's from listening to her quiet phone conversations, the only time she's not talking at the top of her lungs, there's some douche called Jack. There've been others too. I know because she goes all silly and giggly and is even nice to me for a minute or two.

She bellows something about this douche being a real man who can make her come.

I want to vomit. I mean, who wants to hear about their parents' sex life?

There's a crash, and I freeze. It wouldn't be the first time she's thrown an object at my dad. He yells out, then there's a loud repetitive *thud*, like something rolling down the stairs.

I jump out of bed and race out onto the landing. Everything goes dark, and I'm not sure how long I'm there. I might have even passed out, but as I come to, I stare in shock at my dad's crumpled body.

One

"WE HAVE REASON to believe your husband was poisoned." The detective stares directly into my eyes.

Despite his efforts to stir a reaction, I remain deadpan, even if I'm twisting my fingers into a knot under the table.

Having just arrived after a turbulent flight from Florida, I'm jumpy and fighting fatigue. I had a restless night at my mother's, with all kinds of polluting thoughts robbing me of sleep. The last time we slept under the same roof was seventeen years ago, and as I lay staring at the ceiling, I replayed haunting memories of growing up with this woman I called Mother. I went there for a reason. She thinks I went there to make amends. That's never going to happen. *And why am I the one who's supposed to be apologizing? For what? For hating her?*

"He died from a cardiac arrest," I say at last.

"The first autopsy was inconclusive. However, the second toxicology report shows traces of digoxin, which is known to induce a heart attack."

I shake my head. "I have no idea what that is."

"I'm sure you can look it up. Google it." The detective's mouth turns up with the makings of a smirk. The prick's loving this.

"I rarely cook. Erik cooked for himself, largely."

Those pan-sized steaks that Erik favored, sickeningly undercooked, come to mind. His noisy eating, one of many unbearable traits, would make me leave the room. To remain calm, I employed the control of a monk, knowing that the slightest frown would set him off.

The cop's hard stare suggests he's already locking me up and tossing away the key.

"Besides," I add, "Erik often ate leftover takeout without knowing how long it had been in the fridge."

The man's unblinking gape remains glued to my face as lingering silence stretches like a taut elastic, threatening to snap and sting.

"Not that kind of poisoning but the kind that a person would not accidentally take. This is now a murder investigation."

My fingers knit, and his attention moves straight there. This detective doesn't miss a flinch.

"In your sister-in-law's statement, she describes hearing you and your husband often arguing and says she didn't witness affection between you."

"I take it you're not married." I stare at his naked ring finger.

"That's immaterial, Mrs."—he stares at his notes—"Storm."

"My husband and I were no longer in love. I was about to ask for a divorce."

"An unhappy marriage is a perfect motive for murder. I see there are no other claimants in his will." He reads from his notes.

He leans back on his chair and crosses his hands over his blubbery belly, which looks like it will burst a button on that cheap shopping-mall jacket.

"You can't hold me here. You have no proof." I stand up. Worn out after a long flight, I want to go home and curl up in a ball.

He points. "Sit. I haven't finished yet."

His gruff tone virtually pushes me down onto the chair. I bite my tongue and comply. This ugly man's spoiling my party, because I should be popping a champagne cork in celebration of an exciting job offer.

When Jane from the art auction house called and mentioned Italy in a sentence with the word "job," I sat up.

"Just tell me how your husband was poisoned, and we can close the case." He taps his pen against the file.

"I had nothing to do with Erik's death." I roll my lips, which are dry like my mouth. "I wasn't even there when he ate that night. I was working."

"Yes, I've got your statement here, along with the names of your husband's enemies. We've followed those up, and they all have alibis."

A few minutes pass as he stares me down. His eye color is almost nondescript, just like the man. He's hoping to break me with this sudden silent act, which only amplifies the thoughts colliding in my head like a concert of discordant sounds.

"Tell me a little more about your relationship with the deceased."

I wiggle slightly, and the cold metal of that uncomfortable chair digs into my spine. The furnishings are designed to add tension, no doubt, just like the claustrophobic urine-yellow room.

"We married when I was twenty-nine. Erik was thirty-one. I met him after I graduated, and we dated for a few years before tying the knot."

He stares at his notes. "Art history with honors."

"You've done your homework."

"That's my job," he says. "Do continue."

"There's not much to tell. We were married for five years."

"You don't have children, I see."

"I had a miscarriage." I test him to see if he's done his homework.

His eyes roam over his manila file. "Yes. I have the hospital report."

"Then you'll know about the injuries he inflicted on me."

"Yes, it's all here. You didn't file charges, though." He holds my stare again. "Why did you stay?"

I shrug despite the tightening knot in my stomach. "At the time, it was easier than trying to make it alone."

"Were you still intimate?"

"If you call being forced into sex intimate, then yeah, I guess so."

His frown deepens. "Rape is another motive to add to a growing list of reasons for poisoning a spouse." He looks up from his pad. "So he was violent on repeated occasions?"

Responding with a slight nod, I exhale, reminding myself to breathe despite the lack of air. This is a painful subject, one I could barely discuss with a shrink, let alone this cold man.

My mind replays the fatal shove that left me on the floor, clutching my belly. Even the therapist couldn't get a clear answer out of me after asking, "How did it make you feel?"

Is that all they ever ask?

"Apart from physical pain, it made me feel numb," I'd replied. I left out any information about the contradictory spasms of relief and sadness I felt every time I saw someone cradling their newborn. After they'd performed a D&C, the first emotion I felt was relief, a guilty admission that I could never share with anyone, let alone this detective who smells of sour milk.

I'm an emotional puzzle. Enter the therapist. But he kept rolling out every cliché known to psychological analysis, things like the theory that I married Erik because he reminded me of my father.

"That's just trite Freudian crap. My husband was *nothing* like my gentle, loving dad." I rose sharply. "Is that the best you can do?" I charged off and ended up sharing a few drinks with Maggie from the women's shelter instead.

"So, we have a man who abuses his wife. A wife who needs her husband purely for security, and there it is, an open-and-shut case."

I roll my eyes. "Falling for clichés is a rather lazy approach to detective work, wouldn't you say?"

"Clichés are useful markers of human behavior. And in this job, valuable."

"My life reads nothing like a cliché."

If only. Why wasn't I one of those boring but easily satisfied college girls who imagined their heaven in some indistinguishable McMansion?

The detective turns off his recorder. "Okay, that will be all."

I rise and iron out my skirt.

"Don't go far."

"You've got nothing on me." I think about that job in Italy, set for next week.

"His sister's convinced you did it."

"That's hardly concrete evidence. Besides, she never liked me."

After I leave the police station, I take a taxi home. Normally, I ride the subway, but I'm too depleted to face another human being.

I crave a dark room and some strong pharmaceuticals. I smell bad too. Tension makes one stink.

Two

I ARRIVE HOME TO the converted warehouse I begged Erik to buy even though he had his sights set on a home in the suburbs. While I went for artsy grunge, he was more the clean-line type. It's hard to believe that I thought him super cool after meeting him at a Pop Art retrospective.

He was only there, I discovered years later, to meet a woman. He succeeded—he met me. It's amazing how quickly those chiseled features turn ugly after you've been together for a few years only to discover that behind those attractive blue eyes lives a dull mind. Then you find that you have nothing in common with this person you're meant to live with forever and that the man you thought you knew is a monster. A violent monster.

Dull conversations, I can tolerate. That's why friends were invented, and I'm not my mother, who seems to think everyone owes her a good time. Expecting a spouse to be that "everything" person is a tad unreasonable in my book.

"It's a little too trendy for me," Erik had said, walking around the repurposed former warehouse with an open-plan design and ample light, another big plus after living in a dark, poky Brooklyn apartment we'd shared for two years. After Erik inherited two million dollars, I begged him for a new home.

"It's a great investment. Think about the future."

He sniffed. "That doesn't sound like you, Mal. You can't look beyond next week. I tell you what. If you promise to stop taking the pill, I'll agree. How's that?"

Erik was dying for kids. I wasn't. But if telling a lie was what it took to live in that Soho apartment, then I would hide my pills somewhere he couldn't find them. Instead, I forgot to take them and got pregnant but lost the baby a couple of months later.

It's a gray afternoon, and I turn on some lamps while stepping over clothes, magazines, and an empty wine bottle. Take-out cartons and dirty glasses litter the coffee table.

My attention goes to the retro wooden sideboard with the signed baseball sitting like some prehistoric specimen in a glass box. Above it hangs a framed football jersey worn by someone famous. All of it has to go, along with the German beer mugs and hideous knickknacks I trained myself to ignore. I could probably sell the sports memorabilia, which will help, considering Erik didn't have life insurance. At least that's one motive that the police can rule out.

They came earlier and took away some dirty plates and cups and a pot that had been sitting unwashed on the stove for a while. I'm not great at domestics, another trait that riled Eric.

After opening the fridge door, I reach in for the vodka and take a swig straight from the bottle before slumping onto the sofa, where I stare out the window at the glass-walled building in front. During idle moments, and I have plenty of those, I enjoy my apartment façade reflecting back at me from across the road.

I don't have the luxury of reverie, however. I need legal advice.

After another hit of liquor, I decide to drop into the women's shelter where I volunteer, which is only a short walk from my apartment. It's a long story but goes something like this: When I was at college, a friend's mother had to escape an asshole boyfriend, and after she ended up at the women's shelter, I went there sometimes with my friend to help with jobs like cleaning and chopping vegetables. It became a habit. I liked helping in my small way.

Maggie, who's a champion in my eyes, greets me as I enter through the secret side entrance. Wearing one of her sunny smiles, she gives me a big hug. "Hey there. Haven't seen you for a while."

I sit for a moment and bury my head, then tears erupt. Now that, I wasn't expecting. The last time I cried openly in front of others was at my grandfather's funeral when I was seventeen. Seventeen years without shedding a tear. *How is that even possible when all I want to do is bawl my eyes out?*

Warm tears unfreeze my heart. That's what it feels like. I refused to let Erik see me cry. I suspect that's why he kept hitting me, for some kind of emotional response, but I remained stoic, or maybe that's stubborn. Even when I lost the baby, my eyes were dry.

"Hey, sweetie, what's happened?"

I wipe my eyes and tell her I'm now a prime suspect in a murder and how my life has been turned upside down.

Her brow creases. "They found poison in his system?"

"Yup. I didn't do it. I mean…" I sigh. "I was crap at chemistry. Flunked science."

She returns a compassionate smile and takes my hand. "Do they know what Erik did to you?"

I nod. "That's why I'm being harassed."

She shakes her head. "Assholes. They always blame the battered wife."

I accept a tissue and wipe my nose. "I also wanted you to know that I might not be around for a while. I'm going to Italy next week."

Her face lights up. "That should be great. You deserve it. You're a hard worker."

My eyebrows meet. "I'm not, though. Some days, I don't even want to get out of bed. And I drink too much."

"We all get up to no good at times. Don't beat up on yourself."

I give her a tight smile.

"You've studied criminal law," I say. "Tell me, can they stop me from going overseas for work, seeing that I'm a suspect?"

She shrugs. "Depends on the evidence. If it's only circumstantial, which it is, in this case, I can't imagine so. At worst, you might have to report your whereabouts while you're away."

I exhale a deep breath. "Fun times ahead."

She smiles at my sarcasm. "It might only be something like showing your passport to a local police station. But maybe you should contact a lawyer."

"I know. That would be the sane thing to do, but wouldn't that be admitting to something?"

"Not really. You need counsel. And while I'm here for you, I'm up to my neck with work."

I lay my hand on hers. "Hey, it's fine. I just needed someone to talk to. And as you say, they have nothing on me."

Feeling a little lighter following our chat, I head home to call one of Maggie's lawyer friends.

Three

I drag myself out of bed. Just my luck, I finally managed to fall asleep two hours before having to be somewhere important. The trip to Italy is all I can think about, and I won't blow this chance of leaving New York. Even without this interesting if vague job offer, I'd probably still go somewhere, despite that ugly detective insisting I remain close. Well, I have news for him: I *am* going. They have nothing on me, and the lawyer said so. He even fit me in last night. I paid extra for that, but it was worth it since I don't have much time to lose. Italy is only a few days away.

The two million dollars sitting in Erik's account comes to mind. Something he kept from me.

Can I access it now that I'm a suspect?

I'm still awaiting probate, but I do have his credit card with a staggering two-hundred-thousand limit, another secret he kept from me. Asshole.

Some of it, I've already used to pay that young lawyer. The money was well spent, seeing that he put my mind at ease, even though I've decided to discontinue his services for now.

I walk around lost in a haze of thoughts, namely, how to get ahold of that two million before the law shuts it down.

Two hours later, I'm sitting in Jane's office. She owns Artly, an art auction house where I work analyzing art for authenticity, a skill I learned from my grandpa, who could recognize a fake a mile away.

And now, due to my art-appraising experience, I find myself in the company of an FBI agent. They certainly have a way about them. Rigid backs. Serious. Authoritative. Intimidating.

After he flashes his ID, I ask, "What exactly am I expected to do?"

"We've been watching an international art dealer for a while now. Though he travels throughout Europe, he seems to favor Italy. There have been some fakes getting around with his name attached."

"What period of art are we talking?" I ask.

"Mid-nineteenth century to contemporary. The alarm bells were sounded when a Monet was discovered in New York."

"I imagine it came with provenance," I say, suddenly excited, as I majored in art history with Impressionism being one of my main subjects.

"The dealer in question purchased the Monet in France, where an expert verified its authenticity. The work was then purchased by an American private collector, who upon loaning it to a museum discovers it's a fake. The original, we've since learned, is in Prague."

"So this dealer purchases a fake and paid some purported authenticator to pass it. There are crooked authenticators," I say.

He nods. "We are aware of that."

"Is it just the Monet?"

He shakes his head and taps his file. "A Chinese collector recently had his entire collection stolen. All of it ended up here in New York, all fakes."

"I take it they also pertain to this same dealer?"

"Yes. Dylan Hyde's name is all over them."

"Also well-known artists?" I ask.

"Mainly nineteenth to mid-twentieth century, I believe."

"That's my world." Excitement sizzles through me. *Fun at last.*

"We just want to know what Dylan Hyde's up to. What he's buying."

"Why haven't you brought him in already?"

"Because we need to catch him red-handed, so to speak. And this world of art fraud is a complicated one. Who's to say that the person who purchased the art didn't have it faked?"

"That's true. Many like to hide the originals in vaults and hang fakes for show. Especially with art that dates back. The wrong conditions could destroy some of the older works."

He nods. "We were alerted after the stolen works started turning up at Sotheby's and Christie's."

"Perhaps this dealer's innocent," I say.

"Maybe, but his name keeps popping up. There was even a Rothko, I believe." He stares at his notes.

"Contemporary art can be difficult to prove." I look at Jane, who returns a smile.

"So what do you want me to do?"

"You've been called in because you know your art, I believe, and can easily pass as a dealer on a buying spree."

"Undercover, you mean? Don't you have your own team for that?"

"We sent a pair to case him in Prague last year. We need someone less likely to stand out."

"So, you want me to get to know him?"

The agent nods.

"Like a honeypot?" I ask.

"It's hardly James Bond. But we need to know what he's buying."

"But won't I need to buy if I'm there as a dealer?"

Jane looks at me. "You'll be allocated a budget to buy for the auction house."

I've just become that shopaholic about to enter Prada with a limitless credit card. "I like the sound of that."

"Good. We'll put together a dossier on Dylan Hyde so that you get acquainted with his art-buying history, which will inform you on what he's likely to bid on."

I knit my fingers and look from him to Jane while biting my lip. "Um, look, my husband's just..."

"We know about your husband's death, and please accept my condolences." His mouth forms a tight line.

Do they know I'm a suspect?

My stomach knots. Discussing my personal life is the last thing I feel like doing.

"We also know that you've been questioned." His eyes grip mine, and a breath is trapped in my throat. "You'll be away for ten days. As far as the police go, you'll be attending these Italian auctions as an art buyer. All we need to know is what Dylan Hyde is purchasing and anything else that stands out."

Jane nods and gives me a stress-busting smile.

"If that's all you need, just to know what he's buying, then I guess that's easy enough." I shrug and side-glance at Jane, who's there to hold my hand. She's the greatest.

After he leaves us, I say, "I can't believe it. How surreal."

"It is a little." Jane closes a manila folder. "I've had a few of these in my day."

"Really? Did you ever catch them red-handed?"

She shakes her head. "It's not easy to prove. But they know that. Especially with modern art." Wearing a sympathetic smile, she adds, "Think of this as a break. I can't imagine what you're going through."

I nod, and my first real smile in two days stretches underutilized facial muscles. I hug her. "Thanks for this."

I leave Artly with a spring in my step.

Four

After an hour-and-a-half drive up a steep mountain with barely enough room for two cars, I finally arrive at my destination a little sweaty. Apart from the fear of plunging to my death, given there was little room for error on that steep ascent, I'm also a bit twitchy over Detective Sawyer, who is stalking me by sending texts and calls reminding me to report to the local police ASAP.

Bright sun warms my face as I reach into my bag to pay the driver.

"*Grazie,*" I say to the driver, who, having opened my door, sets my case down.

"*Prego, signorina.*"

I step out onto the cobbled pavement and stand before the archway entrance to my hotel. With its honey-colored stone wall façade, the building radiates Old World elegance.

A plush burgundy carpet is rolled out for a grand entrance, which I won't be making since I'm wearing jeans and a crinkled shirt.

The historic city of Matera brims with rustic charm. I feel like I'm in a movie. I read somewhere that it's one of the oldest cities in the world. That's some claim, and I've always had a soft spot for history.

Not mine, of course—I would love to rewrite that. But somewhere in my jaded soul lives a romantic.

The only dark cloud hovering over me is that I have a police station to report to, though that can wait. As can the call to Sawyer.

I start to walk and nearly fall into a heap. Cobbled paths and Louboutins are as compatible as an elephant and a tightrope. Now I understand why I'm seeing women everywhere in sneakers or Birkenstocks.

I walk with my eyes on the ground until I reach the marble-floored lobby, which is smooth and skyscraper-heel friendly as I glide along, absorbing the sumptuous décor tickling my aesthetic fancy.

Five stars, I can do.

As I run my eyes over the opulent lobby with its chandeliers and velvet and finishes fit for kings, I ask myself whether perhaps I ate moldy toast that's now brought on hallucinations.

My phone goes off, snapping me back to the real world, and the shit show back home returns to haunt me.

Before leaving for Italy, I attended Erik's funeral, which was like throwing me into a den of wolves. The dirty stares. The little whispers.

My mother then dragged me to the wake, insisting that it wouldn't look good if I bailed. But then, when it comes to façades, she's a star performer. Pleasantries roll off her tongue like a seasoned Shakespearean actor reciting convoluted language as effortlessly as one might speak second-grade English. Having missed her calling in Hollywood, she even teared up on cue.

I hid behind her veneer of small talk and pleasantries and got stuck in the wine instead.

Chris, my former sister-in-law, scowled at me the whole time. That familiar menacing glare triggered unsettling memories of Erik descending into a rage. It didn't take much to get him going. The dishwasher filled with dirty dishes or clothes on the bedroom floor, and he would erupt.

After two glasses of wine and faking grief for thirty minutes, I left with my mother at my heels. She hadn't flown in just for the funeral; she happened to be there for a friend's birthday.

Still, despite my "What the hell are you doing here?"—a normal response to my mother turning up at my place unannounced—I had to admit it helped having her with me at the funeral. Her nonattendance wouldn't have looked good.

At the service, she whispered something about me shedding a tear or two to make it look real.

Make what look real? That I missed that man? How was I to do that? Glycerin, maybe, as used by bad actors.

I just wore my show-nothing face. I was good at that. Well practiced.

Even when Erik abused me, I would remain blank, which seemed to infuriate him. He wanted me to cry or give some emotional response. He hated that I didn't squeal and moan when we fucked, like they do in porn.

"You don't make me come," I once admitted.

A stinging slap followed, along with "That's because you're a block of fucking ice, bitch."

Now, how could I ever miss that? If it weren't for that nosy detective, I would be pretty happy for the first time in years. I still don't get the whole poisoning thing, though. I mean, it could have been food gone bad. That's the only explanation. I'd been out that day, and have no idea what he ate that night.

At least I managed to transfer funds from Erik's stashed account. A shopping spree followed, of course. That Vera Wang sheath had had my name on it, as did a green Prada handbag, a steal at half its normal price. After that frightful funeral, I needed a lift.

The expressive Italian concierge waves his hands, almost jumping out of his skin. Speaking in difficult-to-follow English, he takes me on a tour of the gym and swimming pool then, speaking my language, tells me about the rooftop cocktail bar, which piques my interest far more than any gym ever could.

He then shows me to my vanilla-scented room with burgundy accents and shows me how to open the balcony doors.

As he leaves, I go to tip him, but he shakes his head as though I've insulted him. Different customs, I suppose.

I kick off my shoes and lay my suitcase on the queen-size bed before walking over to the balcony to slide open the glass door. A quaint table and chairs and a cushioned lounger sit in wait. I visualize sipping a martini and taking in the postcard buildings clinging onto cliffs as though carved from the rock.

Awestruck as the setting sun sprays beams over the golden city's timeless beauty, I breathe in the mountain air and enjoy the warmth seeping into my pores. I make a mental note to thank Jane, or her secretary, for choosing this hotel.

My stomach rumbles, reminding me that all I've eaten that day is a bag of peanuts on the flight from Rome. The auction is to be held tomorrow afternoon, which gives me time later in the evening to study the art for sale and earmark some purchases for Artly.

The contents of my rushed packing don't lend themselves to the rigors of sightseeing, though. I packed only two pairs of shoes, and it took forever to decide what I could live without in my carry-on luggage. Despite this being a ten-day trip, I'm regretting not bringing a larger suitcase. At least I packed a pair of wedges, which are far more suited to the cobbled paths than my Louboutins.

I change into loose slacks and a blouse then wind my long hair, which is crying for a trim, into a messy bun and head out.

The tiny streets are cluttered with cars and scooters, and I try to avoid being mowed down while looking for somewhere to eat. Everything seems hidden in arched tunnels. It's the strangest place in the most unique sense.

This is my first time out of the States, and the air is rich with history. There's this indefinable vibe that's making my skin tingle like some kind of ancestral presence is in the ether.

After climbing a flight of whitewashed steps, I find a restaurant that's set on a terrace high above the Sassi. The waiter finds me a table with a panoramic view of the honey-colored village. With all those serpentine streets, winding stairways, and arched tunnels, the labyrinthine setting reminds me of a time-worn Escher.

When it comes to Italian cuisine, I'm easy to please. I order a slice of pizza, spaghetti with meatballs, and a glass of local red wine. I learned while looking up Matera that this region has the oldest grapevines in the world.

The wine arrives, and I take a sip. Its tangy richness dances on my tongue. A few more tastes, and my imagination fires up. *Could this be the very elixir that once graced the lips of ancient rulers?*

As I take a bite of the most delicious pizza I've ever tasted, I embrace this Italian odyssey like someone entering a beautiful dream, and for the first time in eight days or so, I'm finally feeling good. That is, until my phone buzzes, and yes, of course, it's Sawyer again. *Hell.*

My heart sinks. From a high, the fall is steeper too.

I read the text despite the desire to ignore it. The toxicology report is now available for my lawyer.

Sighing, I wish I had left my phone behind. Talk about one big slap down. All I want to do is forget about what I left behind—for ten days at least. Sawyer is seeing to it that this is not happening. *Jerk off.*

Five

AFTER DINNER, I RETURN to the hotel, shower, then change into my new sheath that fits me like a glove. I undo my messy bun and allow my thickish hair to tumble down to my shoulder blades. It's the longest I've had it for a while.

I stare at my reflection in the mirror and adjust my sea-green knee-length dress.

On my way back from dinner, I spent nearly two hours in a designer shop. It took some willpower not to buy a floral silk wrap-around dress. The clothes in Italy are such a temptation, so instead, I promised myself a splurge in Rome.

Rome. I can hardly contain myself. That heavy book my grandfather had about Rome, Florence, and Venice comes to mind. He described it as his bible when he introduced me as a nine-year-old to the beauty of art. I can't believe I will finally see the place live.

I study my reflection in the mirror and turn around to check my butt. I've lost weight. Anxiety is great for weight loss. Maybe it's not so good for other things like sanity, but at least I'm not having to jump on some fad diet, unlike my mother, who's gone keto. She would have a hell of a time in carb-rich Italy.

Thank God she's not here. I'd hate that. Shaking her off in New York was hard enough. I can't understand why she insists on hanging out with me. She hated me when I was a kid. And even though I'm cold to her, she persists in trying to be in my life.

This is coming from a woman who never hugged me as a child or expressed any concern whenever I fell ill. It was my dad who was at my bedside with face towels and medication.

So no, I will *never* forgive her.

I gape into the mirror, pushing back those provocative thoughts. My eyes look bright despite the lack of sleep on the plane and the long journey getting here. Excitement makes me look good. It makes everyone look good.

I lean into the mirror and apply red lipstick, and after one last look, I collect my new Prada handbag and head off.

The rooftop cocktail bar is dimly lit, and as I search for somewhere to sit, I notice a crescent moon and a dancing star, which I assume might be Jupiter. The night is clear and balmy.

It's a glamorous, cosmopolitan atmosphere. Everywhere I look, I see Rolex watches and designer sophistication. The air's awash with expensive colognes and the scent of citrusy blooms wafting my way in what is almost sensory overload, especially with the valley of golden paths below, lit up by lamps casting shadows and mystery.

With understated jazz crooning in the background, the al fresco bar is a far cry from the manicured bars of New York. Here, the men look like George Clooney and the women like Julia Roberts. Ice clinks, and laughter fills the air.

A tall, broad-shouldered man in a checked designer jacket that looks sewn on is standing at the bar. Though he has his back to me, he arouses my interest. I sense he's chatting up the young woman by his side, going on the spark in her eyes.

I am so lost in that moment that I flinch when a man bends down to ask if the seat by my side is taken.

"No," I return. He's not my type. Not like Mr. Tall, Dark, and Handsome at the bar. Even without seeing his face, I sense he's hot judging by the super-eager expression on the face of the Audrey Hepburn look-alike.

The server brings my gin and tonic, and I sit back and allow my mind to wander, something I haven't done for weeks, even though I know I should be studying the inventory for tomorrow's auction.

"Are you here for long?" the blond male asks.

I shake my head. "Only two nights."

"It's a pretty sight." He points at the honeycombed maze below us.

I nod. "Isn't it?"

"Where are you from?" He sits back.

"New York."

I know I should ask him, but I want to be left alone.

He tells me anyway. "I'm from Australia."

Talking's the last thing I feel like doing right now. I've also developed this unfortunate tick—my foot won't stop tapping. Every time my phone buzzes, I jump. It's awful. All I want is to be free to enjoy this unique experience, but it's like I'm in a glorious mansion haunted by ghosts.

Ignoring my cool reception, the man points at my glass. "Can I buy you another?"

"I'm married." I don't want him hitting on me, so I bullshit, and I hate describing myself as a widow like I should shroud myself in black and go into hiding. Though I wouldn't mind hiding from that douche Sawyer.

And this man is no Chris Hemsworth or Hugh Jackman, for that matter, not that I aim that high.

"I'm married too." He smiles sweetly.

I shrug. "Okay then. Why not?"

He orders another drink, and I pretend to listen as he talks about his life in Sydney. All the while, my eyes are settled on the man at the bar.

Three drinks later, I decide to leave, and Alex or Allan or whatever his name is looks disappointed. I give him one of those "It was never going to happen" looks and head off.

Just as I'm walking to the exit, the handsome man turns around, and as his eyes find mine, my knees go weak.

He is smoking hot. Our eyes lock. He wears a "Have we met?" expression. *If only.*

His *signorina*, meanwhile, looks a little left out as our lingering gaze breaks out into a tango.

After extricating my gaze, which isn't easy to do, since he's managed to mesmerize me with those deep-blue eyes, I walk away.

I sense his gaze warming my backside, turn for a final look, and discover those ocean eyes undressing me.

I wish. It's been an eternity since I enjoyed sex, and I can't recall anyone as gorgeous as that checking me out. Overcome by a burning sensation, I'm stung by desire. Snapping out of that little fantasy, I walk on.

Just as I'm about to step through the exit, Alex or Allan taps my arm and asks, "How about breakfast?"

"I'm not much into breakfast. But look, thanks for the drinks."

I leave before he suggests lunch or dinner and head to my room for some much-needed sleep. I've got a big day tomorrow. It's the day of the auction and requires my full energy.

Six

I PAUSE TO WIPE my neck after climbing endless steps, and it's not only the physical exertion making me sweat but also nervous anticipation. *Can I come across as that cool, calm, and collected buyer?* Taking a deep breath, I push aside paranoid thoughts, like the possibility of this Dylan Hyde seeing through me—a murder suspect being stalked by a tenacious detective. But what I'm doing is legal, I keep reminding myself. After all, the FBI signed off on this.

So just breathe and get on with it.

Getting to the auction is proving a challenge, too, since the villa where the event is happening sits high up. Traipsing through the steep city, with so many steps and sloping paths, feels like I'm in a game of snakes and ladders.

Olive trees dot the surroundings of the whitewashed villa, while grapevines creep over walls. A welcome breeze carries the sweet scent of orange blossoms as I stop to soak in the bucolic locale. Mountain air does wonders for a hangover, I've discovered.

After I left the rooftop bar last night, I ended up raiding the bar fridge because excess is my middle name. And I needed something to drown my sorrows after reading Sawyer's message telling me to report to a police station by morning or face extradition.

Sucking it up, I grew a set of balls, as they say, and this morning, after a double hit of coffee accompanied by a cornetto filled with pistachio cream—the culinary equivalent of an orgasm—I made my way to the police station and spoke to a handsome policeman. They're all handsome here, I'm learning. Or perhaps my hormones are stimulated by their charming smiles and singsong accents.

I rolled out my own charm and smiled sweetly at the policeman. After looking at my passport and itinerary, the officer mumbled something about the Amalfi—one of my destinations—being *bellissima,* and that was that.

Though the auction is set for the afternoon, the viewing is for the morning only, something I should've reminded myself about before emptying the bar fridge last night.

As I step inside the villa, I'm greeted by a man who talks so quickly I can barely keep up. English is spoken everywhere, and I appreciate the locals' efforts. I could have tried to brush up on my Italian, but apart from knowing how to order a drink and say "thank you," I'm clueless.

I do love the sound of Italian, though. It's like I'm immersed in an opera.

The greeter points at a wall of crowded frames. "So, madam, here we have a fine collection of early-twentieth-century art. Signore Battista, the late owner, started collecting in 1920 and had a keen eye for contemporary art."

I look around, and while I don't recognize most of the works, I'd done some homework and marked two works of interest that any worthy dealer would aim for.

The de Chirico had a starting price of five hundred thousand euros, a little out of the budget of our humble auction house, but it would be worth at least two million on the market, I estimate.

I'm drawn to a Cubist portrait of a woman. Despite the naive style of the work, the subject's eyes draw me in. I lean in for a closer look.

"Luigi Pirandello," the man says.

"Yes. He's an interesting painter. I've seen some of his work among New York collections."

He looks impressed.

The starting price being more aligned with my budget, I make a mental note to bid on it. Though a few paintings catch my eye, none compare to the de Chirico. I imagine that's why I'm here. Based on the brief, Dylan Hyde doesn't get out of bed for anything under a hundred thousand.

A few hours later, after a delicious carb-rich lunch that has already added pounds that I can afford, I make my way back to the photogenic golden-rocked villa.

Once there, I'm welcomed by a glass of very fine wine and am offered olives and delicious crusty bread. Unlike the trendy, out-to-impress art scene in New York, there's no champagne or canapés in this bucolic wonderland. A nice change, nevertheless.

I join the crowd milling around on the patio paved with a gorgon-headed mosaic when I hear an English accent that might be that of a royal and turn. For a second time in twenty-four hours, my knees buckle.

It's James Bond from the bar. I can't say why I'm comparing him to the famous spy, but he owns that title all the way down to his gleaming leather shoes. He's dressed in a linen jacket and a blue shirt that makes his ocean eyes pop. There should be a law against that. Beautiful men should not be allowed to dress well. It's too distracting.

Is he beautiful? More like rugged, especially with that tired look in his eyes. I can only imagine what he's been up to. Nevertheless, the longer I stare, the darker he gets.

And that's even more dangerous because I like them dark.

He doesn't smile. Instead, his eyes settle on me, like at the bar. He gives a long, undressing gaze then strides over.

He holds out his hand, and his soft, warm palm touches mine, setting off a spark that travels up my arm. I take a deep breath. This is hardly the time to turn to liquid over a hot guy.

"Dylan Hyde," he says in clipped English.

Bingo.

I remain cool despite the avant-garde percussion solo banging away in my chest. "Mallory Storm."

His perfect mouth curls at one end. "I saw you last night at the rooftop bar. Unless you have a double."

"Guilty." I smile. "I'm staying there. Tonight's my last night." Why I'm giving him that extra detail is best left to my libido to explain.

He nods. "Mine too." He stretches his arm out to the honeycombed ravine before us. "It's quite a sight."

"Isn't it?"

"There's an energy about this place. Very inspiring." He follows my lead and takes a glass of prosecco from a server's tray. "Are you a collector?"

I take a little longer than I should to respond, mainly because his eyes have caught the light, and they're impossibly blue. *Why does this man have to be so distractingly gorgeous?*

"I'm on a procurement tour," I say at last.

"Anything that takes your fancy here?" He tips his head.

Yes. You.

"Well, de Chirico's surrealistic study makes it to the top of the wish list, but it might be out of my budget."

"You've got a good eye, Ms. Storm. That's why I'm here."

"Please call me Mallory." I love the way my name sounds coming from those lips that should be X-rated. "Are you a dealer or a collector?"

"Dealer. I don't collect anything." His perfectly sculptured mouth quirks at one end.

"Oh? You don't get attached?"

"Are we talking art here?" He suddenly turns this conversation into something more intimate.

My heart skips a beat. I'm tripping over myself because this man is messing with my head. "Yes. What did you think I meant?"

He rubs his thumb along his bottom lip, and I suddenly want to lean against a wall for support. "Attachment comes with all kinds of connotations."

I take a moment to respond. "So you prefer to keep your walls clean? You go for the whole minimalist approach."

He shakes his head slowly. "No. Far from it. Minimalism sends me into a panic."

I laugh. "That's rather extreme."

A bell rings, alerting us that the auction is about to begin.

Dylan places his glass down on a table. "Shall we?" He gestures for me to walk before him.

I move forward.

He leans in. "I can leave the Pirandello alone if that's more to your budget."

I stop walking and give him a perplexed stare while trying to figure out if he's playing with me. "That's rather gentlemanly of you. But I'm up for a fight."

He laughs, and I think I fall harder. *Can a man get more handsome?* His tanned features turn his eyes even bluer, and that dark shadow around his chiseled jaw makes his mouth ripe and hard to ignore.

"That sounds like fun," he says with another lingering gaze.

We find ourselves among about forty people. Dylan hangs close and whispers, "They're here for the de Chirico. But Pirandello's caught a few eyes."

"That's hardly surprising. It's a seminal work, his first in the Cubist style. Very collectible."

He looks impressed, which sends a ripple of warmth through me. I'm seeking validation suddenly.

Why I want to impress him, I can't say. I don't normally feel the need to prove myself. *Can it be that I'm meant to be casing him and thus fostering a friendship?* That's the simple reason.

The question that's revolving at the back of my head, however, is whether I can turn myself into a honeypot. That idea has my hormones cheerleading, doing flips and all kinds of rapturous overtures.

I can't be led by desire alone. At least, that's my latest mantra.

And what will I find if I undress this man? Even more importantly, will I get out with my sanity intact?

The auction starts with a striking purple-and-pink modernist vase from Murano.

I send a text and photo to Jane: "The insurance alone will inflate the price. But modern Venetian glass always sells."

"Gorgeous!" she writes. "Up to around $6,000 and we're talking."

That would have been my estimation. "Okay. That's five thousand euros. Let's see."

Stylish in that effortless continental way, a beautiful woman who could be around forty is giving Dylan the eye. Jealousy slices through me.

Ridiculous, I know, but that honeypot role is becoming increasingly appealing.

The bidding for the vase begins at a thousand euros, and I don't like my chances. Not when Catherine Zeta-Jones's look-alike holds up her tanned, bejeweled finger. Her eyes are all over Dylan, who seems to be standing closer to her by the minute.

Recalling the pretty young thing all over him the night before, I imagine him as a modern-day Don Juan. Or maybe he's just the innocent bystander as women fall for his charms. Whichever is true, those bedroom eyes are now directed at the stunning raven-haired woman crashing my party.

I put my hand up nevertheless, and Dylan turns and gives me an encouraging smile. Suddenly, I'm that teenager dying to make a mark. The bid is now at three thousand. It's between me and her. We reach my precipice of five thousand euros.

My heart palpitates. It's exhilarating.

I go for six. She goes to eight.

I've fallen.

And if that's not enough to piss me off, Dylan turns and tilts his head like I just lost something valuable. I feel like giving him the middle finger, mainly for fucking around with my head. *Or am I talking hormones?*

I smile back with a shrug. Indifference beats annoyance any day.

The Pirandello arrives, and I gear up. This one, I want. There's something in the subject's eyes—a hint of darkness and mischief—that speaks to me.

Starting price is one thousand. I can do this. I'm going to win this time, I tell myself.

And then, sure enough, Dylan holds up his hand.

Dick. He knows I want it.

I roll up my sleeves for a fight, and I win at four thousand euros.

I feel like jumping on the spot. I'd bid at auctions before, but this has turned personal.

The de Chirico is last on the program, and Hyde shifts his weight. His shoulders squaring, I know he wants this.

Catherine Zeta-Jones's double leans in, and he smiles briefly before turning serious.

It starts at twenty thousand, and I put my hand up as I chase him up to thirty thousand. He turns and gives me a darkish smile. Yes, two can play this game. I feel like sticking my tongue out at him, but I keep it nice. I haven't had so much fun in years. Nothing like a bit of competition for an adrenaline hit.

The other dealers in the room, who I suspect arrived for this work, are jousting with him as four bids push the price up to two hundred thousand.

At three hundred thousand euros, Dylan wins the impressive surrealist painting depicting a human head on top of a machine resembling the first computer. The auction is over.

I scribble a check for the Pirandello and arrange the delivery, after which I make my way out to the courtyard, where more drinks and finger food are being served.

As I decide whether to stay, Dylan joins me.

"For a minute, I thought you were in for the fight." He smiles.

"You started it with the Pirandello."

"Yes, well, I'm sorry. I'm competitive to a fault."

"Know how that feels. Excuse me," I say. I go to grab a bite and a drink, and instantly, his rich admirer pounces on him.

Dylan glances at me as I chat with an older man who's keen to tell me about a Warhol he once procured for a song. I end up leaving after another drink. I wave goodbye to Dylan, and he comes over.

"Where are you off to next?" he asks.

I take a moment to answer, as I've forgotten the name. I grip on tight to my handbag. This man has me on edge. "A seaside town not so far away, I'm told. Another private estate auction."

"Oh." He looks pleased for some reason. "You're off to Polignano, then? In the morning?"

I nod.

"Then I'll see you there."

My heart picks up again as anticipation flushes through me. "You will."

I walk off with a spring in my step. The fun's just started.

Seven

AFTER WHAT HAS BEEN an eventful afternoon at my first-ever auction in Italy, I'm back in my room. I strip out of my clothes and slide into a floppy T-shirt then set up a Zoom call with Jane.

"Hey, how's it going? Did you buy the Murano?" she asks.

"Nope. Went over budget. But I did pick up a Fausto Pirandello. I'll send some photos later." I adjust my screen to see her better.

"So, you've seen him?" she asks.

I bite my lip. "Uh-huh."

A line forms between her eyes. "Let me guess. He's sexy?"

"Am I giving off some kind of teenage-crush vibe?"

She laughs. "Kinda. So what's he like? Did he buy anything?"

"He's hot. He's like a James Bond of the art world. You know, debonair, sexy Brit accent. Designer jackets sculpted on. Women all over him." I laugh.

"Oh, wow. I look forward to hearing more."

"The Pirandello was a steal, I believe. You'll at least double your money," I say, getting back to business.

"That sounds promising. So what did he buy, speaking of money, and is it legit?"

"It's legit, all right. A Giorgio de Chirico. Three hundred thousand euros, no less. Very marketable. Easily worth triple that."

Jane sighs. "I wish I had a bigger budget."

"The theme's highly relevant now, considering how AI is taking over our lives. It's one of his later works. Painted in the seventies. A fifties computer with a man's head."

"It's authentic?" she asks.

"The provenance looked good to me. I took photos."

"Good. So you're off to"—she glances down—"Polignano a Mare next. A Modigliani." She whistles.

I unscrew a bottle of sparkling water and take a sip. The lasagna I ate is still sitting like a lump in my stomach.

"He'll be there. It's only an hour by car, I believe. And hello, there's a Modigliani."

"It's only a sketch," Jane replies.

"So what? Some of Picasso's lesser works are still worth millions. There are also some appealing contemporary Italian works from the sixties and seventies."

"Great. There's the Mafia guy who comes in all the time asking for Italian contemporary. What's his name?"

I laugh. "You mean Giacomo, or Juk, as he's known? He's not Mafia, is he?"

"I don't know. He just reminds me of Ray Liotta in *Goodfellas*, I guess. He's got that way about him. Kind of sexy."

"Oh, Jane." I take another sip of mineral water.

Now in her mid-forties, Jane swapped marriage and children for a career, not that she's ever admitted any regret there. She's what's known as a serial monogamist, I suppose, though she has this unhealthy appetite for Italian men who are either married or still pining for their exes.

We often went out for a drink, and I would end up moaning about my shitty marriage while Jane complained about some messed-up relationship where she'd become the other woman.

Deplorable record with partners aside, Jane's a sharp operator when it comes to selling art. She possesses the best eye in the business after working for ten years at Sotheby's, where we met.

When she set up Artly, Jane hired me as an art appraiser.

"I'm jealous. Wish I was there among all those sexy Italian men." She giggles then shifts to serious mode. "Oh, I nearly forgot. A Detective Sawyer came in today. Asked a ton of questions about you and your marriage. I kept it brief and told him that we didn't discuss your personal life."

I think about all those conversations we had over coffee or drinks. After witnessing bruises on my arms and cheek, Jane could never understand why I didn't report Erik. I sensed that reporting him would only make him worse, given the police rarely do anything, something I'd learned from battered women at the shelter.

"I guess it was to be expected." My heart sinks as I revisit shitsville back home. "Thanks for not saying anything." I smile tightly. "Hey, I should sleep. I'll send images of anything worthwhile to bid on and keep you in the loop."

"Do so. And, Mal..."

"Hmm?"

"Don't sleep with him. It will only complicate things."

"I wouldn't dream of it." I blow a kiss and shut my laptop.

I do end up dreaming about him, though, before the alarm wakes me for an early start.

Eight

HAVING TO REPORT TO the cops with every new move I make is proving a serious pain in the neck, but here I am, standing at the counter, tapping my foot. I'm irritable and tired. My mood is not helped by the stench of body odor in the station, aggravating my hangover.

After my call to Jane last night, I made the silly mistake of going up to the terrace bar for a drink or five. Disappointed that Dylan Hyde hadn't appeared, I consoled myself, with the help of martinis, by remembering that I'm a serious art buyer and not some desperado who hasn't experienced the passionate embrace of a man for a long time.

Finally, the cop arrives, and after staring at his notes, he scrutinizes me as one might a suspected murderer. I could be reading more into it, but this whole having to relay to the world that I'm a murder suspect makes me shrink to the size of a pea. Nevertheless, I return a blank if unaffected look. The dick makes me wait too. I have to endure the blaring artificial-sweetener equivalent of Italian pop music, consisting of familiar English pop tunes sung in Italian.

I open my laptop and browse the inventory of the estate auction being held that afternoon. As I study contemporary Italian works, my interest settles on a simple ink drawing by Modigliani, one of his reflective long-faced women.

Two thousand euros as a starting price is a steal, and I imagine a bidding war. I wonder why Dylan, a buyer who deals only in hundred-thousand-dollar-plus art, is even attending. Apart from Modigliani, most of the works aren't that valuable.

Finally, I'm free to go. The policeman hands me my passport and traps my eyes with his dark, intrusive gawk.

I hurry out and head for the restaurant by the sea, the one that the concierge recommended upon my check-in.

A few deep breaths of sea air, and I've almost forgotten the past wasted hour.

Even getting to that seaside village situated in the heel of Italy proved stressful. I had to use hand language for the driver to slow down at precipitous sharp bends.

The server directs me to a table under the shade of an umbrella and hands me a menu. He quickly brings water, which I appreciate. I've never drunk so much water before.

It's late May and hotter than I expected, particularly humid and sticky as I readjust my shirt and bra.

I search for seafood on the menu when a voice from behind says, "The *linguine al cartoccio* is to die for here."

I turn, and there's Dylan Hyde, smooth as always in shades, cream linen pants, a loose white shirt, and espadrilles.

He smiles sweetly. "You're following me, it seems."

"More like the other way around," I say dismissively despite a frisson of excitement triggered by his scent, a hint of cedar and sandalwood.

Does he know something?

I can't tell behind those shades what this man's thinking. Even without the glasses, he seems to park his sociable face somewhere in the semi-pleasant zone, wearing a faint, bordering on forced, smile peppered with a smidgen of cynicism. It's enough to make him interesting in an edgy kind of way.

Or is that just a show and what he wants the world to believe? Aren't we all just players in this game of life?

I push those philosophical thoughts aside before I question my own façade and wonder why he's hovering Maybe he wants me to invite him to sit.

The server arrives and pulls out a chair for him anyway. Dylan regards me. "May I?"

"Knock yourself out." I gesture.

"As I'm not predisposed to self-inflicted pain, I'll abstain from that." He smiles. "I do find some Americanisms amusing, though."

"Are we about to poke fun at our once-affiliated cultures?"

"We could." I sense behind those shades a twinkle in his baby blues.

"Let's just say that you have an interesting way of putting things."

"And the English with their silly, at times childish, prattle don't?" I tilt my head.

"You've got me there. It's all just a bit of fun, though. Isn't it?"

I sip water and shrug it off. He's right. Ribbing each other over national quirks isn't worth getting on one's high horse over. And since when was I so patriotic? I wasn't exactly waving a flag back home. Away from home, I'm different, especially after hearing the cop's insulting *Americana* under his breath as if I wouldn't understand.

"I'm just ordering a spot of lunch," I say. At least I can get an insight into this fascinating creature who speaks with a plum in his voice and a hint of derision. It's like the piquancy that an olive adds to a martini.

The server hands a menu to Dylan, who then places his order in perfect Italian and helps me with mine.

After the man has gone, Dylan regards me for a moment. "I must say you stand out."

I toy with my glass. "How so?"

"A beautiful woman traveling alone."

I sip some water, following it with a wipe of my naked lips. I slept in and had no time for makeup. And the white-knuckle journey along skinny, craggy mountainous roads was so bumpy that I feared I might end up looking like a clown had I even attempted to apply lipstick.

Suddenly, I feel naked around Dylan. I know I shouldn't, because why should I care? But that's always been me around gorgeous people. Blame it on my shallow mother, who claimed that showing one's bare face qualified as a mortal sin.

While I look like I dressed in the dark, since my shirt is in desperate need of an iron, Dylan's impeccable presentation could win him a spot on the cover of *Gentleman's Journal*.

"I'm here as a buyer," I say in response to his borderline chauvinistic comment about a woman traveling alone. I remove my purse from the table to make room as the server delivers our drinks, a Campari for me, and a beer for Dylan.

He nods in acknowledgment to the man. "Tell me what brings you into this fine world of art. Are you a painter yourself?"

I shake my head. "My grandfather was a restorer, and he devoted much of his time imparting his passion for art to me. I guess I fell in love with this world then."

"That's a lovely story." He wears a genuine smile. It's a first for him and makes me feel warm and fuzzy.

"And what about you?" I ask. "What drew you into this rarefied little universe of ours?"

"I went to art school and dropped out." He sniffs. "Didn't feel like painting to market, so to speak, and soon discovered I could put my creative skills to better use. Dealing in art is somewhat healthier than inhaling harmful paint fumes."

"There's solvent-free paint, you know."

"It's shite. That's why I don't buy beyond the seventies."

"Not even a Banksy?" I ask.

"Apart from admiring his brash, politically driven sentiments and flawless skill, he's not on my radar."

"So who are you drawn to? Not in terms of selling but for your own tastes." I jiggle ice in the crimson liquid and take a sip. The bitterness is pleasant and refreshing.

He appears to reflect for a moment. It's a difficult question. For art connoisseurs, the broad universe of art is an endless galaxy.

"I'm rather taken with sixteenth-century Flemish artists."

"Oh. Like Bosch, Brueghel?" I sip my water.

"Guessed it in one. You're not just a pretty face."

I roll my eyes. "And you're just a regular guy."

He laughs at my irony. "I'm not, though." His gaze sticks, and I want to slap him. *Why couldn't they have sent me on a mission to spy on a pockmarked greaseball?* Because as much as I want to invite him back for a siesta, I know I can't. It would only complicate things. And he's not exactly flirting. He's playing with me, which is even more arousing in my book.

"I spent my late twenties in Madrid. Getting back to my interest in early surrealism—" He takes a sip of his beer. "The Prado's one of my favorite museums."

"Is that why you were drawn to de Chirico?" I ask.

"Despite my love of surrealism, that acquisition was purely for commercial purposes. All my buying decisions are. I don't get attached." He pauses, and I wonder if we're talking about art all of a sudden.

Our food arrives, and when I see the pasta dripping in red sauce, my stomach does a big leap of joy. "So much for a carb-free lunch." I thank the server, who places the aroma-rich meal in front of me.

"Are you one of those Americans warring against carbs?"

I nearly laugh at that ridiculous notion. But then I think of Jane and my mother's keto obsession.

"No, I'm not, and I'm sure keto and paleo diet fads are not isolated to US citizens."

"Of course not. And look, I'm sorry." He removes his shades, and there they are, those deep-blue eyes with a hint of sincerity.

"No need. I rather enjoy the odd bit of jousting."

His mouth curls slowly. "Don't we all."

After another lingering stare, he wipes his shades and pops them back on. My libido's grateful because this man is ticking a few boxes right now.

I snap out of my inner romance novel and return to the stark reality that Dylan is a shadowy figure entangled in the dark world of art fraud.

That doesn't help either, especially in that setting. Italy should come with a warning about sensory overload. All I want to do is drink, eat, soak up that colorful country's history, and fuck.

I return to business. "Have you seen the collection on offer?"

He nods. "I arrived last night. I'm staying on a friend's yacht." He points at a large, impressive beast of wealth moored off the pier, rubbing shoulders with other fine toys of the superrich.

"That sounds like fun."

"You're invited if you like."

"Oh?" This could get a little touchy-feely if things keep going this way. *An invitation onto a yacht?*

A few drinks with this sexy Brit, who, if I were being honest, is the sort of man one thinks about late at night when visiting an adult fairy tale, and I'm developing an unhealthy crush. Something tells me Dylan Hyde and happily ever after don't belong together.

"There's a cocktail party early evening. Dimitri always knows how to entertain."

"He's the host?" I ask.

He nods. "A client of mine. I've covered the walls of his numerous mansions with art."

I dab my lips with a napkin. "That sounds impressive."

"You should come along."

As we lock gazes, I nod. "Perhaps I will."

Nine

AFTER A STRANGE AFTERNOON, I find myself on a yacht. Holding on for life to the handrails, I'm berating myself. Louboutins aren't practical on a yacht.

Dylan's wearing one of his derisive grins like it's tattooed on. But instead of making him detestable, as it should, it makes him even more desirable. He's with Catherine Zeta-Jones's sister, one who's younger but not by much. *Is that a Botox-straining brow?*

"Have you met Carolina?" Dylan asks, introducing me to said wax model.

"Um, no."

She's not exactly wearing a "Nice to know you" smile.

It's balmy like it has been every night since I arrived in Italy. The nights are so perfect that it's impossible to have an early night.

The auction was strange. Dylan didn't even so much as blink at the Modigliani, which I purchased for three thousand euros. Jane kept asking if it was a fake at that price. It wasn't.

Dylan had eyes for only one work—an oil of the Grand Canal by a painter who didn't even exist on Google searches.

A pretty piece nevertheless, it was in the late-nineteenth-century Impressionist style, and had it been within my budget for such a risky work, seeing as how the artist was unknown, I would have bought it.

I even bid on it, and Dylan cast a "Don't go there" look. That was the closest I'd gotten to seeing his dark side. He was determined to get that painting.

An unknown work? Why?

Anyway, I desisted at one thousand euros, but the bidding rose to a staggering fifty thousand. A woman got into a bidding war with Dylan, who'd swapped his easygoing man-of-the-world persona for win-at-any-cost ruthlessness, and I even detected a note of danger in those hard-to-ignore blue eyes.

An unknown work, which could have been painted by an amateur, for one hundred thousand euros?

That's opened up a few questions for sure. I have nothing to report, however, since it's immaterial whether the picture's real or fake.

As I breathe in that privileged air, thick with expensive colognes and perfumes, I find myself questioning whether the mushroom canapés I'd savored at the auction were of the magical variety because I might just be on a glamorous film set depicting the idle rich at play.

The host, Dimitri, a loud, handsome Russian, has one of those bellowing contagious laughs that drags one along. His backslapping almost qualifies him as that clichéd figure known for downing vodka and breaking out into some crazy gymnastic dance, bopping up and down while legs kick out.

But then, we're all clichés from time to time, especially at social gatherings calling for masks and cheesy smiles. I generally stay away from those. My fun consists of a dark bar at midnight, coaxing some attractive stranger into revealing their dirtiest secret. We all have one or two.

I'm dying to discover Dylan's. I bet he's in possession of a few dark secrets.

I sit on a white leather couch and stare out at the harbor, where neighboring yachts have their own parties going, turning that body of water into a billionaire's playground.

Reflections of lamplights dotting the pier bleed into the water, and when I blur my eyes, a silly habit I learned as a child, the deep-blue water ripples with yellow swirls resembling Van Gogh's *Starry Night*.

As I suck back the sea air, I entertain the idea of becoming a stowaway.

In a low-cut slinky white gown with slits strategically placed on her well-constructed curves, Carolina deserves her own spread in *Cosmopolitan* as that ageless beauty who has it all, including the interest of handsome beasts like Dylan Hyde.

She totters off, and I decide to join him, since he so kindly invited me, but then I couldn't exactly expect him to hang off my arm.

"Your future wife?" I tilt my head toward Carolina, who has her back to us and is chatting to some beefed-up young male.

"Not if I can help it." His cool response coats the air with an aftertaste of disdain.

"You don't like her?"

"That's right. I don't."

"Huh?" I frown. His sardonic chuckle isn't lost on me. "You're playing with me again."

"Again?" He opens his hands. "When have I been playing with you?"

"Stick to your Mr. Coy act if you must." I return his smirk.

"I'm a free agent, Mallory. Always have been. Being attached to anyone or anything is not how I roll."

"That sounds lonely."

So is being married to a brute.

His eyes trap mine, and I see edginess, an alluring if not unsettling departure from his usual confidence. It's like he's granting me a glimpse into another man.

"I like my own company. So no, it's not lonely," he says at last.

He tilts his head as though he's trying to see me from a different angle. "I take it you've been married?"

"I was. My husband died only recently." My stomach tightens. I hope he doesn't want details.

"Oh, so you're a widow?" He frowns as though trying to solve a puzzle. That's been his way with me.

Am I that fascinating?

"You don't strike me as someone in mourning."

"No. I couldn't stand him." My cool if not brash response surprises even me. Must be the three drinks I had before arriving. I needed something to relax my nerves. New places and new faces always make me jumpy.

His mouth curls slightly as though he's debating whether to laugh at my brazen honesty. "I've yet to meet such a young widow."

"No. I guess it's unusual for a forty-year-old American male to die of a heart attack."

He sniffs at my irony.

Determined to steer the topic away from my dead husband, I say, "For someone who's unattached, I must say your dark-haired beauty seems to have claimed you."

"Let's just say I hitched a ride with her. Carolina's married to a wealthy French banker. He's somewhere in the States doing business, and she's traveling around having a little fun of her own." His raised eyebrow says it all.

"Enough of beautiful, bored rich wives. Why that painting of the Canale Grande?"

"Why not? It's a nice piece," he says rather unconvincingly, feeding my curiosity.

"You seemed a little ruffled when I joined the bidding like you just had to have it."

He chuckles tightly. "Aren't we all driven to win?"

"Um, like, yeah, but such an unknown work?"

He shrugs, reverting to his typical nonchalance. "There's an estate in Positano with its share of paintings relating to Venice. In two days, I believe."

He's sidestepped my question. I'm itching to know why.

"I know about it. And yes, I'll be there."

I'm about to return to the question of the Venetian painting when Carolina returns.

I turn to her. "You're also on the art trail?"

She wears a haughty smile, the type that one gives to frivolous questions. "No. I met Dylan on the flight over to Rome."

Dylan gives me that arched-brow look that can mean only one thing. *Mile High Club, anyone?*

As I walk away, I feel a touch of envy. I could easily play the filthy-rich widow seducing sexy males on first-class flights. That two hundred thousand dollars I managed to transfer from Erik's hidden account won't cut it, though. I'm already ripping through it, thanks to this unhealthy penchant for designer clothes.

Taking the sensible route, I remove my shoes and go for a barefoot walk around the impressive vessel. The yacht—fifty meters, I'm told—boasts a wooden interior, white furnishings, and stainless-steel fittings, just like the luxury cruisers I've seen in glossy magazines.

There must be around a hundred guests. Russian, English, Italian, and French words float through the air in a rich mélange of globalized socializing. Nomadic prosperity is on fine display.

I find myself dreaming of what could be. If anything, this trip so far has given me a taste of glamor.

As I lean against the handrail, weed smoke drifts in my direction. A man in knee-length fitted shorts and espadrilles, the favored look of the fashion-conscious European male, reminds me of a young Silvio Berlusconi with that dark peachy tan. He smiles and offers me the joint.

"No, thank you."

He looks disappointed. "Americana?"

I nod. "From New York."

"Uh, not so much Americana."

My brow contracts.

"They're different in New York, I believe," he elaborates. "Like a different country almost." He takes a puff of his joint. "You know Dimitri?"

"I've only just met him. I was invited here by a…" *What is Dylan?* "A kind of colleague, I suppose."

"Oh?" A plume of smoke exits his lips, and I try to avoid breathing as the warm, salty breeze sends it my way.

"Dylan Hyde," I add.

"Ah." He smiles like it all makes sense suddenly. "The Englishman. Yes. He's a player in our little world."

Now I'm intrigued. "How?"

His hand draws a circle. "He's charming. And a good eye for all the beautiful things. And always looking for his next meal."

That last comment makes me flinch. "But he's rich, isn't he?"

He laughs and then holds out his hand. "Massimo."

"Mallory. Pleased to meet you."

"*Molto piacere.*"

He stares out into the night, but I can't leave that comment alone. "He's poor, you mean?"

"You know, lives in the moment. Many of us have to be careful, but not *Signore* Hyde. He's what you call… a free spirit. But he's always doing some business with someone. That's what I meant. As is Dimitri. You've met him, I take it?"

I nod.

"They're all doing little deals here and there. You know my meaning?"

I study him intently. "Like drugs, contraband? That kind of thing?"

He points at the sky. "It's a beautiful night."

I've lost him. Juicy little insight, nevertheless. His not answering me spoke volumes about something dark.

He tries to take my hand, and before he gets too touchy-feely, I say, "Excuse me."

Ten

ALL THE BATHROOMS ARE occupied, and I'm in need of a visit, so I climb up to the top of the yacht only to find it's been cordoned off at the stairs. Never one to follow rules, I climb the steps anyway. I need to pee, and it seems that every bathroom has been appropriated by giggly pleasure-seekers.

I walk past a bedroom with beige-and-white decor, which, going by the size of the room and the art on the wall—a Paul Klee, no less—must be the master bedroom. Next to it, a door opens into an en suite bathroom.

After washing my hands, I apply some hand cream, which smells heavenly, and spray on some Chanel cologne in a pink crystal decanter. Leaning into the mirror, I touch up the bottom of my eye makeup to ensure it's sultry but not overdone. I open my bag, remove my red lipstick, and apply it, then step away to study myself while fluffing my hair.

I hear talking in an adjoining room. Laughter echoes through, and my inner snoop getting the better of me, I turn the doorknob quietly and peep through the tiniest slit.

Just as I'm about to leave, Dimitri holds up the painting that Dylan paid that ridiculously inflated price for.

Another man watches, and I recognize him from earlier. He introduced himself as Stanislav, and when I asked whether he was Russian, he shook his head vehemently, like I'd insulted him, quickly informing me of his Ukrainian nationality.

I'm about to sneak off when Dimitri takes out a small knife and cuts into the back of the frame before removing a key.

I'm starting to understand why Dylan paid such an inflated sum for the painting. That key must open something valuable. Curiosity too piqued to leave, I watch on.

Dimitri holds up the key as though it's something precious, kisses it, and then tosses the rest of the painting in the trash can like it's a piece of junk.

They speak in what I assume to be Russian, with Dimitri strutting about laughing and holding up his prize. Out of nowhere, Stanislav brandishes a knife and stabs Dimitri in the gut.

My breath hitches, and the blood drains from my face.

What the...?

"That's for fucking my wife, you piece of Russian scum."

Dimitri's on his knees, doubled over and clutching his stomach. After reaching into his pocket, he produces a gun.

Stanislav kicks him to the ground before he can fire it and stands on his arm. The gun drops out of the Russian's hand.

Clearly the winner in this fight, Stanislav bends down and digs his knife into Dimitri's neck. "And this is for inviting that evil Russian dictator into your home." He slices the Russian's carotid, and blood squirts all over his face.

My legs buckle even though I tell myself I need to run. But then Dylan enters the room, and I freeze. My heart thumps like crazy. I can't breathe.

It all happens so quickly despite time stretching like film noir in slow motion.

Dimitri's murderer turns and, seeing Dylan, who's staring in shock at the bloodied dead man, reaches into his pocket and produces a gun.

The next few seconds turn into a drug-induced blur, only I'm drunk on adrenaline and not some psychoactive substance.

A glass sculpture, probably Murano, sits on the desk. Even in this heightened moment of danger, trivialities find space in my brain, which is having a screaming match of its own.

Dylan somehow manages to push the gun away and lands a bone-crunching thwack followed by kicking and more punches. He's not just a pretty face, it seems.

Proving too strong for the Ukrainian, Dylan has Stanislav on the ground when the prone man reaches for the pistol lying close by.

That's when I run in and enter the fray.

Without a moment's thought, I grab the lump of glass and smash it over Stanislav's head just as a bullet is fired, narrowly missing Dylan.

My heart is in my mouth as I stand there with my jaw dropped, staring in bewilderment at Stanislav on the floor, next to his earlier victim, blood pouring out of his temple and mixing with that of his Russian enemy.

Dylan looks at me with a "What the hell are you doing here?" expression.

My legs have turned to wood, and I'm speechless. My heart's choking my throat.

While Dylan places his finger on Stan's neck, I finally find my voice. "Have I killed him?"

The words stick to my dry mouth, and still clutching the glass weapon, I drop it onto the floor with a thud.

What have I done?

Dylan answers my bone-chilling question with a nod.

As I lean against the wall for support, I'm struck by a previously unvisited memory when, aged thirteen, I was at school and tossed a large stone at Mikey Smith for calling me a freak. I didn't kill him and only cracked his skull. This is different despite the same irrational, knee-jerk reaction, shock traveling through every sinew, and a dry, bitter-tasting mouth.

Holy shit. I just killed a man. Why did I do that?

It was like an out-of-body experience.

Dylan points to the bathroom. "Go in there," he whispers. "We must hurry before someone arrives."

He kneels and picks up the bloodied key, still in Dimitri's clutch. He wipes it and places it into his pocket. Calmly. I can't believe how cool he is.

He picks up my glass weapon and, with the edge of his shirt, wipes it. Then he presses Dimitri's fingerprints over it before strategically measuring the distance it might have fallen after hitting Stan's head.

If I weren't shaking in fear, I'd be impressed by how he's staging the crime scene to indicate a different choreography.

He follows me into the bathroom and opens his arms, and I'm in them, close to his body. "You shouldn't have been here. I could have managed," he says.

"But he had a fucking gun pointing at you," I whisper loudly.

His eyes show gratitude, but the deeper I scrutinize them, I sense a hint of uncertainty, too, as if he's asking himself what he should do with me.

He smooths back his hair and washes his hands before wiping the faucets with a towel. "Let's get out. I know a private passage."

I do as he says despite a silent voice saying I should call the police.

Before he leaves, he cleans the bathroom doorknob then gestures for me to follow.

With booming music and loud voices filling the air, I can only assume no one heard anything. That's something, I guess. But it doesn't mean I'm feeling light and easy. The opposite, rather.

Once we're on the lower deck, away from the party, he directs me into a cabin, which is a bedroom. Dylan looks for stray guests before closing the door.

While he appears sharp and clearheaded, my neurons have gone haywire, hijacking my ability to think straight.

"Let's wait for someone to walk by so that they can see us leaving together," Dylan says.

We soon hear a couple giggling in the hallway, and he messes up my hair, undoes some shirt buttons, and gestures for me to leave first.

I smooth down my dress and touch my hair while he's buttoning his shirt as we pass the couple, who wink at us.

When they're out of earshot, Dylan says, "Go back and mingle for another twenty minutes and then leave."

I nod. It's like I've walked into a cobweb and spiders are crawling over my squirming body.

Before he walks off, Dylan touches my hand. "You saved my life," he whispers. His eyes hold mine, and I want to cry.

But I can't even talk, because my throat is frozen, like the rest of me.

"Where are you staying?" he asks.

I remove the hotel card from my bag and show him.

"I'll meet you there. In the meantime, act as though nothing has happened." With that steady voice and calm demeanor, Dylan sounds like he's experienced at this kind of thing. He glances at his Rolex. "In thirty minutes or so. Yes?"

I nod, and like a ghost, I head downstairs and go straight for the vodka shots sitting on a tray and gulp down two in a row, which helps clear my throat and numb some of the intense anxiety gripping my body.

Twenty agonizing minutes later, I exit the room, somewhat relieved that the bodies haven't been discovered. Still, any minute, I'm expecting screaming and people running around yelling. Instead, the guests have just grown louder and drunker.

I wish I could get that bloody scene out of my head. The nauseating stench of blood is following me, even though I drowned myself in cologne.

Why did I do that? I hardly know Dylan.

Why was he there?

Shouldn't I go to the cops?

And then more questioning?

My inner pragmatist shakes her head resolutely, and almost staggering, given the numbness in my body, I head to my hotel.

The balmy, still night is the complete antithesis of the storm raging through me, and as the air sobers me up, I stare at the sky and try to erase the past hour.

Eleven

A SHOWER DOES LITTLE to wash away tension. I change into shorts and a loose T-shirt and make myself another drink. I'm glad I'm leaving in the morning for the Amalfi. If I could, I would leave now.

The terror of what just happened grows by the minute. It's like that throbbing ache after anesthesia has worn off.

Could I have done anything differently?

Why didn't I just close the door and walk away?

Dylan would be dead.

So?

But then he insisted he would have managed.

How? With that gun pointing right at him?

I pace about like some crazed being searching for answers and wonder what to do. With each gulp of hard liquor, I slowly arrive at one conclusion: I can't reverse what I did.

I have to suck it up. Get on with things and stop spinning out.

I pour another drink.

My phone rings. I jump and spill my drink. It's the front desk advising me that Dylan Hyde's asking to come up.

"Thanks," I respond.

I take a deep, steadying breath. Had this drama not been pickling my sanity, I would be half-excited. Instead, I'm debating whether to slap him or cry in his arms.

One thing's for sure: I'll never be the woman I was yesterday. It's like my soul's been invaded by a malevolent force, and now I'm a stranger to myself.

He knocks only once, and when I open the door, he nearly falls through.

"Sorry. I thought not to wake others."

He returns a cool smile like a man without a care in the world.

"Drink?" I ask.

"Just water." He steps into the room and drops his leather satchel onto the sofa.

I grab a bottle from the bar fridge and hand it to him then gulp down half of my neat gin.

He removes a pack of cigarettes from his inner lapel and walks to the balcony. "Mind if I smoke?"

"Sure." I follow him. "Can I have one?"

"Of course." He directs the soft pack of cigarettes at me. "You don't strike me as a smoker."

"I have the occasional one when I drink. Or if I'm feeling tense."

He lights me up, and as the smoke leaves my lungs, my head goes into a nicotine spin.

We remain there smoking in silence. I'm speechless for the first time since meeting him. Palpable tension collects in the swirling smoke exiting our mouths.

When we return inside, he bends down and removes his shoes. "Do you mind if I make myself comfortable? I might have to stay on your couch tonight if that's all right. It will make this whole sudden intimate connection between us look more convincing if and when the police arrive at the crime scene."

"If and when?" I ask.

He shrugs. "It's anyone's guess what happens next."

I nod slowly. "What about your date?"

"Oh, Carolina's fine. I introduced her to Sven. He's that tall Swede skippering the yacht."

I shake my head.

"What?" he frowns.

"Are you all morally bankrupt?"

"Probably." He pulls a half smile. "Morality is somewhat subjective where matters of the flesh are concerned." His eyebrow arches slightly.

"What about killing someone?" That pops out without warning because all this casual-like-nothing's-happened chitchat is making me want to throw up.

Dylan turns serious at last as his eyes hold mine. This time, I don't look away. I want to see what's going on in those eyes that resemble the midnight sky. With bare feet and that loose shirt revealing a hint of chest hair, Dylan couldn't look more appealing. But he's stained now, just like I am.

The violent incident has brought us closer like we're partners in a crime. But instead of money, I'm compensated with the promise of endless nightmares.

"What does the key open?" I ask.

He stares at me blankly like he doesn't know what I'm asking.

"The key," I repeat, not hiding my impatience, because he's hiding something.

"Not sure. But for now, let's not keep talking about this." He turns away.

I just killed someone—a stranger. Not that *that* makes it better.

"I want answers, Dylan. Otherwise, I'm going to the cops and will tell them everything."

That stirs him. His tanned brow flinches. "You don't want to do that. You'll open up a can of worms."

He returns an intense, bordering-on-threatening gaze.

"Why are you looking at me like that?" I'm becoming more exasperated by the minute. Enough of this man-of-mystery shit.

"I've got a question too."

"Like what?" I ask, unscrewing a one-shot bottle of gin.

"Why did you save my life? What made you do that? It's not like you know me."

"You've got that right," I mutter then gulp back another shot. Why isn't the alcohol working? By now, I should be well and truly drunk. Instead, I'm still freaking sober.

I knit my fingers. "I keep asking myself that. Subconsciously, I guess, I put two and two together and figured you might be the lesser of the evils. And he had a gun. Any minute, he could have shot me too."

"So it was a form of self-defense?"

"No. I mean, yeah. Why does it matter?" I'm sounding a little shrill.

He finishes the water. "It matters because you saved my life." He exhales. His first display of tension so far.

"I could have managed, though." His mouth quirks into the makings of a crooked smile. "Though I guess you weren't to know that."

"You got that right. From where I was standing, that gun was pointing at your head, about to blow your brains out." I remove another little bottle from the fridge. "You owe me an explanation."

"I know little. All I can say is that Dimitri was part of a crime syndicate that goes deep into the drugs-and-arms trade and that Stan was his right-hand man."

"And your involvement?"

"I'm just his art buyer. I've furnished his many mansions."

"So you've already said. But what about the painting? Did you know about that key?"

He shakes his head. "Like you, I'm in the dark. But going on the inflated fee Dimi paid me, I'd say this key has something important attached to it."

"You don't say, Sherlock."

He laughs. "You're a firecracker, aren't you?"

I pour myself another drink and start to pace. "I just killed someone."

He pats the sofa. "Go on. Sit down, please. You're making me nervous. And yes, this is not a great situation. But it's happened."

"You really didn't know about that key?" I ask.

"No." He stretches his arms. "I'd love a shower. And perhaps you can throw something over this couch. I like to sleep naked." His sexy smile returns, and I roll my eyes.

"I don't shock easily."

He smiles for the first time. "You're off to the Amalfi in the morning. Yes?"

I nod. "I take it you are too? There's a Matisse."

He rubs his neck. "I am. Why are you going, may I ask?"

Because I'm meant to follow your every move.

"The auction house I work for has me hunting for hidden treasures."

"Then let me help you get there. I'm hiring a car in the morning. It's around a four-hour drive along the Mediterranean, and we can board a ferry at Salerno for the Amalfi. Have you visited that southern region?"

I shake my head. For a moment, thanks to the numbing effect of alcohol, I allow the drama from earlier to melt away as I indulge myself in being that excited tourist about to experience an adventure with a hot guide.

I think about the police, to whom I must report in Naples, and clouds drift in again.

Things are complicated enough without Dylan learning of my little problem back home. My threatening to go to the cops is the only thing I have to bargain with here. If he discovers I'm a suspect back home, he'll know the last thing I need is to be implicated in something like this.

It's a dangerous risk because if Dylan is somehow part of this crime gang, he won't have a problem doing away with me, especially if I become a threat.

With that frightening thought rotating in my head, I wonder if I should disappear before he wakes up. Maybe I should take the key and use that as my bargaining chip. He can't kill me when he doesn't know where I hid it.

I store that thought away. And instead, I steal a peek at this man.

Is he capable of murder?

He knows his way around a fistfight. Had Stan not brandished the pistol, Dylan would have taken him down for sure.

As a million little thoughts percolate, I get ready for bed, and in my oversized T-shirt, I pad about barefooted. Though it's now three in the morning, I'm wide awake. I can't imagine getting much sleep.

Dylan saunters out of the bathroom with a towel wrapped around his waist, and desire flushes through me.

That's not going to happen. You just murdered someone.

I have to travel with this man, and I plan to follow him—all the way. Whatever that key opens, I want to know. And if there's money, then I am owed something. That's where I'm parking my resolve.

Besides, he was spotted arriving at my hotel. He's on CCTV. The last thing he's about to do is kill me. And if I were to race out before him, that might also alert the authorities to something.

Would it? Or am I looking for any excuse to go on an adventure?

I find a set of sheets in the cupboard and am about to toss them on the couch when he points at the queen-size bed. "It might look better if I sleep there. After all, if the police come and case this place, which I suspect they might, we need to make it look like we really were intimate."

His raised eyebrow makes me wonder if he means body fluids and all.

Oh boy. My heart skips a beat. *How did I get myself mixed up in this?*

"Don't worry. We don't have to do anything." He smiles sweetly then drops his towel and Oh. My. God. The man's a stallion.

I take a deep breath to still the flood of lust filling my undernourished libido.

"In what sense? And if you're referring to sex, then you're being a little overconfident there," I say, finally finding my voice given the rush of guilty heat. Instead of desire, I should be thinking of how I'll never be the woman I was yesterday. Whoever that woman was.

He chuckles, easing some of the tension.

I keep my back turned because I don't want to look at that perfect specimen of a male. "Do you think others might know of that key and what it opens?"

Hearing him climb into bed, I turn to face him.

"Probably," he says, placing the sheet over himself.

"Then we need to report it," I say.

"Not a good idea. Dimi and Stan are big scalps, which will only fill some dirty cop's pockets."

He's lying under a sheet, making it easier for me to stare him in the eyes, something I keep doing if only to try to understand this man's motives. "You do know more, then?"

"I don't know what the key opens. But I do know that Dimitri was determined for me to get that painting."

"Why didn't he go and bid for it himself?"

"I'm wondering about that too. I suppose he likes to keep a low profile, and he hasn't got a clue about art."

"Didn't have a clue, you mean." I hesitate by the bed as I climb in. How weird this feels. Everything is no longer normal anyway, I tell myself as I climb under the sheet.

"Why were you there? Visiting Dimitri in his study?" I ask.

"He asked to see me."

Was that a note of hesitancy in Dylan's voice?

I roll over and try to sleep.

"This is rare," he says at last.

"What?" I can already guess what he's about to say.

"Me naked with a beautiful half-naked woman sharing a bed and with our backs turned."

"You flatter yourself. In any case, you're not my type." I almost laugh.

Who the hell am I kidding?

He kisses the back of my head and touches my hand. "Thank you."

A tear slides down my cheek. Yes, I saved his life. He owes me something, I suppose. I just hope I can shake off this dark cloud that's swallowing me.

Twelve

THE COASTAL DRIVE TWISTS and turns, with breathtaking views of the Mediterranean. Rugged golden cliffs line the deep-blue ocean, sparkling in the blazing sun of yet another perfect sunny day.

A ship drifts by on the horizon, and I allow my mind to wander.

Spellbound by history, I'm profoundly taken with that ancient body of water, imagining the siren's song messing with sailors' heads as they embark on their wild adventures. Just like me, embarking on my own wild adventure. Only instead of being tantalized by a song, I'm being lured by the mystery of the key and, of course, Dylan Hyde.

"A penny for your thoughts," he asks sweetly.

It's difficult to dislike this well-spoken, considerate man who likes to open doors for me. If only he were more of a jerk, I could at least abuse him for introducing me to his dark world.

But I'm fascinated too. The farther I travel, the easier it gets to place distance between me and the bloodbath in Polignano.

"I'm awestruck by seeing the Mediterranean for the first time."

"It has an impressive history, I dare say."

"I'm visualizing tall ships. The *Odyssey* comes to mind, as do the Vikings."

"That's a leap from 200 BC to the 900s. But sure, it does evoke emotion. For me, Calais is like that. Whenever I journey from Dover to Calais, I think of the French Revolution."

I turn to face him. "Why the French Revolution?"

"*A Tale of Two Cities* had a profound effect on me at college, and after that, whenever I travel by boat to France, I think of that story for some crazy reason. It stirs emotion to channel history and how things might have been."

"Robespierre was the Che Guevara of his time," I say.

"Maybe. Only, I prefer Danton to Robespierre, who, from what I've read, was a bloodthirsty psychopath."

"But he was on the side of the people. A citizen."

"You know your history. I'm impressed," he says.

"Now you're patronizing me."

He chuckles, and I stare out to sea again. The salt air massages my face as I smile, my first since leaving this morning.

We haven't spoken once about what happened. He hasn't even switched on the radio, which I appreciate. I imagine Dimitri and Stan's deaths will be all over the news.

Dylan glances at me before returning his attention to the winding road. "I don't know about you, but I'm rather hungry. Why don't we stop in Salerno for a spot of lunch, and then I can organize a boat for the Amalfi."

"Sounds good to me."

If only last night hadn't happened, then this would be a dream. Miles away from the drama back home, I could almost talk myself into never returning. I have nothing to hold me there.

My phone pings, and on cue, a message arrives from Sawyer. I revisit an inner dark space, and a silent scream shatters my daydream. I ignore the call, and five minutes later, my phone rings. It's him, of course.

As I fiddle with my phone, it occurs to me that if I don't answer, Sawyer will set the cops on me. It's like he's turned it into his life mission to terrorize me. He has nothing on me. I'm innocent, as I keep reminding him.

I send him a text message instead.

I type: *"I'm on the road. Will report to police once I arrive at the Amalfi later today."*

This is becoming a nuisance. He knows I'm back in a week. Only seven days. That thought makes my heart sink.

I think about the key. There could be money. Lots of it.

"Writing to your boyfriend?" Dylan asks.

I sniff. "None of your business."

He laughs. It's like the last twenty-four hours didn't happen and we're off on a romantic getaway.

I wish.

My body lurches forward, and that little fairy tale dissipates like a dandelion puffball in the wind.

The car accelerates as we approach a hairpin turn. My head starts to spin as I look down in horror. There's no room for error here on these steep cliffs.

"What the..." spills out of my mouth as I grip the edge of my seat. My racing heart mimics the engine's sudden acceleration.

"Hold on," Dylan says, turning the wheel like he's used to this kind of thing.

Through the rear window, I see a black SUV close behind us. Too close.

"Holy shit. He's virtually on top of us," I say in a high pitch.

Dylan pushes down on the pedal, and my knuckles are virtually bursting through my skin as I cling on tight.

Hyper-focused, wearing a steely gaze, Dylan navigates the winding, vertiginous road as an expert might as the roar of engines drowns my cries.

With each twist and turn, tires screech, like I've been thrown into a car chase in a movie. Only that would be make-believe.

The edge looks closer. I can't even see the road, only a sheer, sharp drop into the sparkling Mediterranean.

Behind us, the pair in the SUV skid as they take a bend that Dylan just expertly handled. Growling engines echo from ancient stone walls lining the curved road.

My whole life flashes before me. *Is this it? Am I going to die before living my best life, whatever that might look like?*

Dylan's driving like we're fighting for a winning position in a rally race, only this is a race of life and death.

As he swerves with almost reckless disregard past slower traffic and narrowly avoids collisions with oncoming vehicles, he seems oblivious to the looming threat of plunging to our deaths.

Then we come to a deep U-bend. "Hold on," he says.

My teeth are about to pierce my lip as screams explode silently in my head. *Or is that the screeching tires holding on for their lives?*

I have one eye ahead and one behind.

Then it happens. The black SUV loses control and dives over the cliff, leaving in its wake a stench of burning rubber and the squeal of tires ringing in my ears.

Dylan slows down, as do oncoming vehicles.

I experience a mixture of horror and guilty relief as the rolling black car smashes into ragged rocks and falls into the water like a piece of scrap metal.

It's only after Dylan pulls up at a lookout that I'm able to speak.

He rubs his face, huffs, and looks at me. "Are you okay?"

"Holy shit. What the fuck just happened?" My jaw's dropped, and I'm staring at him wide-eyed in a state of confused awe. "That was some driving."

He smiles like I just complimented him on a nice suit. I don't know how he can be so darn cool.

"I was a rally driver in my past life," he quips, stepping out of the car.

I follow him. "Where the hell did you learn to drive like that?"

He wipes his forehead, the first and only sign of stress. "In the backstreets of London. Let's just say I had a misspent youth. Learned to rub wires together to start cars, and we'd go on joyrides evading cops."

My brow contracts so tightly it hurts. "You're kidding! So this 'man of the world' front is just that? You're from the hard streets?"

Dylan looks pensive as he stares out at the sea, and he answers with a slow nod.

I keep staring at him, searching for more.

He faces me. "One can reinvent themselves, can't they?"

I nod slowly, my jaw remaining dropped. *What can I say? That I'm also trying to reinvent myself?* Maybe a day ago I was, but now, it's like I've become a fugitive. Running away from my past is one thing, but from killing someone?

I can't believe how it happened. Like my reptile brain, that fight-or-flight response kicked in. Only I wish it had been flight. Instead, I opted for fight, as if some paranormal force drew my hand like a magnet toward that glass weapon.

I want to cry, scream, and hide under a rock. *What kind of unlucky star has my name on it?*

He points. "The village is just over there."

Despite a million voices sounding at once and demanding answers, I look ahead at moored boats, a long pier, and a bustling town—a reminder that I'm still alive.

"Who was that following us?" I ask him.

He shrugs. "No idea."

"But they were after you. It's about that key. It must be. Or is there something else going on in your mysterious world?"

Dylan studies me for a moment, showing little before a faint smile grows on his face. "Mysterious world? Maybe they were after you."

He cocks his head, and I roll my eyes.

I exhale to clear the tension. I need more than a deep breath for that. More like a stiff drink.

"You don't think we should report it to the police?" he asks.

Another staring competition follows. I can't imagine he wants the law involved. *Is this his way of testing me?*

"Probably not," I say. "Come on. I'm dying for a drink."

"And you're not worried about whether they survived or not?"

"Well, they wouldn't have, would they? And it was either them or us." Frowning, I study him closely. "Why do I get this feeling you're testing me?"

"Maybe I am. Come." He gestures for me to get into the car.

I'm too tired for further questions, despite having a mountain of them.

Ten minutes later, we arrive at Salerno and find a quaint trattoria with a perfect view of the sea. The server directs us to an outside table with a red-and-white-checked tablecloth and brings a carafe of water. Dylan fills our glasses, and I'm so parched I gulp mine down.

"Aren't you curious as to who they were?" I ask.

"Sure. But they also could have been nutters."

I pull a face of disbelief. "Oh, come on."

"Mallory, I have no idea. Now can we let this one go? I need some downtime."

Despite his abrasive tone, I can't help sympathizing. After all, that was some driving. It required balls of steel. I also recall that almost-demonic expression of survival in his eyes when battling Stan in the cabin. That was the same look he wore while steering us out of danger during that hair-raising drive.

Who is this man?

His knowledge of art qualifies him to be an art dealer. But the way he's managed to deal with dangerous situations suggests another life somewhere.

What's even more disturbing, even defying logic, is that my libido is acting up big-time.

I've always had a soft spot for alpha males. But Dylan, with his man-of-the-world bearing, is beta on the outside and, now that I've seen the way he uses his fists, alpha on the inside.

"Hey, thanks." I touch his soft hand. That's not the hand of someone trained in combat fighting. There's also bruising from the punch-up in the yacht. "You missed your calling as a race car driver."

Dylan chuckles, and his handsome face offers me something new, something almost personable. It's like I've known him for longer than our short time together.

I'm alive. That's all that matters, a realization that's just taking shape. For some strange reason, I feel energized as I push all of what's happened out to sea.

Lounging back, I enjoy the postcard view of that busy harbor with fishing boats, market stalls selling fresh catch, and tourists climbing onto ferries.

I could easily settle into a village life, and I watch with envy as Italian women carry baskets of veggies and fruit. Smiling, they give Dylan the eye. In his designer shades, linen slacks, and blue shirt flapping in the breeze, the man is an Adonis.

The stress of that car chase has done little to ruffle his features. All that testosterone has only made him hotter.

An hour or so later, Dylan's hired a boat with a driver and we're heading for the Amalfi coast, passing islands along the way.

Capri is the busiest of all. Despite the natural beauty of that rock-carved paradise, seeing the turquoise water lined with luxury yachts like Dimitri's triggers unpleasant emotions.

A knot curls in my stomach, and Dylan touches my hand. The man's a mind reader. Even when he's not looking, he notices things, like he's got eyes on the side of his head.

"Are you okay?"

"What do you think?" I point at a yacht identical to Dimitri's, filled with guests partying to loud thumping music.

The lifestyle of the rich is everywhere to be seen on that sun-drenched island, and a woman in a bikini dives into the sea.

"I'd love to jump in," I say.

"Did you bring your swimsuit?"

"No. I might buy one, though. I'd love a swim. It's so darn hot."

He goes to the fridge and removes two bottles of beer. "Can I tempt you?"

I nod. We drink in silence until we finally arrive at our destination.

Built up to the clouds almost, Positano astounds me. I point up at the villas built on the cliff's edge. "How did they manage to build those?"

"By donkeys, I'd say," Dylan responds.

I stare at him. *Should I chuckle?* I feel like doing that, but deep down, I'm a bundle of nerves. I have a flashback to that night in the hotel. Nothing happened in bed between us, despite my body wishing otherwise.

But I do wonder about him and those furtive stares. He checks me out when he thinks I'm not aware. I'm aware of everything about him, only I have no idea who or what he is.

Dylan Hyde doesn't give much away.

Thirteen

BURSTING WITH VIBRANCE AND dazzling the senses, Positano is a feast of color. Endless steps, winding cobblestone paths, and hidden alleys weave to great heights, where balconies decked in blossoms cling to rocky walls.

The hotel I'm booked in is halfway up the mountain, while Dylan's staying somewhere even farther above. Or so he tells me.

"I'll see you at the auction," he says while carrying my luggage, which I'm capable of doing as I told him, but he insisted, to the foyer of the marble-floored hotel.

Yes, he's a gentleman and back to playing his sweet beta role perfectly. That is if this is an act, which I think it might be.

I get little hints here and there, like his evasive answers and clear dislike of questions.

I linger. "You're not going to run away, are you?"

His head lurches back. "Me, do a runner? What do you take me for?"

I roll my eyes again. Lots of eye stretching is going on around this man.

"Look, Dylan, we can drop the formalities at this point. I'm in this all the way. You owe me something."

"I owe you nothing, Mallory." His cold response makes me start. From Mr. Nice Guy to something dark, that's Dylan Hyde, I'm learning.

"And your life? What of that?" I bite back. Enough of the niceties.

"I didn't ask for your help." He stares me down, then his eyes soften. "I am grateful that you saved my life. However, I would have found a way. I *know* how to protect myself."

"I've noticed," I return dryly.

Did I allow my instincts to get the better of the situation?

If I hadn't, I wouldn't be stained with a stranger's blood—or this growing, uncomfortable attachment to Dylan Hyde. Then there's the key.

"Did you train in the Special Forces or something?" I ask.

He smiles as though I've asked a childish question. "Nope. Never served. Let's just say I had a rough upbringing."

"You don't strike me as someone who came from the ghetto."

"Haven't we already discussed this?" Dylan rubs his neck. I can see he's tired. "We'll catch up at the auction later. Okay?"

We lock eyes again for that staring competition we've become so good at.

"What's to stop me from going to the police?" I ask.

He rolls his eyes. "I'm not going anywhere, Mallory. For now, I need to freshen up before the auction. I'll see you there."

"You'll tell me everything?" I ask.

He shakes his head, looking frustrated. "There's nothing to tell. It would be better at this stage if you go back to whatever you were doing." He goes to walk away, then pauses. "What was *that* again?"

Touché.

He leans in and kisses my cheek. His soft lips leave a warm damp mark on my face, and I draw in his scent like a sun-drenched rose.

It's early evening, and after a packed afternoon, visiting the police and even fitting in that swim, I finally find the villa hosting the art auction, which is tucked away behind a sweetly fragrant orange orchard.

The villa's perched perilously close to a cliff with a magical view of the sapphire ocean and scattered islands that remind me of stone-carved creatures.

The afternoon breeze is like a gift from the gods, an almost palpable concept seeing that I'm in Homer's land. Everything about the Bay of Naples and its cavernous enclaves whispers of history.

I wish I could be that innocent, awestruck art lover, but I'm no longer her. I just killed a stranger and am crushing on a man who might be involved in a crime syndicate.

A question keeps revolving in my head, like one of those perpetual rolling neon signs: *How was it he freed the blood-soaked key from Dimitri's hand without a moment's thought?*

Does he know what it opens? But then, why not take it from the painting in the first place?

I recall a couple of security guards at the auction.

Were they Dimitri's minions to ensure Dylan returned with the painting?

Pushing away those lingering questions, I paste on a smile as I'm welcomed into the throng of art buyers.

I find Dylan standing on a roomy balcony overlooking the sea and staring at a glorious turquoise twilight.

Dylan takes the lead and introduces me to a few of his collector friends. Their names exit as quickly as they enter. If ever I needed proof that he's in thick with the European art-dealing scene, I have it right there. Just like in Matera and Polignano, he seems to know most of the buyers on a first-name basis.

I stand close enough to hear him discussing the toxic nature of pigments used in Renaissance art, a conversation my grandfather would have been in his element sharing.

I end up buying five paintings for the auction house. This time, I don't consult Jane beforehand. We haven't spoken since Matera. I think I'm worried she'll read my face because when I look in the mirror, I'm now seeing a stranger.

The 1970s Italian oil paintings are fresh, colorful, and commercially on point, even after using all my budget for this leg of my buying tour.

Buying tour? Is that what this is?

"Good choices," Dylan whispers as I go in hard and make sure I win an abstract that looks like it was painted under the influence of magic mushrooms. Ah, the seventies.

Very marketable these days. Maybe not so much back then.

That's art for you. New and unknown works often incite tomato-chucking from critics, especially if the art's hard to pigeonhole. Fast-forward a couple of decades or so, and art dealers froth at the mouth to get ahold of the once-mocked painting.

An unsigned work piques Dylan's interest. Though it's a pretty Tuscan landscape, there's nothing extraordinary about it, and I wonder why he's even bidding.

I give him a mystified look, and he smiles. "This is why I'm here."

"Really?" I frown.

He cracks a crooked smile, which brims with self-satisfaction that, on anyone else, would be detestable but not on this man. Oh no. He's that guilty desire that you try to keep hidden, even from yourself.

I'm about to head off to pay for my acquisitions, and to take photos for Jane, when he bids again and wins. I ask myself if I've missed anything about that unknown work.

I have to ask. "Please don't tell me this has got some hidden message or code?"

His eyebrows flinch slightly before they smooth out, and a faint smile grows. I might have just struck a nerve.

Since arriving at that auction, it's the closest he's come to lowering his polished man-of-the-world mask. It's like that car chase this morning never happened, not to mention the bloodbath in Polignano.

I wish.

I'm still digging into my palms unconsciously, like anxiety is bubbling away, waiting for that dark hour to erupt, whereas Dylan is all twinkling-eye smiles and charm.

After I've supplied the requisite paperwork and paid for my paintings, I rejoin Dylan, who has his painting wrapped up to take away.

"You're not having that delivered to some UK or Parisian mansion? Or wherever you base yourself?"

He smiles at my dry comment. "I'd like to show you something since you're intrigued by this unknown work."

"I'm wondering why you didn't bid for the Matisse."

"Come." He gestures. "All mysteries will soon be revealed."

I pause. "All?"

He raises an eyebrow. "Now where would the fun be in that?"

He opens the door, and we step out into the night. I'm half expecting him to leave me, but there we are, side by side.

"When are you leaving?" I ask, getting back to the pointy business of that key.

"I haven't decided," he says.

"Oh?"

His silence screams to me. I want to bring up the plan, given that I'm in for the ride, but I'm too mesmerized by the night's fairy-tale setting. My nerves demand some time out.

We walk through an archway that leads into a dimly lit tunnel. If Dylan wasn't there, I'd be spooked. That village has a network of secret passageways.

"Are we off to some secret society?" I take small, careful steps.

He chuckles. "You've got a vivid imagination. No, these passageways go back to the time of Caesar. Secret tunnels for escaping the enemy, I imagine."

"It smells like a urinal." I hold my breath, as there is a stench of something having died in there. As we walk along the creepy tunnel, I ask him again about the Matisse.

"It's a fake." He sounds so matter-of-fact we could be talking about a cheap vase. But that painting went for a whopping twenty million.

"What?" I stop walking. "The provenance was rock-solid. I saw it."

"Then you aren't up to speed at how sophisticated provenance forgeries have become."

That hits hard because I closely studied the oriental-themed Matisse along with its flawless, thus unquestionable, provenance.

"But how? It's not a fake. Surely?" I persist.

"Because I know who painted it."

That brief about unveiling Dylan Hyde and his dealings comes flashing before me. "How? I mean, who?"

"You've met him," he answers.

I think for a moment. "The art restorer you introduced me to at the auction? What was his name again?"

"Yes. Elliot. An old friend of mine."

"But he bid for it."

Dylan leads me out of the tunnel. Welcoming the open air, we enter a piazza, where a woman with a cart sells lemon-infused refreshments. Limoncello is poured out for us, and we take a seat on a cool marble bench overlooking the sea.

It's after nine, and twilight is entering its nocturnal phase. Normally, I would linger over the Prussian-blue sea blending with a delicate turquoise sky, putting Rothko to shame, but I'm too filled with suspense.

"That was Elliot's Hitchcock moment," he says at last.

My head jerks back. "Huh?" Then the analogy clicks. "Oh, I see. He likes to make a fleeting appearance at the scene of his creation." I sniff. "Nice one." Snapping out of that little digression, I face him. My frown intensifies. "But why bid for it?"

"He likes to warm things up and takes great delight in watching the mob squabble."

"My. How audacious." I shake my head and chuckle. "I can't understand why you'd fork out so much for that chocolate-box piece."

Dylan stretches out his hand. "Come. Let's see if my gamble's paid off."

"Do you make a habit of this?"

"Of what?" he asks as we ascend steep steps leading to a domed cathedral.

"Scattering crumbs and teasing one's appetite for answers."

A deep guttural chuckle drags me along. Even his laugh is sexy.

"I only do it with you," he responds. "I like the spark you get in your eyes. Mystery suits you."

His comment is a compliment on one hand and maddeningly frustrating on the other. "And you take delight in subterfuge. You're a teaser."

"I've been called worse."

I want to slap him, especially when his eyes twinkle with humor.

His gaze shifts to something a little darker and lustier, and he pushes me gently against the wall. He kisses me, and I melt. I feel him. All of him.

I want to head to my hotel and rip open the buttons of that crisp cotton shirt, but duty calls. What that duty looks like is becoming increasingly murky.

We separate, and his eyes hold mine.

"Whoa. What was that for?" I ask, taken aback. Talk about not seeing *that* coming.

He shrugs as though it's a normal response. "You're a beautiful woman."

By this stage, I'm almost floored. My legs are close to buckling.

"And... well... I couldn't resist." His lips curl into a faint smile.

Speechless, I struggle to think straight, let alone talk as our eyes lock.

"Um, what were we saying?" I take a deep breath and return to the question of the fake if only to dilute an inflaming wave of desire robbing me of reason. That kiss beat five years of ordinary sex with a husband from hell.

"Where's the original Matisse? And does the estate know it's a fraud?" I ask and we start to walk again.

"No. Elliot replaced it when they weren't looking."

"You're joking. Are you involved? I mean, do you deal in frauds?"

There it was. *And why aren't I recording this?*

I can hardly think straight, let alone scheme, with my lips smoldering from that kiss.

"Too many questions," he says.

As we move along, I fumble with my phone on the pretense of checking a message and press Record.

"He won't be able to sell the original, though. Ten million goes into the pocket of the estate. Or are they in on it?"

"No. As I said, he swapped them over."

"So, what's in it for him? He can't exactly sell the original while its fake exists."

He stops walking. "Call it a noble cause. Elliot plans to hand the works over to a public gallery where the work cannot be sold so that anyone can enjoy them. He hates how the rich procure works only to hide them in vaults."

I also hate that but stay quiet on my opinion, despite admiring this Robin Hood approach to collectible art. "But the estates of the forged works will reclaim them as theirs, won't they?"

"That's why lawyers were invented. A good art lawyer will argue that the person selling the fake sold that work in good faith."

In my busy mind, I rummage for that semester of art law. "If the person can argue that they were misled, surely they have some recall."

"As I said, the right legal counsel can weave miracles."

I pause for a breath. The steps seem endless. "So, you *are* entangled in this world of fraudulent art?"

My heart's racing. Thank God it's dark out there. I'm sure he would be able to read my face.

His silence speaks volumes. He didn't deny it.

A few steps later, we arrive at a Gothic-style villa looking all mysterious as Victorian lamps illuminate an overgrown garden dancing in the breeze, while deep down below, the dark sea is resting after a day of endless visitors.

Fourteen

ELLIOT PLACES THE PAINTING of the Tuscan landscape under a microscope, and after tweaking a knob, he says, "Check this out."

Dylan peers down the lens, and a big smile grows on his face. "I told you."

"Well spotted, old boy."

Their Englishness sneaks out, and I can't help but smile.

As I stand around in the cavernous basement that smells of linseed and oil paint, summoning touching memories of my grandfather's studio, it feels like I'm on an acid trip that started the moment I laid eyes on that handsome beast of a dealer.

"Okay, enough of the lovefest. What is it?" I ask.

They exchange a smile.

I'm invested in the moment, if only for the nostalgia that's warming my universe. Who would have thought a restorer's messy workspace could elicit so many warm and fuzzy feelings? While the horror story between my cold mother and sweet father played out, my grandfather's studio was my sanctuary.

It's ten in the evening, and I'm wondering where the night will lead.

With Dylan in my bed?

Honeypot or call it what you like, I'm due for some pleasure. It's been years.

I push that thought aside and indulge in a moment that will end up in my "finer memories" journal, should I get out of this in one piece.

"Have a look." Dylan steps away from the sophisticated piece of equipment that my grandpa would have mortgaged his home to own had my practical grandmother allowed.

I peer down the lens, and beneath the landscape are the makings of a female portrait.

"How did you guess that?"

Elliot and Dylan share a moment again, and I'm suddenly drowning in condescension. "And drop the self-satisfied smirks, will you?"

They laugh.

"I like this woman," Elliot says.

Dylan points at the sky. "The Tuscan hills are not well blended. There's an abrupt, protruding line leaving a textural overlay. Something you see—"

"When the artist has painted over another work," I interject because it's as plain as daylight with the help of the microscope.

"Yes. Right. And there you have it. Gentileschi," Elliot chimes in, looking pleased.

"Artemisia?" I ask.

"I wish." Dylan has stars in his eyes.

His genuine love of art is moving and somewhat redeeming for this man of many masks, because I also can't forget how he cleaned that blood-soaked cabin as soberly and unaffected as a forensic officer might.

"Her father, Orazio Gentileschi," Dylan adds. He turns to Elliot. "So can I leave it with you to restore it to its former glory?"

The older man nods. "We'll discuss terms later. Not now. Not around magic."

His tone is that of someone who's just stumbled on an exquisite jewel. I'm taken aback, for the longer I stare at the work Dylan so astutely chose, I kick myself for not recognizing it.

He turns to me. "You look a little off-color."

I shake my head. "I'm just pissed off with myself for not seeing it."

"Quite a coup. I do say, this will keep my account healthy for a while."

As will whatever that key delivers. *It's something insanely valuable, or else why kill for it?*

I'm holding on to the banister as I descend the endless steps after stumbling a couple of times. The last thing I need is to be stretchered out of that mountainous village. Fired up, I'm using all the control I can muster to take careful steps. All I want to do is run, scream, and punch something. My emotions have hit fever pitch.

While I was admiring Elliot's forgeries, Dylan left, leaving me there startled. I recorded it all, of course, even the part where Elliot goes on about how Dylan has known about his operation for years. Whether that means

Dylan was palming them off, I can't say. But it's on my phone, and I plan to use it.

I hate that man. He's ruined my life.

Not as much as my mother. No one will ever come close to that, but still, the fire in my belly is about as destructive.

Why kiss me? Why screw with my head?

Elliot just shrugged after I flooded him with questions like "Where's he gone?"

He spread his palms, wearing an apologetic—*Or was that sympathetic?*—smile.

So here I am, holding on for my life as I navigate the pathway to my hotel. There's no other way, I'm told, to get back there.

At eleven in the evening, nothing's easy to find. Especially with all the crazy shit going on in my head.

I pause at a bar and order a neat gin. The waiter points me in the direction of my hotel. I open my bag to tip him when I see a note.

Sorry to rush off like this. But this is becoming too dangerous.

PS: That was some kiss.

I keep reading the note over and over like there might be a secret code.

My heart sinks to my feet as I head to my hotel. Trust me to book a place that's a little off the beaten track. There aren't even people about, and it's not that late. Not for Italy, at least.

Sensing someone behind me, I turn, but there's no one. Somewhat jumpy, I move along, gripping on to whatever I can find. Peering over my shoulder, sensing someone close again, I nearly run into a man.

Picking up my pace, I'm using contradictory muscles, ones that give flight while others try to avoid having me tumble down as sweat trickles down my arm.

In the distance is a square with a lit-up bar, and my mood brightens, despite feeling like shit about Dylan's disappearance.

Just as I'm close to the piazza filled with people eating and drinking, I hear a noise echoing from one of the many tunnels. I stop to look when a hand lands on my shoulder.

I'm dragged from behind into the dark. My heart pounds. I'm gripped around the waist by a powerful force, and panic surges through me as I kick and claw, struggling to free myself from a relentless show of strength.

Gripped by terror, my mind races, searching for a way out. Fear tightens around my throat, and I just manage to scream, my cries echoing off the walls.

Battling for survival, I unleash force I never thought I possessed by thrashing about as the man tightens his hold on my waist.

Then I realize I'm cornered by a pair of menacing thugs.

"What do you want?" I cry. I pass them my bag. "Here, take everything, just leave me alone."

They're not interested, it seems, in what I possess. Just me.

I try to run again, and one of the men grabs my arm, nearly removing it from its socket.

Stifling my cries, he covers my mouth with his rough hand, which stinks of tobacco. Adrenaline ignites my every nerve.

Frantic, I thrash about, desperate to break free, mustering every ounce of willpower I have. I punch his chest and manage to bite his hand, but he's proving too strong. The more I fight, the tighter he holds me, and excruciating pain runs through my body.

Tears pour down my cheeks as I scream into the hand smothering my mouth. Life flashes before me for a second time in one day. I'm not ready to go.

I stand on his foot and knee him in the balls, but his partner punches me in the face, and I see stars. My body goes limp.

Expecting death or something worse, like rape or torture, I prepare for the horror that awaits me as I'm dragged off like a rag doll.

Out of nowhere, a man enters the fray. In that tunnel, it's so dark, I can't see who it is.

He's swooped in and punching and fighting the pair as though they're half his size and strength. They certainly don't look that way.

One of the men brandishes his pistol, and my savior deftly kicks the gun out of the thug's hand, while the other man is on the ground under his foot.

He's a force of nature. They don't stand a chance, especially after he picks up the gun and pistol-whips the last standing attacker, knocking him out.

The muggers are on the ground, out cold.

Meanwhile, I lean against the wall, tongue half-hanging-out and at a loss for words. A throbbing ache vibrates through my body, reminding me that I've sustained some serious bruising.

But thanks to Dylan and his almost superhuman fighting skills, I'm still alive.

I gaze at him, not knowing whether to scream or hug him. "I guess that makes us even," I mutter as I follow him out of the tunnel.

Fifteen

HE HELPS ME INTO an SUV, and when he starts the motor, I face him. "You came back."

Remaining silent, he drives off, and I become vigilant again given that he's having to navigate that large vehicle around tight pebbled streets.

Nevertheless, I sink into the seat, ignore the sense of danger pounding away in my head, and try to breathe normally again.

"Why did you do that?"

"I wanted to make sure you were okay." He steers around a tight, risky bend.

Everything screams of danger, including the man at the wheel. My life's in his hands all of a sudden.

"But you ran away," I press.

"We'll talk later. Right now, I need you to get your belongings. You have five minutes."

This is another man. His face is steely, with a sheen of sweat. It's a result of the humidity and him flooring two men. The testosterone is almost palpable, as are the sinews in his neck, still inflamed from a do-or-die situation.

I'm not going to argue. If he wanted me dead, he could have let me be. "Okay." I open the door.

"Wait." He jumps out and, always the consummate gentleman, helps me exit. "I'm coming. Just in case."

"Just in case? You think I'm being followed?"

"Can't be too sure." He whispers something to the security guard at the entrance and tips him.

"Okay, let's hurry," he says.

When we're in my room, I'm rushing about, throwing things into my suitcase, dirty underwear included. I blush as he returns a little eye roll. The man can read me like a book. Whether that's a compliment or a concern, I can't decide.

He carries my stuff again, but women's rights have gone out the window. Had he not saved me, I would probably be in a dark room being tortured, raped, or even murdered.

Once we're off and driving, I ask, "Where are we going?"

"Rome."

"Like, now? It's close to midnight," I say. "And you were leaving without saying goodbye."

"I thought I might. But after seeing you followed, I think it's best if I keep you close."

"Oh, you're scared I'll talk. Like, keep your enemies close? That kind of thing?"

"You're not exactly an enemy. But sure, something like that. And I'm sure whoever's on my tail will send another lot on the hunt."

"How would they have found me?"

"They've probably been casing me and saw you leave Elliot's. I noticed them after I left and then destroyed my phone. But once I picked up the car, I realized you would be their easier target."

He remains quiet and focused on the road.

I'm too tired to discuss the ins and outs of this midnight mad dash. But I'd be lying if I didn't admit to being pleased to be there.

We're on the autostrada, heading for Rome. I'm exhausted. We've already stopped twice for coffee. Dylan takes the exit to Cassino.

"I need to sleep," he says as we drive into a small city with a lit-up medieval castle poised on a mountain.

We stop at the first hotel we come to, and ten minutes later, I'm in the shower, washing away the tension of the past few hours.

When I get out of the shower, Dylan is on the bed asleep. He's managed to remove his shoes and jacket, and there he is, quietly snoozing like a man who hasn't been through a death-defying car chase and a bone-crunching punch-up with a pair of heavies.

I notice his bruised knuckles, and my heart goes out to him. Something else jumps out at me, though—his leather satchel.

I know that once we're in Rome, he'll dump me again, and I want in. I want to see what that key opens. We're in too thick for that not to happen.

I'm tempted to search for the key, but something tells me he'll look for it, and right now, I need him as my ally, not my foe.

We'll be sharing the bed because there's no couch, and this was the only room left. My hormones broke into a tango at that thought.

Dylan just shrugged and gave me the first hint of a smile for hours, and here we are.

He's in a deep sleep while I debate whether to remove his slacks, given that he'll be more comfortable, but instead, I jump into bed and lie there. In the dark, my eyes are on the ceiling, thoughts revolving around and around.

My heart sinks at the thought of having to report to the police. If ever I needed an excuse to escape my former life, it's now, if only to get that smelly detective off my back, something a good lawyer could do in their sleep.

They have nothing on me. It's all Erik's sister's doing. She's the one who insisted on an autopsy. Determined to make my life hell, she's always hated me. And now I have this horrible detective running this investigation like some textbook case of an angry, unhappy woman getting back at her husband. Well, I've got news for them: I refuse to be anyone's cliché. I'm innocent. I just don't feel sad about Erik's unexpected passing. That's my only crime here.

Between the pair of them, they're out to crucify me.

With money, I could buy a good lawyer and clean up loose ends so I can move forward with my life and become a better person. The person I could have been had my disruptor mother not pushed my dad down the stairs.

The lack of justice over my father's death is like a heavy weight I have carried for years. Try as I might, I can't shake it off. But I do have one trump card up my sleeve where my mother's concerned. I push that thought aside since I have other, more pressing matters to contemplate. Namely that key and its potential to provide a life reset.

Then there's Dylan.

What do I do with him?

I've got enough evidence to have him questioned, at least.

But do I want that?

He saved my life. Not to mention there's this insane chemistry between us.

One thing's for certain. Despite the obvious danger, I wouldn't miss this situation for the world. It sure as hell beats catching up with friends in New York and talking about the same old things.

Sixteen

We sit on the balcony, enjoying a late breakfast and coffee.

I soak up the view of that medieval castle and its rustic beauty, photographing it in my mind for those times when I'm confined to the ordinary push and shove of New York.

A hint of depression floats over me, despite the afterglow of the best sex I've ever had. Yes, we just had sex. And oh my, it was better than I could've ever imagined.

"So what will we call this?" I ask.

"What?" He sips his coffee.

"What we just did."

His mouth curls divinely. "You mean fucking?"

I nod.

"Does it need defining?" His brow creases slightly.

"No. I guess not."

He studies me for a moment. "Try not to overthink it. Life's easier that way."

"Oh gee, thanks, Sigmund."

He laughs. "Like I said in Positano, you're a very beautiful, desirable woman. I think I made my attraction obvious." He arches an eyebrow then looks ahead pensively. "And we now share some history."

I sigh. "I'm not letting you out of my sight until I discover what that key opens."

"So you've said." He holds my gaze.

His cool response acts as a sobering reminder that any minute, he could run off, just like he did in Positano. Those thugs did me a favor, even if I've developed a nervous tick of looking over my shoulders and jumping at shadows.

Dylan didn't have to save me. I wonder why he did.

"So how does this work, then?"

He shrugs. "We'll leave for Rome later today after I've picked up a burner phone. Isn't that part of your itinerary?"

I nod hesitantly. *Did I tell him that was my next stop?* So much has happened that all I can recall are the bigger moments, like killing a man and us fucking our brains out.

All I know is it was the hottest sex I've ever had. No booze was involved. Just morning sex with me biting into his neck to muzzle moans and groans unleashed from the most intense orgasm I've ever experienced.

I follow him into the chaotic-looking room where my clothes lay strewn while his satchel and overnight bag sit unopened.

"Did I tell you I was going to Rome?" Jane enters my thoughts. I haven't contacted her about my latest acquisitions.

"How else would I know?" He turns on his laptop.

Maybe I did say something on the drive here. I was too focused on how he saved me from those thugs and a growing mountain of questions.

He goes to his overnight bag and pulls out a clean shirt. "Nice yellow bikini, by the way."

"Huh?" I shut down my phone and give him a puzzled look.

"I saw you having a swim yesterday."

"Oh. You were at the beach?" I have to think back. I've almost forgotten where I was yesterday. So much has happened. I did find time to buy that bikini and have a swim at Positano as I'd promised myself, and Dylan was there. It's not surprising I didn't see him, though, as it was a quick dip among lots of tourists.

"I'd just gotten out of the water when I saw you arriving." He looks into my eyes, and my resolve to keep a distance vanishes. Suddenly, his lips are all over mine.

I drift off, allowing him to hold me tight against his firm chest. My body's making the decisions by shutting down all those inner rumblings.

Rationality finally kicks in like that finger-pointing adult crashing in on a pair of hormone-drunk teenagers. I force myself to pull away, despite my body heating up as quickly as a Ferrari's speed climb.

"This is not a good idea," I say with hesitancy, because any other time, this would be a great idea.

He stares into my eyes, and my resolve buckles again.

He moves away, and disappointment clouds my emotions, which are already gearing up for another round of passion with this ridiculously handsome man.

"What were you doing at the police station in Positano?" he asks.

A bucket of cold water wakes me out of my sensual dream.

He sits in an armchair across from me and crosses his legs.

Despite it being barely midday, I pour a little bottle of gin into a glass and gulp it half down. His eyes burn into me like the liquor in my chest.

"I can see I've made you nervous." He pulls a tight smile. "Did you tell the police about Polignano?"

I shake my head.

Scrambling for excuses, I say, "I'm having to report my whereabouts to NYPD over traffic infringements and unpaid bills."

A line forms between his brow. He's not buying it.

Tough. I don't owe him the truth.

It's three in the afternoon, and I accompany Dylan to buy a burner phone, after which we return to the hotel to prepare to leave.

"We're only two hours at the most away from Rome," he says as we enter the room.

I'm almost packed, and despite looming questions about his plans in Rome, I'm feeling a little looser.

The recording I made of Dylan has become my trump card, I tell myself as I hear him talking on his phone in the bathroom.

When he returns to the room, I smile at him. "Talking to your girl-friend?"

"Nope. Don't believe in them." He puts his phone inside his satchel while I scan his face for more insight. "Mallory, I'm a reprobate. I make no apology for that. I eschewed monogamy a long time ago."

"But don't you fear growing old alone?" I clip down my suitcase.

"If an antidote to the fear of loneliness necessitates being chained to a person whom one cannot even stand the sight of, let alone sleep with every night, then give me the anchorite's life any day."

My jaw drops, and a strained laugh follows. "That's such a cynical and bleak outlook."

"What about you?" He slants his head. "You're not exactly painting rainbows."

What kind of vibe am I giving?

I think of my suburban upbringing in New Jersey. Dark and difficult memories surround that sad home, especially after my father fell down those stairs to his death.

That's when, aged fifteen, my life took a dramatic turn.

After my father's death, I ran away and stayed with my grandparents. My grandfather's workshop became my refuge, where he made me what I am.

Who that is remains inchoate—a work in progress. Right now, however, I'm a widow who's fallen big-time for an art dealer involved in selling fraudulent art. I'm even starting to sympathize with those who fall for criminals.

Is he a criminal?

I snap out of my reverie and return to Dylan's comment. "I married the wrong man, that's all. But I'm sure there's a good match somewhere. I can only hope."

"What constitutes a good match?" he asks.

"A couple that share the same passion."

"Okay, a friendship. And what else?" he asks.

"Um... well, great sex, of course."

"That goes without saying." He smiles. "What about if he or she enjoys the art of flirting and undressing mystery?"

"You mean cheating?" I ask.

"If you want to call it that."

"If I love someone, I'd probably get jealous," I admit. Strange, because I can't say I've ever been jealous of other women. Not that Erik gave me any cause, other than his porn habit. But even that didn't rouse the green monster.

"And that's the problem right there." He looks victorious, as though he just checkmated me.

"You don't get jealous? You don't fear losing someone you love?"

"I don't do love. I don't do jealousy. The pair are twins, a mirror of each other. Like Lucifer, once divine, now destructive. To covet is to want to own. And that goes against the free spirit I subscribed to a long time ago."

"Are you happy, though?" I ask.

He shrugs. "I have my moments of basking in the sun. But it's unrealistic to expect to be happy all the time. Lows intensify the highs. As a lover of art, you surely recognize that grays make bright colors pop. Look at a woman in red on a dull day, and she will stand out more than on a sunny day. Ups and downs make for a dynamic existence."

"But no one likes to be sad, do they?"

"Of course not. But I detest how sadness has been pathologized. One doesn't need a shrink when a pint with a friend or even a good book is all that's required."

"I don't subscribe to having a psychologist on speed dial."

He laughs. "That's why I like you."

"Oh? Why exactly do you like me?" I need to milk his compliment, if only for my own sanity. *Or is that vanity?*

Both.

He presses his chin on his finger. "Let me see. Your long legs. The fact you don't wax your pussy."

"Huh?" My eyebrows fling up. That, I wasn't expecting. "And that's it?"

He joins me at the window and runs his hands over my waist. "Your perky breasts."

"Small breasts, you mean."

"They're perfect. And then there are your pretty eyes and how they spark when looking at art. That's rare for sure. And a turn-on."

"Okay, I'll take that as a compliment. Though that Brazilian is on my to-do list." My lip curls slowly.

"Save yourself the agony."

His droll response makes me chuckle.

Dylan pauses and stares deeply into my eyes. "Aside from your substantial feminine charms, the biggest allure for me is that you're hiding something. I find mystery an aphrodisiac."

"As it is for everyone, I imagine." I give him a thin smile despite the rumbling in my chest.

Seventeen

"How do I know you won't run away?" I ask as we're about to drive off to Rome.

"I can't have you running to the police. Remind me again why you were there?"

His eyes narrow ever so slightly. He must have noticed my fingers knitting together.

"As I said, a few unpaid fines back home. Nothing that interesting."

He gives me a strange smile.

I bring up the yacht incident just as he starts the car. "Why haven't they reported the murders? I've scoured the internet."

"I'm wondering the same thing. I have a theory, though."

"Being?" I ask.

"Sven, the skipper, was part of Dimitri's inner sanctum. He might have cleaned up the mess and decided to keep the vessel and the collection. Knowing Dimitri, he would have had a stash of drugs, cash, and lots of gold jewelry on board. Russians love their gold."

"Don't we all," I say under my breath. "How is it you arrived at the cabin at that crucial point?"

"Stan asked to meet me there."

A sharp turn creaks my neck. "I thought you said it was Dimitri?"

He shrugs. "Like you, I'm a little off-kilter."

I study him closely, trying to figure out whether he's taking me for a ride. The more I get to know him, the more questions arise.

"What was your connection to Stan?" I ask again.

"He was Dimitri's right-hand man."

"I know that," I say with a huff. "But why would he want to shoot you?"

He accelerates as we hit the autostrada and pass a sign that reads Roma 146.

"Perhaps he thought I knew about the key."

"Did you?"

He shrugs. "I had my suspicions. The painting meant something more than just decoration to Dimitri."

"So what did Stan say to lure you to the office?"

"He told me he had something that would interest me. A project of sorts."

"Okay. And that's it?" I ask.

"You're quite the interrogator." He changes lanes and accelerates. He's a lead foot, but after that impressive rally-standard driving, swerving along the corkscrew coast, he's proven himself competent behind the wheel.

"You owe me answers since my hands are covered in blood. Wouldn't you say?"

"That's all I've got. I don't know why Stan wished me dead."

"Why were you so quick to lunge for that key?"

He shrugs. "I saw Dimitri clutching something. I thought it must belong to something important."

"So why didn't Dimitri go to the auction himself, seeing as that painting was so valuable to him?"

"He always sent me off to do his bidding. That's how Dimitri rolled."

"You must have suspected something. The fact he was willing to go so high for substandard work."

"He told me he loved Venetian art. I didn't query it."

I can't help but feel something's amiss with his story. It's the ease with which he answers like he's well rehearsed.

"So how does this painting end up in some obscure seaside village?"

"What I do know is that Dimitri had art stolen from his Como villa two years ago, and since then, he's had me tracking down this particular work. He told me that the painting held sentimental value."

I leave it at that. Dylan's explanation sounds plausible at least, although my thirst for answers is still unquenched.

It's six in the evening when we arrive in Rome. We've checked into our hotel, and I've watched Dylan like a hawk, expecting him to dump me somewhere. Instead, he surprises me by suggesting we unwind and become tourists for a few hours. The irresistible proposition has my heart fluttering like a teenager around the most popular boy at school.

The Colosseum sits against the turquoise sky like a decayed golden crown worn by one of those titanic Pagan gods they once worshipped. Despite its crumbling outline, the former amphitheater still breathes immense charisma, just like Rome itself.

As we walk through the ancient ruins at the Palatine Hills, I peer down at remnants of ancient Rome. Massive marble columns stand impossibly high among sprawled ruins, telling stories of emperors and gladiators. Goose pimples prickle my skin as I stare in wonder at a whole world of history.

My heart pounds against my ribs, and I'm dizzy suddenly. I'm unsure whether it's due to seeing Rome for the first time, which has had me oohing and aahing for hours, or Dylan's breath on my neck.

His pine cologne wafts my way, and all I can think about is how good he felt buried deep inside of me. The scratches on his back are a testimony to that. Drunk on orgasms, I could barely utter a word, let alone remember my name.

Maybe the memory of that steep drop threatening to swallow us up on the way to Amalfi is triggering something too.

I cling to the railing for dear life when a whoosh of wind or a ghost or something threatens to send me over the edge. Like a tap or a touch.

Is it that?

Panic tightens my veins, and I stumble. With barely an inch of ground, I'm teetering over the edge all of a sudden.

I reach out to Dylan. His grip confuses me.

Is that a shove, or is he trying to stop me from tumbling to my death?

As doubt gnaws away, I ask myself whether Dylan is pulling me up or pushing me down.

Everything slows to a crawl. It's an out-of-body experience, like one of those nightmares where you want to scream but can't. My jaw is tense and my throat tight when a scream finally erupts.

Dylan's eyes meet mine, but I can't read him as chilling ambiguity paralyzes me with doubt. The line between trust and danger blurs.

I struggle in his hold.

"Hey, hold still," he says as he leads me away from the edge of a steep drop.

A tangled mess of neurons are sending confusing signals. Covered in sweat, I cry out, "Let go of me!"

Tourists turn to watch as I beat on his chest, and he grabs my hands to stop me.

"What just happened?" Dylan looks concerned.

Or is he pretending?

"You just tried to push me." I take a breath and try to calm myself.

His head lurches back. "Are you crazy? I felt you losing your balance and pulled you back. You must have felt that."

Tears fall down my cheeks, and he holds me as I unleash a torrent of emotion.

"It looks like you might have been having a panic attack. Are you frightened of heights?" he asks.

Memories of the stairs at my childhood home enter my thoughts—the same stairs that killed my father. I recall a dizzy spell and having to hold on to the balustrade while staring in shock at his lifeless body below. I recall trying to scream and not being able to. Just like now.

I step away from him. "I need a drink."

He exhales audibly. "I think that might be a good idea."

We find a bar overlooking the Tiber and choose to sit outside and give the waiter our order.

Dylan offers me a cigarette, and I take it. As I draw back on the smoke, the nicotine seems to restore some equanimity.

"What happened back there?" he asks just as the waiter sets down a Peroni for him and a gin and tonic for me.

I shrug. "I'm not sure." I study him closely. His blue eyes show me little, which only adds to my angst.

"Have you had a panic attack or a dizzy spell before?" he asks.

"Maybe once. Or twice." I gulp back my gin and tonic like it's a soda on a hot day.

As a curl of smoke exits my mouth, I watch a pair of women in skyscraper heels, dressed to the nines, gliding along those cracked, cobbled paths without a care in the world.

I return to his question about panic attacks.

Perhaps there've been a few. Emotional breakdowns act like amnesia, I was told by the shrink I visited once.

Erik used to accuse me of being crazy all the time. But instead of talking it out, like Dylan's attempting here, my husband would knock me about.

I stub out my cigarette and look into his eyes. "I thought for a minute you were trying to push me over."

He studies me closely, so closely I feel naked.

"That's plain paranoia, Mallory. I might be many things, but I'm not a murderer."

"Oh? Then what do you call that car chase? Those men died. And what about the fight? One of those men ended up on the ground, blood pouring out of his head."

"It was either them or me. Or you, for that matter." His stare grips mine, and I'm asking myself again whether I can trust him.

Is he dangerous?

"Are you involved with some kind of crime gang?" I keep staring into his eyes, searching for a reaction. "Or some kind of spy, even. That would be better, I suppose."

He laughs. "You've got some imagination."

I'm shaking again. Perhaps he's right. I'm having a panic attack just thinking about what's happened in the past four days.

"I mean, who are you? You drive like a rally driver who's done circuits at the Grand Prix and fight like a prizefighter."

He shakes his head, and his mouth curls ever so slightly. "They were chasing us, remember? The SUV swerved and missed the tight corner. And you're here in one piece. Remember that."

I nod slowly. He's right. I've got to stop thinking the worst.

"It's just that I don't know what you're about to do next."

"Try not to overthink it." He tilts his head. A shimmer of warmth touches his eyes, and I just want to fuck him. Which is nuts, given how unsettled I've become.

Eighteen

OUR HOTEL ROOM OVERLOOKS Piazza Navona, one of the numerous aesthetic jewels in this eternal city, with Bernini's Fountain of Four Rivers in clear view from our balcony.

As I unpack my suitcase, I look for something to change into. I'm bored with my clothes and dying for new ones. Also, a Zoom meeting with Jane is overdue. I've also got a progress report I need to put together for the FBI. Now that's a troubling thought. *Should I tell them about Elliot and Dylan?*

I decide to keep it neutral.

At least I sent Jane, and also Sawyer for that matter, a ton of messages, making all kinds of excuses, while we drove from Cassino. The thought of the stalking detective sends a dark cloud floating in again.

Dylan types something on his laptop. He's checking his emails, he tells me.

I still can't believe we're sharing a hotel room. It's something about keeping me close, he admitted yesterday evening during that deep and meaningful conversation at the café following my panic attack at Palatine Hill.

Was it a panic attack?

The jury's out on that.

Dylan thinks I'll blab to the authorities about what happened. That's why he's keeping me close.

Is that why he's pleasuring me too?

I wasn't about to demand my own space. As soon as we entered the room, he pushed me onto the bed, virtually ripped off my clothes, and made love to me like a man starved of sex. My orgasms were so powerful it now feels like I'm losing my mind to this man.

"I have an estate auction to attend tomorrow evening. Will you be there?" I ask as he packs away his computer and removes his phone from the charger.

"There are a few pieces worth bidding for. So yes." He combs back his dark hair peppered with the occasional gray.

Dylan's one of those men who improves with age. Tall and with just the right amount of muscle. Hollywood's next James Bond? He seems to possess acting skills. Or is he for real? At this stage, it's anyone's guess.

"How about the key? I take it you know where to find what it opens?" I hold his eyes.

"We're being followed." He scratches his temple.

My eyebrows collide. "Oh?"

"Yesterday on the autostrada, I noticed a black BMW SUV. It's now here in Rome."

"And you were going to tell me when?"

"I'm telling you now. And you weren't exactly in a good place yesterday." He gives me a tight smile. "I didn't wish to sound the alarm bell. I noticed the same vehicle earlier this morning."

"Oh? You were out?"

He nodded. "While you were getting your beauty sleep, I went out for a walk. Rome at dawn is a spectacle."

"Rome anytime is a spectacle."

There. You see, he could have run away. Why didn't he?

He's not exactly telling me a lot about his plans.

At least I have that tape. The trouble is if I threaten him with blackmail, Dylan will learn of my assignment.

"Are you certain they're following us? There are a ton of black SUVs getting around." I rummage through my suitcase, looking for a clean T-shirt.

"Not so many in these tight little streets, though," he says, scrolling on his phone.

"How do we go about this, then?" I try not to sound panicky.

"We'll just give them the slip somehow. That's not difficult to do in Rome."

He walks to the balcony and stares out at the crowds hovering around the fountain and taking selfies. "I have a female friend."

"Oh?" *Why doesn't that surprise me?*

"Sophia knows about the key and where I need to go." He walks back inside.

"I want to be around for the grand opening." I set down my hairbrush and stare him in the eyes.

After he doesn't respond, appearing lost in thought, I reiterate, "I'm coming along for the opening."

I remove my T-shirt, which smells a bit, and swap it for another shirt as I stand there half-naked before him as though making a point.

He looks away. Whether that's so I don't distract him, I can't say, but Dylan can't seem to take his hands off me. One can't fake *that* kind of attraction.

"Going in different directions is the best way to lose them."

"What if they follow me? Won't that put me in danger?"

"Not if you visit the police station." He tilts his head. "I imagine you have to report to them again."

I give him a faint nod, and that knot in my stomach tightens.

"So how will this Sophia help?" I study him closely. "I mean, yesterday, you didn't know what that key opened, and now suddenly, you've got a contact?"

He holds my eyes again. "I've only just spoken to her. She knew Dimitri. She knows about the key and the location of the vault."

I nod slowly. "Won't she expose you? Us?"

"She's someone I can trust." He pulls a tight smile. "She's the closest thing I have to family here."

Dylan rubs his neck, a subtle gesture of his whenever he shares something personal. "Sofia's a sixty-year-old widow who's got a doctorate in Renaissance art, and well…" He shrugs. "I recently saved her money on a pair of Botticelli fakes she was about to pay millions for."

He picks up his satchel. "I'm just going out for an hour or so." He stares at his Rolex.

"But what if they stop me? They might torture me."

He walks to the door. "They won't."

"How can you be so sure?" I knit my fingers.

"Because their end-game relates to the contents of the vault. The danger zone's afterwards."

"Then why try to kill us on the road to Salerno?"

He nods reflectively. "Good question. No idea."

"You will be back?" I ask.

Pointing at his overnight bag and laptop, he says, "I'm leaving those here. And if you think you can crack into my password, don't bother. It's thumbprint recognition only."

I shake my head. "Ye of little faith."

Well, okay, I was going to try to take a peek, but he doesn't need to know that.

The door shuts behind him, leaving me with my nails digging into my palms.

I want to scream for becoming attached to him, because the more mysterious he becomes, the deeper I fall.

For now, a coffee's calling out to me, so I fix my face, grab my bag, and head outside.

The concierge gives me a warm smile and a wave, and I exit through the rotating door, wishing I were a blithe tourist and not suddenly caught up in some Russian crime syndicate's cat-and-mouse game.

After a coffee and a stiff drink, which is all I needed to get a grip on things, I return to the hotel. The concierge informs me my laundry has been pressed and ready. Grateful for that, as I'm running out of clothes, I ask for them to be delivered to my room.

Once I'm there, I set up my laptop for a Zoom meeting with Jane.

She comes up on my screen and waves. "Hey, stranger."

"Hey," I huff.

"Are you okay?"

I smile. "I'm fine. Only…"

"Only?"

"Oh, it's just that annoying police investigation. I have to report every time I move to a new city. It's a serious pain in the butt."

She returns a sad smile. "I bet. Um, look. That detective returned the other day, asking to see your work computer."

"I don't know what he's expecting to find." I sigh.

"I told him you'd be returning by the end of the week. He said he'd wait. But if need be, he'd return with a warrant."

I bite into my lip. "I'm sorry to put you through that. It's crazy. I'm completely innocent. You know that, don't you?"

"I do. And hey, don't worry about me. It's worse for you. Can't you just get a lawyer to plead your innocence?"

"I plan to."

Whatever's in that vault, I'm hoping it will buy me the best lawyer in New York. I've already sourced one who's dealt with similar cases. She comes under the lugubrious title of the widow's lawyer. She also comes at a hefty cost.

The outcome hinges on two things: money and whether this protracted booty call continues with the man who's quickly becoming the love of my life.

"I love the art you've procured so far. And under budget. I'm impressed."

"I thought you would be." I smile. "There are a few abstracts I've seen in the catalog for tomorrow's auction that are strong contenders."

"I can't wait to see the Modigliani. I've already got a ton of interest," she says.

"I bet."

"So what have you found out about Dylan Hyde?" She sounds like that girlfriend who's dying to hear about a sexy night with a hot guy.

"He's got the Midas touch when it comes to art. So far, he's bought original art from what I can see. I'm not seeing anything illegal."

If only the authorities knew about Elliot and the fake Matisse that makes Dylan guilty by association.

"So have you gotten to know him?" Her eyebrow arch isn't lost on me.

"I have."

"What's he like?"

"He's gorgeous. And charming in that British kind of way."

"Oh..." She has stars in her eyes. "I bet he is. You do think the work's commercial, don't you? Do assure me. This has been a tough year."

"The Modigliani alone will cover what I've spent so far, Jane."

Her face lights up. "Great. And you've still got Rome, and then there's Venice. I've got a client who's obsessed with anything Venetian. So go mad. Signed masks from the sixties and earlier."

Anticipation sizzles through me at the mention of Venice. "I'm on it. I've studied the catalog and am certain you'll be pleased."

After I tell her about the sights I've seen, we end our conversation.

Nineteen

ICONIC IMAGES HAVE SUDDENLY come to life, and I've traveled back in time. Only with Dolce and Gabbana and Dior designer shops close by, not to mention the throng of tourists holding up their phones for that special photo, I'm snapped back to the present.

Standing at around twenty-five meters, the statue of Oceanus makes me gasp with disbelief. Every sinew and muscle is defined to perfection as though blood is flowing through the creature's veins. Michelangelo's marble masterpiece sits as a testimony to the artist's superhuman ability to give birth to something so impossibly lifelike. Famous as it is, the Trevi sculpture is just one of many structural marvels gracing that eternal city. It's like a theater of marble. The sheer scope of human ingenuity blows my mind, a reminder of what got me hooked on art in the first place. As my grandfather told me once, art reveals our soul and, along with science, is the ultimate gift to humanity.

I wish he could have been here with me. That thought brings a tear to my eyes as I recall the angel sculpture on the bridge to the Vatican earlier. I stroked the sculpture's feet while asking my grandfather to protect me, something I used to do whenever Erik fired up. The angel's intense gaze seemed to be staring into my eyes as though she understood.

After traipsing around doing the tourist thing and buzzing from witnessing live versions of images I'd only ever seen in books, I drag myself off to the police station with a heavy heart.

I negotiate a tiny lane, taking small, careful steps so that I don't fall into one of many cracks when my phone beeps.

It's Dylan, and he suggests meeting at Piazza Venezia at two for a spot of lunch. My face cracks into a smile as I respond with a thumbs-up emoji. That moment in the sun soon fades when I step into the station and a uniformed policeman peers up.

He's handsome and well-presented. They all are in this city. Even the men at newsstands look elegant.

His unexpected smile puts me at ease, and I explain the situation then hand over my passport, anticipating his welcoming vibe turning stony. To my surprise, he merely nods and then returns my passport.

"I can go?" I kick myself for not remaining cool.

He nods, and off I go, thanking my lucky stars. I can only conclude that as such a big city, Rome has seen it all. After all, the women behind famous emperors were notorious for dishing out poisons.

Speaking of black widows, my mother calls. It's not her first, and with half hour to kill, I head for my favorite café in Piazza Navona, order a stiff drink and a coffee, and call her back. It's a rare call from me, but I'm sick of all her messages.

"Finally," she shrills.

"I haven't had a lot of free time. And I sent you a text."

"What's it like over there? Is the weather nice?"

The sky's falling in because I haven't called, and we launch into the weather?

"It's sunny."

"Lots of handsome men, I bet."

It baffles me that I even allow our relationship to continue, considering how I shut her out. She's thick-skinned—that much, I do know about my mother— given my angry tirades when I was younger, followed by radio silence. Yet she insists on being in my life.

Hate is exhausting, and some days I just give in, like now, which isn't to say I forgive her. That will never happen.

I ogle a façade with carved angels and listen to my shallow mother babbling on about her neighbors.

"When are you returning?" she asks.

"My fare's booked for Monday."

"That's five days away."

My heart sinks. *Only five more days?*

"I bet you've seen some lovely shoes," she says. "I mean, you *are* in Italy."

"I haven't had a chance to shop."

"Really?"

She sounds so amazed I almost laugh.

"But you're in Italy."

"Some of us have to work, Mother."

"Mm, you sound agitated."

"I have to go." I end the call abruptly.

As always, I question my mother's need to connect with me, despite her obvious disinterest in me growing up and how she barely acknowledged me when I was forced to move in with her and my stepfather following my grandparents' death.

I know she had a stunted teenage life, and despite her tendency to talk endlessly about anything, she remains quiet about that time of her life. Her brother once hinted that she'd been touched inappropriately by a family member, but he didn't go into detail.

All I know about my mother is that she was a small-town girl who grew up quickly and ran away to the city, where she met my father at twenty. Her history starts there.

Her parents died when I was young, so I didn't know them that well, but I do recall my grandparents as being distant. They were seriously religious, cold, and strict. I preferred my dad's side of the family, noisy Irish Catholics into partying and who stepped into a church only for weddings, baptisms, and funerals.

To clear my mind, I click a link on my tablet and check out the art being auctioned later this evening. I remove a notebook from my bag and jot down a few items of interest, all the while pushing away bad vibes. Just hearing my mother's voice brings a heavy, dark mood. I must stop taking her calls.

Nestled in one of Rome's ritziest neighborhoods, the auction is being held in an opulent two-story villa. As I wait at the filigree gate under a towering canopy tree, enjoying a respite from the sweltering heat, I soak in the old-world ambiance of that elegant leafy avenue.

Once inside, I see a large crowd of art collectors. Here, it's all about unfussy elegance, a departure from the over-the-top "look at me, I'm different" patrons of the New York art scene.

Designer dresses. Gold everywhere. Handsome men in well-designed jackets.

I walk about looking at the works on offer, sipping Prosecco, while looking over my shoulder at Dylan. He leaves the woman he's glued to and comes over at last, just after I've arranged payment and details of delivery for my acquisitions.

"Nice choices," he says rather sweetly.

"I'm glad you approve."

His grin at my cool tone fades quickly as he leans in. "We have to go separate ways, you do realize?"

I nod. "I guess that means you're staying with Monica Bellucci's twin."

He smiles. "She hasn't invited me."

I roll my eyes. I'm annoyingly affected by him.

"You've been chatting to Freddie, I see," he says. "I've seen him around. He's loaded. Or he must be. He bought a Manet at an auction I was at for five million a few years back."

"So? Am I meant to jump up and down all over him like a happy penguin?"

He laughs. Even his humor is infuriatingly contagious as I squeeze my lips to suppress the curl. "He can be so lucky. I found your bouncing up and down this morning rather a delight."

I roll my eyes. "Now you're being lewd."

His lips curve. Dylan loves to joust. So do I.

"I'll catch you at the hotel later," he says. "Be sure to catch a cab straight back to the hotel."

During lunch earlier that day, after I questioned why he hadn't visited the vault so far, Dylan explained that Sophia would be the one to obtain the case tomorrow.

"The case?" I asked. "So you *do* know what it opens?"

"I have a hunch."

"Oh?" Questions kept sprouting up like weeds after a heavy rain. This not knowing about the key's purpose is starting to wear thin.

"You'll be remunerated. Can't tell you exactly how much but enough to see this to the end."

"To the end? Or my end?"

He threw me a "Don't be so melodramatic" look. "Let's just get to tomorrow." His penetrating gaze held. "In any case, if I wanted you dead, I wouldn't be here enjoying your beautiful baby blues, now would I?"

That experience at Capitoline Hill returns, the one where I was close to tumbling to my death. *Was he saving me? Or was he about to push me?*

"When exactly is this happening? I'm to be in Venice the day after tomorrow," I say.

"Early morning. Very early, in fact."

Twenty

I LEAVE THE AUCTION and find a cab, but since it's a perfect night, I get him to drop me off at Via del Corso for some window shopping. There are way too many people around for me to feel vulnerable, and after a few drinks, I'm tipsy and high on beauty.

For an art lover, Rome is what a candy store is to a sugar freak.

It's when I enter a back street on my way to the hotel that I sense a figure in my periphery. I steal a glance, and sure enough, it's that bearlike creep again.

I speed up then twist my foot but move on anyway despite a throbbing ache. My racing heart pushes me on, especially now that the heavyset man's gaining on me.

I'm regretting not taking a taxi. *What was I thinking?*

He's getting so close I hurry toward a main path where I see a crowd. With eyes glued to the ground to avoid stumbling, I run smack into a bulky figure in black and scream. The next few seconds are a blur as I push against his hard body.

He grabs my arms, and I try to wiggle out of his grip. "Let go of me," I cry.

The first thing I notice is his subtle rich-man cologne, then I peer up, expecting the worst as the man releases me, holds up his palms, and shakes his head. He's not the stalker, who now seems to have vanished.

"I'm sorry." My body slumps, and tears burn at the back of my eyes.

He shrugs and smiles. "No worries." And off he goes, an elegant man whom I was about to punch in the face.

With no time to stand around feeling silly, I continue to a busy little piazza. The stalker is nowhere to be seen, and I release a trapped breath. Maybe I imagined him. If only.

A ton of tourists are taking selfies, and for once, I almost feel like hugging them.

I sit on the edge of a fountain as welcome sprays of water cool me down. It's so humid that tension seeps out of my pores.

In a bid to find my location, I check my phone, but I'm too wound up to understand it. Most tourists speak English, and after I've asked a few, none can direct me to Piazza Navona, but an older man, a local, crooks his finger. "*Vieni,*" he says.

He's offering to show me the way.

"*Sì?*"

He nods and gestures for me to follow, so I do.

I keep looking behind me, and sure enough, the Hulk in black has returned. My heart jackhammers again as I move close to the Italian man. Lucky for me, we cross a main road, and it's back to noisy crowded streets. I'm too wound up to look behind me, so I stick with the throng instead.

I open my bag and give the man a ten-euro note. He shakes his head, but after a little coaxing, he takes it.

My hotel faces that busy square, and while it's noisy at night, I'm glad it's there.

As I scan the crowds, I can't see the man in black and take a deep, stilling breath. I step through the glass doors and see a security guard, whom I want to hug, but I smile at him instead.

"There's a tall, heavyset man in a black suit. Please don't let him know where I am if he comes in."

"*Non si preoccupi, signora*. I'm here all night. No one can pass."

After popping some ice on my ankle, I raid the bar fridge, which has been restocked following my last session. I sink into an armchair, down the gin in one gulp, and let out a big sigh.

As I slowly unwind, I stare at the window to see whether the man in black is out there. He's easy to spot. You would think they'd make them a little less obvious. But if he was sent to scare me, then it worked.

Two shots, and I'm finally breathing normally. I look at my phone, but there are no messages. Good. The less to think about the better.

I step out onto the balcony, and as garlic and herbal aromas come wafting in, I watch the crowds fill the place like the night's only begun despite it being midnight.

An hour or so later, I've managed to polish off the entire white liquor collection from the bar fridge. There wasn't much to begin with, and this is hardly the time to go on a health kick, so I set my sights on the scotch by Dylan's bedside.

The bed is smoothly made, folded in that inviting way that only hotel staff know, unlike my messy bed back home. I never make my bed. I just pull the comforter over me, generally after falling into it. Erik resented having to confront an unmade bed, staring at it like it was my fault the damn bed was in that state.

I'm too wound up to sleep, and it's nearly two, and there's no sign of Dylan. I can't say what disturbs me more: the fact that he might fall into danger or that he's fucking that pretty Italian.

Since when do I get jealous?

Since falling hard for an enigmatic man who's still like a stranger to me. That's when.

The worst part is I'm not sure if he's only keeping me close because he wants to kill me. And whenever I bring up being owed something from the vault, he goes quiet. My inner romantic likes to think he's into me just as much, but the realist doubts that. Dylan Hyde has an agenda, just like I have. Mine is to fall into money so I can rewrite my life. While he's so vague and evasive, I swear, I'm close to losing my mind trying to guess his motives and what he's thinking.

In between casing the piazza for the Hulk, I start to pace. I think about how Dylan held me last night while he slept. Normally, I need space, but it felt nice. I look over at his side of the bed and decide to raid his liquor.

Then I cross a line and open the drawer.

It's not a Bible staring back at me, as one finds in hotels back home, but a gun. I pick it up and look at it as though it's a rare sight. Shocked, I'm left gaping at the pistol like it might have fallen from a distant galaxy, when, much to my horror, in walks Dylan.

I jump back, holding the weapon.

He puts up his hands. "Hey. What are you doing?"

"What's this?" I ask.

"It's a Beretta. And why are you going through my things?" He sets down his satchel.

I take a deep breath and bury my head in my hands and want to cry. *How do I answer that?*

"I don't know anything about you, and I..."

"Decided to snoop," he says, finishing my sentence. His eyes burning a hole into my face, he removes the gun from my hand. "In my business, this is necessary."

"So you *are* part of some Russian crime syndicate?"

"And you might have murdered your husband," he returns just as sharply.

He strolls casually over to the sideboard and pours liquor into two glasses then turns and faces me.

Speechless, I take the glass from him. After draining the glass, I ask, "How do you know?"

"Because I've done my own snooping, and there were two things that came up."

"Two things?" I gulp.

He stares coolly into my eyes, like an accuser about to hang a noose around my neck. He turns his back to me and stares out the window in silence as he sips his drink.

"So, are you going to leave me hanging?"

The air's so heavy with tension that I can barely breathe.

He comes and stands close and stares into my eyes without blinking. Time stretches as his blinding gaze traps mine.

I search for a hint of something familiar in those blue eyes that suddenly look black under the dim lamplight. I've never met this man before. He feels dangerous, and my muscles tighten like they might snap.

"Tell me what you know!" I'm almost screaming.

"Keep your voice down," he says sharply.

Despite his sudden intensity, he remains unruffled. He keeps scrutinizing me like he's holding back on purpose to break me.

"Are you going to put me out of my fucking misery or not?" I say in a stressed-out whisper.

He releases an audible breath. "Tell me, did you murder your husband?"

I sigh with exasperation. "No. Of course not."

He nods slowly, and his mouth quirks into a faint grin like he's taking delight in my anguish.

"So, you've discovered I'm the prime suspect."

"Yes. I'm sleeping with a potential black widow. You wouldn't be my first."

I pick up a pillow and throw it at him. "I hate you. And don't call me that! I'm fucking innocent."

He picks up the pillow and sets it back on the bed, Mr. Smooth again. I want to kill him or scratch his eyes out. And what's worse, his grin's growing. The bastard's enjoying himself at my expense.

I gulp down my drink and stare into space. Broken, I'm too jaded to heap abuse at him. Then it occurs to me that there was more. "What's the other thing you discovered about me?"

"That you're casing me." He pushes me onto the bed.

I freeze. I grip my arms and stare up at him. Memories of Erik pushing me onto the bed come flooding back, and I start to tremble. "How?"

He gives me a long hard look. He's back to being dark and potentially dangerous.

"You left your laptop unattended."

When did I do that? I've been so careful since we've been sharing the same space. Or at least I thought I had.

It becomes a staring competition. All my former concerns about him fucking some pretty girl turn into teenage nonsense compared to this. We've just entered a space where only adults with an ax to grind play.

I get off the bed and place distance between us.

"How stupid of me." The meek reply betrays just how out of my comfort zone I've become.

"Tell me everything. All the details." He steps onto the balcony and lights a cigarette.

It's around three in the morning. The air offers a breath of comforting coolness. Below in the piazza, the crowds have thinned to groups of young men laughing and pushing each other, couples smooching, and street cleaners.

I turn my back to him so he can't read my face. Dylan doesn't miss much, I've discovered. "I'm *not* a black widow."

"I don't care about your husband. From the little you've told me, it sounds like he deserved it anyway."

My neck nearly whiplashes as I turn to stare into his eyes. They return the same intense scrutiny, only this time, I don't feel as intimidated.

Resigned to making a full confession, I take a deep breath. Describing my mission, I explain how a fake Monet turning up at Christie's, among other faked works, alerted the authorities, who've been keeping an eye on him ever since.

He draws back on his cigarette and frowns. "My name was attached to a Monet?"

Dylan's disturbed—or perhaps confused—expression surprises me.

"Your name as the last purchaser was on the provenance. I saw it."

"What exactly have you told them?"

"I've told them nothing. *As of yet.*"

At that last comment, his eyes trap mine again. I think he gets that suddenly I'm armed with more ammunition.

Am I now in danger because of it?

Or will this mean he'll keep his end of the bargain?

I shake my head. "How did you find out?"

He seems lost in thought again and takes a moment to answer. "I discovered it this morning. While you were in the shower, a message came up on your phone about reporting to the police."

Me and my long fucking showers.

"Why not expose me? When you had it right there in front of you with the Matisse," he asks.

"Because this has become fucking complicated, hasn't it? And you're forgetting that I killed someone..." I choke back tears. "To save you" pops out of my sob as I stand and turn away to hide my face.

He stands close, so close I can feel his breath on my neck.

Dylan turns me around and gives me a warm, lingering hug, and my tears pour out like I've sprung a leak from an emotional faucet, saturating his shirt.

I untangle from his hold, and he passes me a tissue.

"I'm not normally this emotional." I swallow back another sob.

He wears a sad smile. "Don't worry. I've seen worse." He strolls to his bottle and tops up our glasses then passes the tumbler to me.

I think I've fallen even deeper in love with him. My heart has suddenly made an appearance. I didn't think I had one. After my father's death, I buried it deep in this pit of bitterness and cynicism.

Why am I allowing myself to get so close?

Does he feel anything for me?

His body language would suggest that, but then he could be stringing me along.

Is that paranoia or intuition?

Naturally suspicious, I learned not to trust a long time ago, at the expense of possibilities. Paranoia sabotages. It hijacks the potential for happiness. That, I do know. But I also need to exercise some control here.

I fall into the armchair, wipe my face with a tissue, and ask, "So what now?"

He sits opposite me, crosses his legs, and returns to that smooth, devilishly handsome Brit wearing his signature half smile. "You tell me."

I sigh. "I was followed."

He nods slowly. "Same here."

"Oh? I'm surprised to see you back here, to be honest."

His eyes plow into mine again for one of those speechless conversations we seem to share. "I came back because I wanted to."

"And getting back to being followed," he adds, "I managed to lose the wanker. But we must watch our step."

"Then you should at least carry that pistol around."

"I carry a Beretta all the time," he says. "That's a spare."

"So that was really a gun in your pocket?" I smirk. "Here I was thinking you were happy to see me."

He laughs. "Both."

Dylan takes my hand, and I fall onto his lap.

We kiss, long and passionate, and I forget everything, including my name.

"Why don't we go to bed?" I say, unbuttoning my shirt slowly.

Wearing a smooth smile, he tilts his head. "That's the best idea you've had all night."

As I'm lying in his arms, waiting for my breath to return after he made me see stars not once but many times, I say, "I recorded it, you know."

He moves away from me. "What?"

"The conversation between you and Elliot regarding that fake Matisse."

Though it's dark, the lights filtering in from outside reveal his brow lowering. "And?"

"Well, I thought you should know that in the morning, if I'm not with you, I have instructed Jane to send that recording to interested parties."

He unravels from my arms and says nothing.

I play with my fingers. "I still don't know if I can trust you."

"I've noticed. Go to sleep. We've got a big day ahead."

"You're not going to run before I wake?"

"Not now."

Whether he would have run or not, I'll never know. At least I've got a trump card in this game of cat and mouse.

"It will trash your reputation as an art dealer," I reiterate.

"Go to sleep."

Twenty-One

WE BREAKFAST AT AN outdoor café, and though I'm looking over my shoulder a lot, I'm not as wound up as yesterday. I'm not hiding anything anymore. That's a big relief despite persistent questions about Dylan. They'll never stop coming, I sense. The man does not like talking about himself.

"Our stalker's getting his beauty sleep."

Dylan laughs. "He'll be back, I'm sure."

I shake my head. "How can you be so relaxed? I'm a nervous wreck."

"There's no point in stressing out." He sips his coffee like a man without a care in the world.

How the hell does he do that?

Mr. Super Cool again. Still, I can use some of his easy confidence, if that's what it is, given he's acting like we're about to visit a museum.

I wish.

"So what's happening with the key?" I ask.

"Mission accomplished." He dabs his mouth with a napkin.

"Huh?" My brow contracts.

He finishes his orange juice and asks the server for another round of coffee, to which I nod.

"And you were going to tell me when?"

He smiles. "That's such poor grammar."

I roll my eyes. "Oh, for fuck's sake. Pull your head out of your ass, will you?"

He laughs. "That's cute. If not impossible for even the most flexible yogi."

"Stop poking fun at Americanisms. I mean, I could go on about you being some tosser knobhead."

"I've been called worse."

"Tell me about the vault." Now he's annoying me, despite my desire to smile at his nonsensical evasiveness. "Where is it now?"

"The case is safe with Sophia. She visited the vault early this morning." He looks at his watch. "We're to meet in an hour for the exchange."

"The exchange?" I ask. "She's opened the case?"

"No. I instructed for the case to remain unopened."

"How do you know they didn't follow you to her place?"

He shakes his head. "There was no one around. We met inside the only Gothic church on the Vatican side of the Tiber so I could brief her."

He sips his coffee and signals to the waiter. "*Un Cognac, por favore.*" He looks at me, and I nod.

"Did she contact you? They might have intercepted the call."

"She had my burner phone number."

"What's inside the case? Aren't you curious? It could be a bomb."

He sniffs. "You've got a dark outlook on things."

"Hello, Russian mafia."

"Dimitri wasn't in the mafia."

"Well, that's a relief." As irritation builds, I roll my eyes.

"Don't worry. I'm certain there's something of high value. Otherwise, why follow us?"

"You tell me?" I hold his stare.

"This discourse is getting a little tired." His expression hardens as he gulps down his Cognac, and I feel a bite of tension again.

"So how will you retrieve the contents?" I ask.

"There's a tunnel. Sophia is to meet me in an hour."

My mouth curls. "Right. A real cloak-and-dagger scenario."

"It is, rather." He toys with his demitasse. "After that, I've arranged a boat. Along the Tiber."

"Oh?" I'm loving how I'm still in his plans.

He passes me a number. "That's my burner phone. Just in case."

"In case of what? Aren't I accompanying you?"

"I just said so, Mallory."

His abrasive tone makes me wince. Taking a deep breath, I remind myself that this is a tricky transaction that requires a steady mind.

"Where will the boat take us? I'm meant to be in Venice."

"We'll get to Umbria, or somewhere we can hire a car, and we'll drive."

That idea puts a smile on my face, easing the heavy anxiety shadowing me. The inclusion of "we" in all his plans cheers me right up.

We hail a cab in Via Del Banco di Santo Spirito, and in perfect Italian, Dylan gives directions.

There's no stalker to worry about, and I even take time to breathe, realizing how I've been almost hyperventilating since checking out of the hotel. Once we arrive at the other side of the river, he asks the driver to stop.

Just as I'm about to climb out, Dylan shakes his head. "Wait. Here."

Scanning his eyes, I ask, "What if you don't return?"

He huffs, clearly frustrated by my relentless if justified paranoia. "I'll be back soon."

Dylan then says something to the driver, and there we are, in a backstreet somewhere close to St. Peter's Square. I wonder where this tunnel is that he's referring to.

Five minutes or so later, though it feels a lot longer, he returns with an attaché case, and I sigh. My relief is such that when he's there in the taxi, I hug him.

He gives me a puzzled smile. "What's that for?"

"For returning, and..." I swallow a lump in my throat and feel prickling at the back of my eyes.

He tells the driver where to take us then regards me again. "And?"

I sigh. "For not being killed."

He places his arm around my shoulder, draws me close, and kisses the side of my head.

I have to swallow a flood of emotion as I point at the case. "That looks heavy. Do you really not know what's in it?"

It takes a moment before he responds with a subtle shake of the head. Yes, he's back to his inscrutable best, but I'm done trying to figure out whether he knew all along about this case. I sink into the seat and stare vacantly out the window before the driver drops us off by the bridge of the angels.

As we disembark, Dylan says, "The pier is just over there." He points at a jetty. "The boat hasn't arrived, though."

"Oh? Was it due now?" Just as I say that, a boat arrives.

"That's it. Good." Dylan points, cocking his head for us to hurry.

We move along swiftly under the canopy of shady sycamores that seem as ancient as Rome itself. Whether it's a bad omen or not, we pass a large gull digging his beak into the belly of a pigeon. My breath hitches at the murderous creature goring the helpless bird. With red-rimmed eyes, the predator sees us, wearing the satisfied look of a conqueror. Blood drips from his bent beak.

"Shit," I gasp.

Untouched by this Attenborough moment, Dylan takes me by the arm, and we hurry along.

Still haunted by the gory sight of avian cannibalism, I startle when, out of nowhere, a pair of men jump out of a black car. Before I know what's happening, they're grabbing at the case in Dylan's clutch.

It's early. At seven in the morning, no one's around.

I watch in terror. My heart's pounding, and my breath's stuck in my throat.

It's all so sudden as two heavyset men pounce on Dylan. One brandishes a gun, and a gasp of horror rumbles in my chest, which builds into a scream as I cover my mouth with my hand.

Grunts and growls from the skirmish before me deafen my cries. My senses are so acute I can smell the thugs' sweat fusing with cheap cologne.

Dylan kicks the gun away and then lands a king hit, sending the large man onto his knees, followed by relentless pummeling, while somehow managing to elbow the second man in the ribs just as the would-be assailant reaches for his gun.

I yell, "He's got a gun!"

I circle them, standing on the periphery and looking for an opportunity to help. It seems as though Dylan's winning, especially after he kicks the second weapon from the other man's hand.

With one eye on the gun and one on Dylan, who stumbles back from a sickening blow, I take a step in. Instincts are pulling me in two directions, one screaming for me to help while the other is telling me to run.

Just as I step in, Dylan knees the man who's on top of him in the groin and smashes into him. Crunching bones and agonized grunts echo through the air.

Each blow seems to reverberate through my body as I grip my arms.

While Dylan's on the ground, rolling around with one of the pair, who look almost like twins, the other writhes around clutching his gut.

Time stretches despite it being only a matter of minutes. The onslaught is merciless. I'm deafened by their gut-churning growls and blinded by shock and horror.

But then I notice the man on the ground reach for the case, and a sharp hit of adrenaline surges through me. I kick the case away and stomp on his hand.

"Get the case!" Dylan yells.

Just as I'm clutching the handle, the thug grabs me by the leg and drags me to the ground.

Things go blurry as my breasts scrape along cold concrete. Gulping back suffocating fear, I cry out.

Dylan, coming to my rescue, frees me from the heavy man's claws by punching him to the ground.

Amid this violent chaos, he yells, "Get the case. Run!" His voice, raw with urgency, slices through the air like a knife as Dylan points toward the boat, which is about a hundred yards away.

Every fiber of my being screams for me to stay and help, but the panic in his eyes acts like a shove forward.

I turn and bolt, clutching the case like my life depends on it.

Each step is weighed down by uncertainty, however, and my mind is heavy with concern for Dylan. But survival instincts impel me forward, nevertheless.

I hear gunfire and pause for a second, turn, and Dylan's still standing.

He'll make it. He has to, I tell myself.

Twenty-Two

DRENCHED IN SWEAT WITH a thundering heartbeat and my tongue hanging out, I charge onboard the boat, where I'm met by a pair of beefed-up men. *Can I trust them?*

Taking a steadying breath, I have little choice in the matter. It's either me here or back there, being shot at.

I point to where I've just come from, but the black car has gone, along with Dylan. I'm clutching the case so tightly my knuckles hurt. I even somehow managed to drag along my carry-on. How I did that remains a mystery, since everything became a blur from the moment I made a mad dash away from that gut-wrenching fight scene.

The skipper joins us and, looking a little concerned, touches his cheek. I imagine he's referring to how disheveled I appear.

He welcomes me, and still somewhat breathless, I explain, "My partner's been taken away by those men." I point at where they were.

He nods slowly, looking sympathetic, then takes a notebook out of his skipper's jacket. "You are talking about Dylan Hyde?"

"Yes. I believe he booked this boat to take us somewhere." I'm exasperated at how vague and desperate I sound.

"That's correct."

What's happened to Dylan? My heart's screaming louder than my thoughts.

He reads his notes. "You are his plus-one, I take it."

Okay. Plus-one. I suppose I can remain nameless.

Can I trust this man?

I have very little choice.

He looks over my shoulder, and a car has pulled up. The same two heavies I saw earlier are heading our way.

"Right. Yes. We need to go. Like, now," I say.

He leaves me there on the deck and starts the boat. I nearly stumble when one of the security guys takes my arm and guides me to a safe place.

A gun fires, and the boat takes off while the heavies are left standing on the jetty.

Where's Dylan? Is he dead?

One of the two men directs me down some steps to a tiny cabin. He hands me a bottle of water, and I thank him before taking a long, thirsty sip. My throat is so parched from anguish it's burning.

My heart races again. *What if Dylan's been murdered?*

I call his burner phone. No answer.

I'm experiencing claustrophobia in the windowless cabin and head up to talk to the skipper. I join him at the helm as he steers the vessel into the center of the river where, during happier times, I would be dazzled by the ancient bridge with the ballet of angels. Their intense expressions seem to mirror my frazzled emotions.

Here I am on this boat with three mysterious men, and we're going where exactly?

The sun's beating down on us, and my hairline is drenched from stress as we travel under the arched bridge.

"Where are we going?" I ask.

Turning the wheel, the skipper replies, "Orte."

One of the men joins us and points at something while speaking in rapid-fire Italian.

Looking over his shoulder, the driver says, "*Signora*, it is better that you go below and stay calm."

My eyebrows collide. "Stay calm? Why?" He accelerates, and I fall back, and the security guard grabs me before I fall.

"*Per favore*, go!" the skipper yells.

I look behind us and see a boat pursuing us.

My heart picks up speed like our boat as I head back down. Clutching a rail, I'm thrashed about and fall onto a bench.

I sit and bury my head. There's a shit show on acid in my brain, which ends with me at the bottom of the Tiber, tangled among relics of busted corpses.

It occurs to me that my phone is potentially being tracked. As though reading my thoughts, one of the guards enters, removes the phone from my hand, and destroys it.

I hear a gunshot, and my eyes bulge. The guard brandishes a gun and heads up.

We're moving at such a speed that I vomit all over my T-shirt. I'm a mess. I wipe my mouth with the clean part of my T-shirt then rummage through my bag for the pistol.

After I hear another shot, I decide to see what's happening. I feel vulnerable hidden away in there.

I sneak up the steps one by one until I can see the river. Clasping the rail tightly, I notice both guards are still standing. I start to breathe a little. At least there's no bloodshed.

Yet.

Another round of shots arrives, and I duck for cover. This time, the firing's coming from our side.

A few minutes later, just as I'm hyperventilating, there's nothing but silence. No yelling, no shooting.

Or has the gunfire deafened me?

The boat reverts to its normal speed, and now I'm hearing my heart thumping against my rib cage.

I return to my cabin and remove my filthy T-shirt, toss it into the bin, and change into the first thing I can find from my carry-on.

One of the guards knocks and enters. "All is good. They're gone."

"Who were they?" I'm in my bra, and he looks away as I shrug into a fresh T-shirt.

"Not sure, *signora*."

"The name's Mallory. And yours?"

"Pasquale," he replies. A gentle giant, it would seem. His brown eyes shine with that kind of reliable support you'd expect from an older brother.

"I can't breathe in here," I say.

He gestures for me to pass, and I climb to the upper deck, where his partner is on the phone.

Pasquale opens a fridge door and offers me a Coke. I take it. He removes a bottle for himself and one for the skipper.

When he returns, he sits by my side and wipes his face with a tissue.

"So what was that?" I ask.

He shrugs his large shoulders. "I cannot say. I imagine you have some enemies."

You think? Why didn't they see it to the brutal end?

The Coke helps, and as the sugar works its magic, despite residual tension, I'm finally breathing evenly again.

He offers me a cigarette, and I take it and then join the skipper.

"That was pretty intense," I say.

"*Si*. Your phone, I imagine, must have alerted them."

He steers toward an embankment. "We are nearly arrived."

"Are you a friend of Dylan's?" I ask.

"No. I was hired."

"And you brought security with guns?"

"Those were my instructions, *signora*."

"Mallory's the name."

"Okay." He smiles. "No worries. We are close."

Twenty-Three

I FIND MYSELF IN a mountain village, in one piece at least, but I'm frazzled too. My priority is a new phone, and after asking around by using hand language and poor Italian, I find a shop where a helpful young guy using broken English helps set the phone up.

There aren't too many hotels to choose from, but I take the first one I can find. I'm not expecting five stars, and it's clean.

After dumping my stuff on the bed, I strip out of my clothes and take a hot shower. Slowly, I come back to life, but only just. My heart's aching from not knowing what's happened to Dylan.

He can't call me either.

I think about how those men arrived in the black car.

Where was Dylan? Tied up in the back seat? Or dead?

I want to scream. There are too many unanswered questions, like who was behind that boat chase.

I stare at the case for the first time. The last thing I felt like doing on the boat was opening it. Now here I am with this coveted item, and I feel like throwing it against the wall.

Dylan's more important to me than this damn thing, despite it being responsible for so many deaths.

As I fumble around with the metal case, I soon discover it requires a key.

"Of course it does." I sigh with frustration.

And it looks as solid as an armed vehicle. I imagine it will need some heavy equipment to crack it open. It's heavy too.

I go to shake it when I decide that's not such a great idea, just in case it detonates. By now, my paranoid imagination is so full of blood-soaked fatalities, I could give Tarantino a run for his money.

Sitting on the edge of the bed, I stare into space. At least I'm no longer being pursued. That's a small mercy, despite my frozen spirit.

I want to cry but can't. My emotions are constipated, clogged by a ton of unanswered questions, fear, worry, and intense longing.

When I lost my father, I was plunged into this same dark, catatonic state. I wanted to cry but couldn't. Nothing could be worse than losing a father, but I'm in that dark space again anyhow.

I change into a pair of sneakers that have become my favorite footwear, something I would never have thought possible. But then I'm full of surprises, like falling madly in love with a man I'm meant to be casing and who might be lying at the bottom of the Tiber with all those decaying relics.

I try calling him again, but it rings out. Though I want to scream from sheer frustration, I grit my teeth instead.

The boat chase replays in my mind.

Why did they stop firing?

Was anyone killed?

Or were they just sent to scare me?

It's nine in the evening. The sky's putting on a show with a breathtaking turquoise-and-pink twilight as I sit outside a café, waiting for my pasta to arrive.

I'm not hungry, but I haven't eaten all day.

The hotel staff informed me there's a train that connects to another going to Venice, only a forty-five-minute taxi ride away. So I plan for that trip in the morning.

The air is crisp and awakening with a fragrant earthy scent.

The food arrives—lasagna. It smells delicious, and after managing to eat half a plate of food, I push the dish aside.

The waiter looks dismayed as he comes to remove my plate. "You don't like?"

"It was lovely. Just too much," I say. "Can I have another glass of wine?"

He nods. "*Subito, signora.*"

It's about time I enter the real world again, and I call Jane. "Hey."

"Hey, stranger. I've been trying to contact you," she says.

"I lost my phone." I sigh. "I'll be in Venice by midday tomorrow. The auction's later in the afternoon. Can you do me a favor and contact the FBI and tell them their report's on its way?"

"I will. They contacted me this morning, concerned you might have absconded, and were even considering sending someone."

I inwardly groan. That's all I need. "I'll contact them tonight."

"Do that, just as a formality. As I told them, you're back in a couple of days, and I'm sure you'll have more to report once you're here. Is Dylan there?"

"No. I'm in a mountain village somewhere outside of Rome. It's a long story, and I promise to tell you all about it."

"I look forward to it. You sound tired."

"I am. Anyway, I'll talk to you when I'm at the airport on my way back. Promise to send pics of the spoils from Venice."

She giggles. "That sounds cool. Take care of yourself, sweetie."

I can barely say goodbye as I end the call. The sound of a warm, familiar voice chokes me up.

The protective shield I've spent years fabricating has finally cracked.

This Italian trip has turned me into an emotional wreck. I forgot to pack that stoicism I've often relied on through tough times.

Could I have done things differently?

Would I have preferred never to have met Dylan?

Never to have experienced the best sex ever, not to mention our little adventures?

The long drives, quibbling over silly things like music choices and cultural quirks.

I've loved every minute, though I could've done without that murder scene on the yacht, that steep and winding coastal car chase, and yesterday.

What about Dylan? Would I have preferred never to have known him?

The answer is a resounding no. At least Dylan showed me that I had hot blood in my veins and what passion really felt like. For a while there, I started to believe I was that cold, heartless excuse for a woman that Erik accused me of being.

And now the man who's stolen my heart might be dead.

The question of whether he's still alive has turned into an earworm hounding me like tinnitus on crack.

Pushing endless pesky thoughts aside, I need to think about the morning and open my laptop to check for train times to Venice.

A woman shrouded in black, who looks like she's just stepped out of a fifties-era biblical movie, limps to my table and shows me her trembly, unwashed palm.

I've given a lot of cash to the beggars of Rome. Men too. Normally, my rule in New York is to give to female beggars only. Sexist, I know, but that was during my man-hating period.

Ignoring the sad creature before me is not an option. Her intense black eyes reveal a tragic story. As I reach into my backpack, the waiter shoos her away, but I lift my hand for her to wait then hand her a ten-euro bill.

Her wrinkled face lights up, and she bows and mutters her gratitude. After she shuffles off, I ask the waiter for a translation.

"She said that God will bless you with love, good health, and luck."

For some reason, that buoys me more than some platitude uttered by one of those late-night TV gurus with blindingly white teeth.

Twenty-Four

AFTER LEAVING THE SANTA Lucia terminal in Venice, I come face-to-face with Canale Grande, and my breath hitches as I gaze in wonder at a domed church rippling in the water. It's an image I've seen often in many famous works of art. And here I am standing before it.

There's a tussle for the Vaporetto, resulting in a long queue. As I look around for another option, a man approaches offering a water taxi, and I take it.

The heavy metal case, despite a few broken fingernails and improvising with tweezers and a nail file, remains stubbornly locked. I imagine I'll have to employ the help of someone discreet.

Something has to happen because I can't exactly take it on board a plane without knowing what lies within. Customs won't have a bit of that.

My flight home is booked for late tomorrow. The thought of that alone makes me jumpy. I somehow have to open the case, go to an auction, and visit a police station within six hours while quashing a barrage of emotions. My heart is snapping, but I need to keep moving forward. Standing still only makes me relive everything over and over, especially those special moments. I'm avoiding the darker bits.

All I see are Dylan's eyes on mine, showing me something about myself I never knew or never had validated—that I'm an attractive, intelligent being whom he liked to hold close.

Or was I manipulated?

If so, strange how I ended up with this weighty, sought-after case, which was the end game, after all.

Tears arrive unannounced. And here I was thinking I'd forgotten how to cry. Even beauty, something I once analyzed with an academic brain, makes me want to cry. I've become super sensitive.

Finally, we speed off in the boat taxi, and memories of the harrowing boat chase are triggered. But after a night of wallowing and thinking endlessly about Dylan, I refuse to fall into another slump.

I breathe in the salt air and cast my attention on the dazzling spectacle of the Grand Canal. It's like I've stepped into one of my art books. Curvaceous buildings. Domes. Façades painted in Art Nouveau. Guggenheim Museum. Balconies and arched bridges and gondoliers in striped T-shirts and caps, all of whom are singing their hearts out.

Spray from the water wakes me as the driver asks, "San Marco, *si*?"

Ten or so minutes later, after basking in the beauty of that water-bound city, we arrive at my destination.

The bliss of being there, however, is soon short-lived as that thorny question re-emerges: *Will those heavies find me?*

Why didn't they finish what they started on the boat?

After all, I had the case with me and hit men are known for their tenacity. Or so the movies tell us.

"*Siamo arrivati.*" The driver points at the sign, San Marco.

I pay him, and he helps with my bags. I show him the address of my hotel, and he directs me in broken English that I half understand. It's not easy focusing on what he's saying as the famous winged lion and the Doge's Palace catch my eye.

Suddenly, I'm at a theme park with only a dime to spend. I'm overwhelmed. Even a week wouldn't be enough in Venice. Pushing that frustrating thought aside, I drag my luggage along, grateful for the smooth path that soon changes as I enter one of the many cobbled alleyways.

If I thought Rome, which is on a grid, posed a nightmare for someone with poor navigational skills, then the labyrinthine network of Venetian alleyways is sure to challenge me. And it's difficult to concentrate when surrounded by photogenic sceneries of snaking canals, not to mention avenues of designer shops filled with nothing but temptation.

I spot a gondolier leaning against a wall smoking, and after I ask for directions, he points at an arched bridge.

Finally, I find my hotel, and once I've checked in, I change out of my sweaty clothes, have a quick shower, and as it's hot and humid, I slip into a cotton skirt and a loose blouse and tie my hair up.

It's two o'clock, and I'm starving. There are so many restaurants it's impossible to choose one. I head toward the Grand Canal and walk along the esplanade, passing the famous Hotel Danieli, and drool at its timeless beauty.

I settle for a restaurant close by, dining alfresco, of course, where I order pasta and salad. Soaking in the ambiance of the crowded esplanade, I see, farther ahead, hundreds of tourists spilling out of a cruise ship.

Venice is choking with tourists, and I fear for this magnificent city's future, as many locals understandably do. But then, I'm one of the many, and I need to be here. If not for the business of buying art, for the sake of my soul.

What a contrast to yesterday. Last night in that quaint mountain village, I cried so much I no longer identified as stoic. It wasn't just about Dylan or that day's drama but shit from my past, too, gushing out of me like pus from a fetid sore. I'd never bled so many tears before. Ever. By morning, I was raw with red, puffy eyes.

I've put that behind me, at least for now, because talk about the healing power of beauty, Venice in all her mind-boggling splendor has managed to put a smile on my face.

I know I need to report to a station, but I refuse to bring myself down again. After opening my laptop, I study the auction's catalog and make notes. Apart from masks, there are some well-rendered oils of Venice by unknowns. I think of the billionaire stockbroker client of Jane's who's obsessed with Venetian art and note paintings to bid on.

After polishing off my plate, I sip excellent wine and watch the show before me.

A male wearing a linen jacket grabs my attention. *Could it be?* Even his smooth, easy gait is familiar.

I call the waiter for the bill, but I can't wait. I can't let the man slip away into the crowd. "I'll be back," I say and leave him my phone.

I push through crowds, my breath close to hitching, when I spot him about to step onto a boat. I tap him on the shoulder, my heart in my mouth with anticipation. When he turns, I see a stranger.

My shoulders slump. "Sorry, I thought you were someone else."

I return to the table, inches shorter, pay my bill, and leave.

The queues for the Doge's Palace and San Marco's medieval basilica are so long I don't even bother. I'll return one day, I tell myself, and instead buy a silk dress, which is a perfect fit and so light and airy I almost feel naked. It's ideal for the humidity.

Now I need to find someone to open that case. *But how?*

Twenty-Five

It's seven in the evening, I'm in an apartment overlooking the canal, and the auction's about to begin.

A room full of masks put on a show, and I'm met by a bunch of twisted actors hanging on the walls. All the famous Carnivale characters are there, like the long-nosed Scaramouche and the delicate Pierrot.

The guide waxes lyrical, waving his hands like he knew the artist personally. Something I've encountered during hurried visits to museums throughout Italy is that there's this intense passion for art, expressed through their words and gestures.

Another message arrives from Sawyer, and I'm dragged down to reality again. I wonder how he got my temporary number and can only assume Jane gave it to him. That's what I hate about the digital world— you can't escape.

Pushing that dark thought aside, I enter the auction, bid aggressively, and win a collection of six masks along with four oils of the Canale Grande. As I'm paying for them and arranging delivery, a man taps me on the shoulder.

I turn, and he asks, "Mallory?"

Studying the short Italian man, I nod hesitantly. My shoulders tense, like I'm expecting him to pull out a pistol. He passes me a note. I take it and head to the bathroom.

My hands tremble as I unfold the note.

"Meet me at Danieli's. The concierge is expecting you. As am I." D.

My heart jackhammers like that teenager about to go on her first date with a boy she's been crushing on for ages.

He's alive. He's here.

As I stare into the mirror, I notice my cheeks have suddenly fired up.

After I finalize the paperwork for the art, I make a mad dash for the exit. Knocking into people, which is easy to do in the crowd, I can't get there quickly enough. Anticipation dripping down my arms, I remove a tissue from my bag and wipe my neck.

It suddenly occurs to me that I need to get the case and so I head to my hotel, which is close, first.

Once inside, I grab my belongings and the all-important case. I'm not sure what I'm expecting, but at least I'm prepared.

I pause for a breath.

What if it's a trick?

My heart races again as I start imagining all the things that could go wrong. I can't believe how emotionally raw I've become.

I try calling his burner, something I've done repeatedly, and wonder if burners can trace my call. I keep moving since I have no other choice in the matter.

Five minutes later, after pushing through crowds on the esplanade, I arrive at the glorious hotel and indulge in the decorative curves of Art Nouveau. My attention moves from ceiling to floor. It's like I've stepped into a storybook castle with flourishes of the Orient, ornate décor, and lush velvet surfaces.

Snapping out of my wow moment, I head straight for the desk. "I'm Mallory Storm, I—"

The manager nods before I can finish. "*Sí.*"

He signals for a staff member before a young man arrives, takes my luggage, and beckons for me to follow.

When we arrive at the second floor, he points at a carved wooden door. My legs tremble as I knock. Expecting the worst after everything I've been through, I'm close to fainting.

Dylan opens the door, and air trapped in my chest exits in an audible sigh. His face is bruised, which comes as no surprise, considering the battering he sustained. He takes my hand and draws me into the room before locking the door.

"Thank God. You're alive." I collapse into his arms.

He holds me for a moment, and his body softens slightly before he winces.

Dylan steps away. "I'm in a little pain, I'm afraid."

"You must be. My God." I shake my head as I struggle for words.

Dylan strolls to a bottle of whiskey sitting on a marble-topped side table, pours some into a pair of red crystal tumblers, and passes me one. He offers me a cigarette and then lights it before moving to the balustraded balcony.

"How did you manage to escape?" I join him on the balcony overlooking the seemingly endless body of water.

"It's a long story."

"Did you kill them?" I ask.

His nod is slight, like it's a difficult admission. "It was either them or me." He gulps down his drink and returns his attention inside. "I take it you have the case?" He points at my suitcase.

I stub out my cigarette while maintaining eye contact, looking for something more than a pat on the back.

He's become so remote I'm stressed again. "I take it that's why you're here?"

Silly question. *What am I expecting?*

"Well, yes." His mouth twitches into a strained smile.

"Tell me, did you know about the case all along? The key?"

He rubs his neck and winces. "This conversation's getting tiresome, Mallory."

"Have you seen someone?" I ask. "They have doctors here, I'm sure."

"I'm fine. Just a little sore. But I'll live." His smile is warmer this time.

I snap open my luggage and pull out the case. "I had to get rid of some of my clothes to fit this thing in. So at the very least, you owe me a new wardrobe."

He removes the metal case. "It's a little heavy. Again, well done." He strokes my cheek affectionately, and I become that young girl being complimented by someone she holds dear. The problem is I can't read Dylan.

Of course it's all about the case. I can't imagine he would come all this way just for me, but I need to know that those nights we made love meant something to him.

Am I a bad judge of body language? Perhaps he's just good at faking.

Women are better at faking sex than men, I remind myself.

Pushing that needy nonsense aside, I watch him reach into the inner pocket of his jacket and produce *the* key.

The key now figuratively, though originally, soaked in blood.

"I almost expect it to glow."

Dylan looks tired. His normally trimmed five-o'clock shadow is now a short beard with the odd gray hair. He's still the hottest man on this planet, especially with those deep-blue eyes that are even more pronounced against the blue sky.

I collapse into a velvet armchair and cover my face as tears swell up, threatening to burst into a sob. "I've been through hell. I ended up in this village..." I think about that crone-like woman. Maybe her blessing did come true.

He takes my hand and gives me a sad smile. "Yeah, well, it didn't go to plan. And I'm here by sheer force of luck."

After topping up his drink, he shows me the bottle, and I nod. We're both good drinkers, it would appear. Codependency has never looked so alluring, especially with someone like Dylan.

But is this a trap?

As suspicion percolates, I hold his stare, searching for some answer.

"What is it?" he asks.

"You're not going to try to have me murdered?"

A slow, enigmatic smile grows, and he shakes his head. "I think there's been enough killing for a while, wouldn't you say?"

I'm back to that borderline-panicked state again. While I'm not expecting him to push me onto the bed and show me how much he's missed me or worried about me, I wouldn't mind a little more of something.

What is that? I can't say.

But he's darker than I remember.

Or am I now seeing glimmers of the real man?

He still hasn't answered my question about the key.

"Did you know about this case all along? Is this some kind of mission? I mean, you need training to fight like that."

"I grew up in a rough neighborhood."

"So you've said."

"The less you know the better." He lights another cigarette.

"I think I preferred it when you were putting on an act," I say.

He stands close and strokes my cheek. "It wasn't an act, Mallory."

His scent—that complex mingling of pine, tension, and masculinity—reaches me. I draw him in. My hormones are on fire again.

This man has me eating out of his hand.

Turning away like he's trying to hide his feelings, he stands with his back to me, staring out at the final vestige of twilight. Dark streaks of blue mingle with turquoise and fiery reds, painting a watercolor background against a domed cathedral that looks like it's floating on water. Its rippling reflection looks like the famous Monet depicting that same scene.

"I came here for the case. Of course. But I came here for you too." He faces me again.

His gaze digs in deep, and my heart blooms again like a rose in the sun.

Pushing aside all these fluffy romantic feelings, I finally show some spine. "I have a lot of incriminating evidence against you. Like Elliot's forgeries, for example."

"For someone accused of killing her husband, I would have thought you'd want to stay as far away from the authorities as possible. And you wouldn't anyway." He touches his bruised jaw, moving it subtly before flinching. "I saw that look on your face after hearing about Elliot's grand plan for the art to return to the public, something only those passionate about the preservation of art can understand. You're one of us, Mallory."

Tears burn in my eyes. It's all too much for me, and I want to howl. But I suck it back and take a deep, steadying breath instead.

"Anyway, we're here. And I'm relieved, to be honest." He exhales.

"Not for a lack of drama. They chased the boat, you know, with guns firing," I say.

"Guns firing?" He frowns. "Was anyone hurt?"

"No. But their boat stalled. A bullet must have blown out the motor. There was no ball of fire. Sadly."

His head lurches back. "Why sadly?"

A nervous laugh exits my mouth. "Well, then I could have had the whole Hollywood treatment. You know, a testosterone-charged skirmish. Men bludgeoning each other and then a boat chase. The boat losing power is a bit of an anticlimax, wouldn't you say?"

He searches my face. "I'll take the anticlimax any day. Unlike Hollywood brawls, in real life, having one's face smashed in is far from fun."

Taking pity on him because his face is black-and-blue, I frown. "Are you sure you don't need a doctor?"

He shakes his head. "You're sure they didn't follow you here?"

"I haven't sensed anyone so far. And what about you? Are you being followed? How did you get here?"

"Like you, I haven't noticed anything. But I'm not hanging around to find out."

"Oh?" I ask.

"I'm leaving early in the morning for the Greek Islands. I've hired a yacht. Interested?"

What? Did I hear that right?

I frown. "I'm meant to be leaving for the States."

"Rewrite your life."

My brow aches as a million thoughts rush in like peak hour on the subway. My life in New York flashes before me. I don't have too many nice memories to linger over, just awful ones. Especially that dank, claustrophobic police station and Sawyer. My mother. And not much else. There's the shelter and Jane, but apart from those good souls, who else is there?

Can I leave all that behind?

I would become a fugitive. Or I could just buy a great lawyer from afar.

What of the FBI?

Good legal counsel can help me there too. I could argue I was being pressured about a crime I didn't commit and chose the chicken's way out. Besides, Sawyer's already convinced I did it. He's searching for anything to nail me to the wall despite my incessant pleas of innocence. As I kept telling that misogynistic detective, not all toxic relationships end in murder.

With money, I can at least get a decent lawyer. Maybe I can solve my problems while soaking under the Mediterranean sun. Money can do anything.

Buy love?

Is that what this is?

Dylan stringing me along under the pretense of love?

Despite ongoing questions about his character, I'm suddenly looking for reasons *not* to go.

Pleasure, of course, is winning over responsibility. I mean, I've been acting responsibly since my father's death, and look where that got me—a degree that pays little, an abusive marriage, and now I'm a murder suspect.

While this inner dialogue takes place, Dylan has the case in hand while gesturing for me to follow him into the bedroom. In spite of the old-world opulence and a balustraded balcony overlooking the shimmery canal, my attention gravitates to the metal case.

I watch with great anticipation, my pulse racing like the excitement of opening Christmas presents but on steroids, as Dylan sits on the bed and faces the case.

"We almost need a drum-roll," I say as light relief because I'm almost frothing at the mouth. "The shit storm we've been through for this case."

He peers up, and a tight smile forms.

"How can you be so darn calm?" I shake my head.

He shrugs. "I'm British."

"Shit-poor excuse." I gesture. "Come on. Do it, then. Open it."

He slides the key in, and after a bit of jiggling around, the case snaps open, and *voila*, it's filled to the brim with thick wads of euros.

My eyes widen. "How much is there, do you think?"

He rubs his bottom lip. "They're one-hundred and five-hundred-euro notes."

I lift one bundle of the larger notes. "There must be at least a hundred thousand euros here alone. No wonder the case was so heavy."

I point at a red-velvet drawstring bag. "What's in there?"

After reaching into the bag, he produces a white enamel-and-gold-crusted egg and lays it on the satin bedspread like there's a photo shoot for some collectibles magazine.

My jaw drops, and I point. "Is that what I think it is?"

"A Fabergé egg, no less."

"The goose who laid the golden egg. Holy shit." My eyes light up in wonder, and as I go to touch it, he stops me.

"I'm concerned it could come with a boobie trap."

"Oh." I frown. "Like, it might detonate?"

He scrapes his head and appears on edge. "Let's leave that for now."

I study him, sensing something more to his response.

"There's all of this, though." He points at the cash. "And half of it is yours."

I nod, lost in thought. I leave the mystery of the egg for a moment and say, "That's, like, around ten to fifteen million euros."

I fall onto the bed and laugh. He joins me, and we hold each other. I'm gentle this time, aware of his bruises.

As I soak in his warmth, his lips meet mine. Despite this fiery urge to tear his shirt off and feel him buried deep inside of me, I draw away to avoid causing him pain.

"Did you mean that earlier? About me rewriting my life? And with you?" I stumble around, searching for the right words as the thought of owning all that cash while traveling with the love of my life, who gets me—at least it feels that way—is slowly sinking in.

My hormones are throwing a party. *Who wouldn't want to tag along with a man like Dylan Hyde?*

He nods slowly as though the idea's growing on him. "I think we're good together."

"What happened to that man who changes his women as regularly as his sheets?"

"I don't change my sheets," he replies dryly.

"That's rather unhygienic."

"That's why hotel staff were invented."

I toss a cushion at him, and he catches it.

"Sleep on it. You can decide in the morning. Early, though. I'm leaving at eight. The yacht departs from Lido."

"How will I get a new identity? And won't they need my docs before I disembark?"

"You can stay on board while they're organized. And you're already in Europe, so they won't need to stamp your passport, I imagine. However, it would be safer to get that before you disembark."

"And this can be done in a short period?" My head spins with all kinds of scenarios while my dull-as-dishwater life back home flashes before me in monochrome.

He nods, short on detail as usual, but who cares?

I'll do anything to be with him. Even shed my identity and ditch my past. It's a crappy past.

I don't really need it anyway.

Twenty-Six

THE YACHT IS THERE waiting for us, and we're welcomed by Ron, the skipper, and three staff members aboard the large, gleaming vessel.

"How long will it take?" I ask as we place our bags in the cabin.

Dylan sets his laptop down. "Around thirty hours, all going well."

"You mean if we don't get swallowed by a wave or taken by pirates?"

He laughs. "I see you remembered to pack your paranoia."

I have good cause to be jumpy. I'm leaving my life behind, and the thought of the unknown is both terrifying and exhilarating. I'm also grappling with trust issues while trying to ascertain whether Dylan's legit. "It's best to be prepared."

"Ron tells me the conditions are perfect with a favorable weather forecast. Might even get a swim in." He unclips his carry-on suitcase and unpacks. He stores our precious cargo in a safe and sets the code.

"Do you know someone who can get my passport?" I ask.

"I do know someone."

I study him again. To my way of thinking, the only people who know about passport forgers reside in the dark corners of life.

I push that thought aside, given that I'm not exactly a model citizen considering how I'm already embracing my new status as a millionaire thanks to ill-gotten wealth.

"You've done this kind of thing before?"

"No. But I have my contacts."

In search of that elusive insight into this man's true intent, I scan his eyes. There's a lot about Dylan I don't know. But then, there's a lot about me he doesn't know.

We're lounging back sipping juice and eating olives, fresh crusty bread, and cheese.

"Who would have thought such simple food could be so delicious?" I say, munching another piece of bread. I think I've consumed almost half a loaf.

Stress might be bad for one's health, but it's great for shedding pounds.

Dylan is just as ravenous, it seems. "It's all about freshness. I could almost live on olives and fresh bread."

Wearing knee-length shorts, Dylan is bare chested and looks ripe and delicious, despite the yellow bruising on his rib cage. He must read my mind because he gives me one of those lingering bedroom smiles.

"What?" I ask.

"Just thinking how gorgeous you look in that bikini."

The warmth of the sun combined with his undressing stare makes my nipples tighten.

We've been sailing for three hours. It's afternoon, and instead of counting cash or discussing business, we're sunbathing and lounging about for a much-needed break. My body, mind, and spirit are pleased, especially after the past few days I've had.

"I think I'll take a dip first. It's boiling." He rises and tilts his head. "Coming?"

"But I've just eaten." I follow him anyway, dusting off breadcrumbs from my thighs, red from the sun, and crying out for some sunscreen.

"You haven't had a heavy meal," he says.

Though I can swim, as I look out at the endless stretch of water, doubt creeps in. This isn't exactly a swimming pool.

We climb down steps, and after walking around the large, impressive vessel with a shiny wood interior, we arrive at the lower deck, where we find towels, robes, and flip-flops.

"They've thought of everything," I say, impressed by how we've been catered for.

"It's top-of-the-line." He wears his signature half smile that dimples his cheek and makes him seem a little shy like he's going out of his way to avoid vanity. "Nothing but the best. That's my motto."

"If one can afford it."

"We can, Mallory."

Dylan's use of "we" again brings a smile to my face. It's hard to believe this is happening, but I'm happier than I've been for a long time. If ever.

He performs a perfect dive. Of course Dylan can swim like a pro. Everything about this man exudes effortlessness.

I dive in after him, and the coolness of the water steals my breath.

While floating on my back, I regard the sky, which is bluer in this region than back home. "This is fantastic."

Dylan floats by my side. "I think so. There's a pool for laps, but nothing beats the healing power of the sea."

"I hope there aren't any sharks."

"You've got more chance of being killed by the human variety."

We're now treading water and facing each other. That comment triggers memories of Polignano.

"I wonder why they haven't investigated Dimitri's murder?" I ask.

"They found the bodies."

I frown. "You know how?"

"I saw it on the news report online."

"When?"

"Yesterday," he says, unfazed as if he's talking about a football score.

"Why didn't you tell me?"

"I didn't feel like talking about it." He takes me into his arms and holds me. "I was more interested in fucking you than distressing you."

If he was trying to woo fear out of me, it worked.

"Come on. Let's get out," he says after squeezing my butt.

Though his racy affection manages to defuse a rise in emotion, that stomach knot has resurfaced.

I rub my hair dry while watching Dylan, with just a towel around his waist, counting money.

"How much is there, so far?" I ask.

"Ten million. And that's only a third of it."

Shaking my head, I sigh. "That's a lot of cash. And there's the egg. What are we to do with that?"

"What am *I* to do with that, you mean?" His cool response acts like a takedown. From attentive and personable to cold and remote, Dylan switches without warning.

As our eyes lock, a ton of thoughts enter my head as rapidly as a stadium fills with keen spectators.

"What did the reports say about the bodies?" I switch subjects to the crime that delivered this jaw-dropping bounty.

"They were discovered at the bottom of the sea, just as I thought. Sven obviously cleaned up the mess." His brow arches. "A diver found their anchored bodies."

He licks his finger and continues to flick through the notes, making a note on a pad as though this sudden finding is just fluff.

"How can you be so cool?"

Wearing reading glasses, he peers up from the table, which is covered in wads of cash. "Unless they find your fingerprints or have CCTV footage, then you have nothing to worry about."

"But won't they check some guest list for that night?"

"A guest list? Dimitri invited all kinds of untraceables."

"Untraceables?" I shake my head. "Are you all tainted in this scene?"

He looks up wearing a faint smile. "No more than you."

"I wasn't until I met you," I say under my breath.

Lost to counting money, he doesn't so much as flinch at that comment.

Dylan places the money in the safe, locks it, and then rising, stretches his arms. He drops the towel and changes into a pair of drawstring linen pants and a white shirt, then he slips into a pair of deck shoes, and I've forgotten what we were saying. He's so naturally handsome I'm lost for words.

"Come on. Let's have a pre-dinner drink, shall we?" He smiles. "It's a lovely evening, and I'm told that the calamari are to die for."

I change into a gypsy-style cotton skirt and a tank top. The night's warm, and nothing beats bare arms and feet on a summer night. Being out to sea in such a balmy, perfect night is feeding my soul, which, prior to this little adventure, was malnourished.

Dylan's right. I've got to quit stressing over things. But after almost a lifetime of being told to always have a plan, that's easier said than done. Without a plan going forward, I'm a nervous wreck, but then with one, I can't help wondering if I'm missing out on the fun, spur-of-the-moment stuff—like right now.

We make our way onto the main deck with its pristine white-leather furnishings. The first stars are sparkling in the turquoise twilight.

I stare at the heavens and shake my head in wonder, especially at how the sky bleeds into the dark-teal horizon.

"I wish this cruise could last forever." I sink into the comfortable leather armchair.

After that swim and warm shower, I feel cleansed and refreshed, and the Dimitri episode is filed away in the dark zone of my brain reserved for anxiety attacks.

Dylan passes me a drink he's just mixed at the well-stocked bar.

"Do you think that's a genuine Fabergé?"

He takes a moment to answer. "I can't imagine Dimitri would stash away a fake."

"What about provenance?"

His lips curl slightly like I've asked a naive question. Yes, the smile is patronizing and a little arrogant, but it becomes him nevertheless. Perfection is rather tedious when it comes to humans.

"I can't imagine provenance will be an issue."

"Of course. How silly of me."

His brow shifts slightly, then he smiles at my sarcasm.

I stretch out my legs. "I *am* coming with you, you realize."

"Let's just see how things travel, shall we?" He stubs out his cigarette in an ashtray and finishes his drink.

My eyebrows gather. "Are you suggesting I won't be able to get that promised passport?"

"That does enter into the equation, sure."

"You said you knew of someone." My blood pressure rises again since I've basically escaped my former life. *Or have I?* I've been AWOL for only two days. And yes, that message from Jane asking where I am caused me to question this crazy spur-of-the-moment decision to escape my life.

"Where are we going again?" I ask.

"Thira. It's part of Santorini. You'll love it." Reverting to not-a-care-in-the-world, Dylan's confusing me again, but I breathe it away.

"I have to trust" is a mantra that's perpetually rotating in my head. Only time will tell whether he's dangerous. Dylan so readily offering me half of the cash has aroused my suspicion.

Fifteen minutes later, dinner is served, and despite a glimmer of concern about the passport, I am famished. The calamari's tender like nothing I've ever tasted.

"You were right about the cook. This is delicious," I say.

"Isn't it?" He gives me a warm smile, and I'm putty again.

"Tell me about your family," I say, realizing we've never spoken about his life in London.

"Your brief didn't divulge?" He dabs his lips with a napkin.

I search Dylan's face for a hint of cynicism because he has a right to be pissed off, but he appears unaffected.

"My brief was minimal. Nothing about your background. Only that you're a hotshot dealer whose name's been consistently linked to forgeries."

Dylan's mood has dimmed. At least it's some response. The man shares emotion only when he's climaxing or viewing art. Anything else—including that blood-drenched scene on the yacht or the car chase—and Dylan's cool, calm, and collected attitude prevails.

I rattle the cage. "Why, Mr. Hyde, I can see you're a little ruffled."

He tops up my wine. "Why would you think that, now?" He cocks his head, and his signature half smile returns.

"Just that you looked a little shaken by that comment, that's all."

"No one likes to be spied on."

He's got a point there.

"So, do you have siblings?" I ask.

"I have a brother."

"Are you close?"

"No."

"Are you fighting or just different?"

"Different, I'd say." He takes a deep breath, which makes me wonder if there's a family issue there.

"Are your parents still alive?"

"My mother is. My father, I don't know nor care." He pushes his plate away and stretches out his legs.

"Oh, they're divorced?"

"They never married. He did a runner when I was young."

"You've never asked after him? Or gone looking for him?"

He pulls a face like I've suggested something preposterous. "Why would I do that?"

"He's your dad, I suppose."

"He was a sperm donor of sorts," he says.

"Oh, you're an IVF baby?"

"I'm forty-two, Mallory. I don't think it was a popular form of conception back then."

"He wasn't around even when you were a kid?"

Dylan shakes his head. "Single-mother upbringing. All I know is he's involved in petty crime. Someone who'd steal your grandmother's silver."

My eyes widen. "He did that to you?"

He tilts his head with a mock smile. "I'm being ironic. The last time I saw him, I was ten or something. He turned up late one night, looking for money. Not a nice man. As they say, you can choose your friends but not your family."

I nod slowly. *Boy, don't I know it.* "Do you still keep in touch with your mom?"

"I do. I bought her a nice cottage in Cornwall, and she's happy there with her garden."

"That sounds idyllic."

"What about your father?"

"My dad died when I was fifteen. That kind of broke my heart."

A hint of sympathy softens his eyes. "I'm sorry. How did he die?"

"My mother killed him."

His eyebrows rise. "How? And was she convicted?"

I shake my head. "There wasn't enough evidence. But she pushed him down the stairs."

"You saw it?" His frown deepens.

"Kind of." I toy with my glass as I think back on that scene. Only through hypnotherapy have I managed to relive it.

"What does that mean?"

"Though I blacked it out of my frontal lobe, it registered in my subconscious."

"Right." He looks puzzled. "Sheer speculation, then?"

"According to my mother, it is," I scoff.

"So you dreamt it, and one day, you woke up with that verdict?"

"Now you're sounding like her." I don't hide my annoyance. "I relived it after a few sessions of hypnotherapy. When my mother pushed my dad down the stairs, I stood behind them. I just had a dizzy spell and passed out. I remember it all." I gulp back my drink. This is not an easy conversation. "My mother hated my dad and always put him down, accusing him of hitting her. I never saw him raise a hand toward her. He was a good man. He was the one who made me breakfast and got me to school. And then one day, he was gone, and within a month, I had a new stepdad."

"I take it you didn't take a shine to him."

"I actually grew to like Mike. He was always kind to me. And I couldn't blame *him* for murdering my dad. Could I?" I smile tightly. "He was filthy rich. That's why my mother married him. What a cliché." I sniff. "We moved into a nice big McMansion in New Jersey."

Dylan pulled a face as though I'd described visiting hell. "Oh. Not nice."

"No. It was awful. I still remember the smell of new furniture. Plastic, artificial smells. Bad for your health, and my mother was bad for Mike's health because he didn't last either."

The crease on his brow deepens. "Oh? He died?"

I nod. "She poisoned him."

Dylan's jaw drops. "Goodness, your mother's sounding like the proverbial black widow. And the police?"

"He had a heart attack. Couldn't be proven."

"Then how do you know she poisoned him?"

I stare at my drink, reliving the crazy scenes the evening he died. One hour after dinner, poor Mike was frothing at the mouth.

"One night, my mother was drunk, and she pointed at her favorite book for dealing with problems. It was a book of herbs with the poisonous herbs section dog-eared."

"But it's pure speculation, surely. He had a heart attack."

"Mike was one of those health freaks. You know, clean living. He didn't drink. He wasn't overweight. He went to the gym regularly. His family couldn't understand it, as there were no heart issues in his family. But they accepted the doctor's final verdict and left it at that."

Lost in thought, Dylan lights a cigarette. I can only assume he's digesting the Hollywood domestic thriller that easily defines my family history.

"How did your husband die?" he asks.

"Heart attack."

His prolonged stare says it all.

"I know what you're thinking."

"Well, yes..." Dylan keeps looking at me as though I've suddenly grown a set of horns.

"Why are you looking at me like that?" I gulp back my drink.

"I'm just trying to establish whether you killed your husband."

I rise and walk to the barrier and gaze at the rippling sea. It is now night, and the sky has become a blanket of stars.

"I think my mother did it," I say quietly.

"Your mother?" He sounds baffled.

I nod. "I told her how Erik used to hit me, and she told me to leave him. Which I would have, but I didn't have a dime, and New York's tough without money."

"But your mother had money after the death of her rich husband."

"His family contested the will, and she hadn't been married long enough."

"So you were too poor to leave your husband?"

"You could say that. But I did try separating, and he just came back and found me and would knock me about. It was easier being there than not, despite his violence."

"I'm sorry." He pulls a sad smile. "Then why are the cops on your back?"

Picking at my nails, which are looking worse for wear after the week I've had, I shrug. "I guess I'm the obvious target. You know, battered wife and all that."

"You don't want to snitch on your mother. Is that it?" His brow creases again as he scans my face for answers.

I shake my head. "They'd never believe me. There's no evidence."

"Right. Well, you're in a ripe old pickle, aren't you?"

Dylan sounds so English I can't help but smile, despite the conversation turning the calamari into eels squiggling in my gut.

Twenty-Seven

IT'S MIDNIGHT, AND WE'RE on the highest deck, cloaked by night and a full moon. I'm feeling a little lightheaded as I lean against the railing.

The discussion reverted to the egg again, and Dylan went all mysterious and evasive on me, so I kept at him and drank more, and now he's dark on me.

I'm ten million euros richer, I remind myself, and that should be enough to keep me going for a while. I need to let it be. But I'm too inquisitive for my own good, as I sense there's more than Dylan's letting on, especially considering how he steers the topic away from the egg each time.

Suffocated by all these unanswered questions and with building paranoia, given that when I'm not in this man's arms, I have no idea who or what he is, I search for inner calm. Only, with the yacht rocking at my feet, my head is spinning.

Or is it the sheer drop, since we're so high up?

Dylan suggested we have a midnight drink, and while the moon, sea, and stars are putting on a spectacle, I'm on edge, literally, as I grip the railing. I'm too scared to let go because my legs are barely holding me up.

The reflecting moonbeam paints silvery waves below, lapping against the yacht. My head spins the more I look down.

Is it the bottomless expanse of the sea or something sinister lurking in the shadows? Or is it just my mind playing tricks?

Dylan joins me and stands very close. His breath on my neck sends a shiver through me.

I picture his pinched expression—like he'd just sucked on a lemon—after I asked about what happens next for us, or for me, specifically. His silence sliced through me like an icy blast.

Have I become a thorn in his side? A burden?

Pushing those thoughts aside, I remind myself it was Dylan who invited me along, but then he made a "keep your enemies closer" comment about something or other, and that keeps resurfacing, adding to this sudden fear.

He steps beside me. "Are you okay?" He strokes my arm.

I can't speak. His fingers unleash a jolt of electricity through my veins. Growing panic makes it more of a threat than a pleasure.

The line between what's real and paranoia has blurred, and my legs weaken as my body sways. I grip the railing for my life because if I let go, I sense he might push me over.

If he did, no one would know. He could just tell them I fell overboard while he slept or something equally plausible, and the crew are tucked away down below.

Another wave of dizziness washes over me, threatening to floor me. I have to look ahead, but the need to vomit is real.

Dylan grabs me. It's a strong clutch, not the gentle hold of a lover.

I sense danger and struggle in his arms because I can't tell if he's trying to help me or hurt me.

Clinging to the railing for dear life, I cry out while pushing him off me. "Are you trying to kill me?"

I somehow manage to run to the stairway, but then I slip over.

The next thing I know, Dylan's behind me, grabbing ahold of me as I squirm about the floor. I push him away. "Leave me alone!" I scream.

He lifts his palms in defense. "I'm only trying to help here. I think you've had too much to drink and—"

"No, I haven't. You're trying to hurt me." Tears stream down my face.

I see him for the first time. He looks worried, whether for himself or me, I can't say.

He helps me up. "Mallory, you're hallucinating. I would never try to harm you."

Yorgis, the cook, arrives on the scene. "Is everything okay? It's a little rough, I'm afraid. The wind's picked up."

While I can't talk because I feel too nauseated to speak, Dylan says something in Greek and then helps me to the cabin.

I run straight to the bathroom and vomit.

After I've cleaned up, I return to the bedroom, plonk down on the bed, and bury my face in my hands.

A memory of the night I had a similar reaction while at the Met enters my thoughts. As I stared down the stairs, Erik nudged me, and I had to grasp the banister to keep from slipping. After that experience, my heart rate accelerates whenever I'm somewhere high up.

When I related the Met incident to the shrink, he connected my acrophobia to witnessing my father tumble to his death, even if it registered only subconsciously, considering I'd passed out. That was a logical conclusion in some ways, but the question of whether Erik was trying to make me fall still haunts me, since we'd just argued. He'd been drinking, and I recall seeing in his eyes the same anger and frustration he got during a violent tirade.

Now I find myself just as confused. I can't tell whether Dylan wants me or whether he's stringing me along.

Am I being paranoid, or am I sensing something sinister?

I just wish I wasn't so damn attracted to him. My desire for this man has made me irrational. I mean, here I am, running away from my life. It's the kind of radical decision I would never dream of. I'm not a natural risk-taker, but yet I'm taking the biggest gamble of my life. *Hoping for what ,exactly—*A happily ever after with a man who makes me see stars one minute, and then the next makes me wonder if I'm to be one of his victims?

He joins me on the bed and strokes my head. I wonder why he has to be so tender. It confuses the crap out of me because I've seen that secretive, sizing-up gaze of his like he's trying to figure me out. Or maybe he's wondering what to do with me.

For now, his hands feel like a soothing balm as I sob warm tears.

I seem to have left my mask of indifference behind in Italy. More specifically, in Polignano.

Twenty-Eight

WE'VE BEEN MOORED AT Thira for a day now. Itching to feel solid ground under my feet again, I stare with longing at the dreamy island scene—charming white buildings, crystal-clear turquoise waves, and sun-kissed sandy shores. All are calling out to me.

A male visitor took photos for my passport in the morning, and then Dylan left with him. It's late afternoon, and I'm becoming increasingly fidgety. I keep telling myself that Dylan can't flee while the egg and cash are in the safe.

I'm still confused where Dylan's involved. Despite that, we made love before he left, and it felt very real. He's a man of few words, but as they say, actions speak louder, and he is a voracious lover and does things to me that no man has ever done. It's heart-pounding bliss. The more intense this adventure becomes, the more intense our passion.

Maybe Dylan's right—it *is* all in my imagination, and staring down from the heights of the top deck is what triggered my panic attack, just like it did in Rome.

I can believe nothing else because right now, my freedom is in his hands.

Erik often accused me of being irrational and said I liked to indulge the dark corners of my mind by thinking the worst of everything. Catastrophizing.

But maybe we can take only so much trauma in our lives before that line between safety and danger becomes unreadable. The drama back home is never far from my thoughts either.

Jane's a friend, and I'm sure she'll be worried about me. I couldn't care less about my mom or anyone else for that matter.

It's early evening when I spot Dylan strolling along the pier. I almost rush at him.

He opens his hands. "What's the matter?"

"I thought you'd never return."

Wearing a cute smile that makes me want to slap him, I can't tell if he's humoring me or genuinely sympathetic. *Who can tell with this man?*

"I was always going to return." His gaze locks onto mine.

My jaded side knows that it's the contents of the safe, not the contents of my heart, that have drawn him back. We enter the cabin, where my bags are packed and ready to go.

"It's hot." He wipes his brow.

Wearing a blue polo T-shirt, knee-length shorts, and yachting shoes, and sporting the tanned features that accentuate his blue eyes, Dylan Hyde is a man who can name his pretty girl.

I turn away and toss that thought aside. I have no idea what lies ahead for me, but I have two needs: to get off that boat and to crack that egg open. I know there's something inside because I've felt it rattle.

For some reason, Dylan's holding off, and I want to know why. Although he's claimed the egg since I've now become a millionaire, I can't exactly complain, yet curiosity has gotten the better of me.

We leave at last. The passport is in my hand, and I'm now Melanie Johnson.

"So, Melanie." Dylan stops and turns. "The hotel first?"

I nod with a bright smile. I've just passed the immigration check and had to use all my inner control to stop trembling, despite the chaotic scene in my brain that was almost making my head wobble. As it turned out, there was no need for any of that anxiety because my passport's rock-solid.

This new identity has freed me. I'm being given a second chance, and all the crap I left behind is a distant bad memory.

Dylan takes my bags like the gentleman he is.

What will this new life mean for us? I ask as I watch his arm muscles flex while lifting my case.

We make our way to the hotel, which is on the waterfront and close to where we disembarked. A five-star luxury hotel is just a sample of what awaits me. Buoyed by that thought, I smile. "This is perfect."

The whitewashed hotel with its azure shutters and cascading bougainvillea overlooks the Aegean Sea.

Ambling along and soaking up my freedom with the hot sun beating down, I can't stop smiling. A weight has been removed from me. I feel free.

I'm Melanie. A new chapter. A new me.

We enter our room, a blend of rustic charm and luxury in turquoise accents with watercolor scenes of the island on the walls, while air-conditioned comfort provides relief from the heat outside.

As I look around, I get this childish urge to bounce up and down on the queen-size bed. It's firm and comfortable, just as I like it.

I take a deep breath and release all the tension I've been carrying for the past few days.

The early-evening sun warms my face, and a garlic-rich aroma wafts onto the balcony, stimulating my appetite as I sit with my legs up, sipping a gin and tonic.

I'm surrounded by blues of every shade—rooftops, the sky, the ocean, and a glistening swimming pool, where I see myself sipping a cocktail in my new bikini.

"Dinner?" Dylan asks.

I nod. "Can we order here? I love it so much. Good choice, by the way."

He runs his thumb along his lower lip. "I think so." He then places the money—including my bag full of cash—into a safe.

A few minutes later, room service arrives with the menus, and I leave the ordering to Dylan.

Unable to stop smiling, I feel like dancing on the spot. I'm rich. I'm sharing a room with a hot guy, and I've never felt so good.

We've just eaten the freshest fish I think I've ever tasted along with a crisp white wine that got better by the glass. I stretch my arms like a sated cat. "When are we going to open the egg?"

He holds my stare and remains silent.

"We *are* going to open it, aren't we?" My brow tightens.

He saunters to the safe, removes the satchel, and splits the cash into two piles. "Take yours."

I stare at my future.

"It's all there. Ten million euros," he says.

That breaks the sudden tension, but the air has thickened between us.

"Keep it in the safe for now, I think."

He returns it to the safe. "Treat it with respect, Mal, because Europe's expensive."

He's talking like we're about to part, and I feel vulnerable again, which pisses me off. I hate how attached I've become.

"Are you about to leave me?" I'm a little drunk, and my fears come tumbling out.

He lights a cigarette and stands on the balcony. "I've got a buyer in Paris."

"I'd love to go," I say. "I've never seen Paris."

"It might be better if we aren't seen together for a while." He wears a tight smile.

"Why?" My eyebrows knit.

"Just until the dust settles."

"But the authorities wouldn't be aware of the vault contents, would they?"

He stubs out his cigarette. "Somebody must know something. Why else were we followed?"

I nod slowly. "There are lots of questions, I guess. Like why Stan would want to murder you." I stare him in the eyes but get nothing in return. "Can you trust this buyer in Paris?"

"He's an old friend. I'm not concerned."

"But won't he be curious about its origins?"

"He doesn't care about that kind of detail."

I study him. His answers are short and clipped.

"Then at least let's crack it open. Give me that satisfaction. I'm dying to see what's inside." A faint smile trembles on my lips. "Will you still want to see me after the dust settles?"

He strokes my cheek affectionately. "It's not my style to stick to one woman, but you've gotten under my skin a little, so I imagine I'll miss you."

The tenderness of his gaze makes my eyes prickle with tears. Trouble is I don't know if he's the good guy or the bad guy in this story.

I fall into his arms, and we make passionate love again.

We lie in bed in each other's arms, our hearts beating together. "Are you always this virile?"

"No. I'm lucky if I can fuck twice in a day. Let alone three times."

"Then you must like me." I hate how needy that sounds.

"Oh, that's undeniable." He squeezes me tighter. He's not just a great lover, but Dylan's always so tender afterward.

In our early days of marriage, before he became a tyrant, Erik would always roll over and sleep. No cuddling. Nothing. I should have guessed that marrying him would lead to loneliness. But I was young and stupid.

Poor excuse, I know.

Our eyes meet, and I read conflict in Dylan's eyes—a suggestion of confusion, some inner struggle. Maybe he does have feelings for me but doesn't know how to process them. Or maybe that's what I want to see.

Am I seeing a mirror of my emotions in his dark-blue gaze?

At least his isn't an empty gaze. I've witnessed enough vacant looks to know a deeply conflicted, complex man when I see one.

I want to ask a million versions of the same question. I want to hear him say he wants me, finds me beautiful, all those silly affirmations. Silly because the responses might only be appeasing bullshit. It will only piss him off if I hound him with soppy questions.

One thing I know: Dylan's a lone wolf, just like me. Maybe that's why we've connected.

I draw him in like I would a soul-healing elixir, his faded cologne and masculinity all rolled into one alluring scent. I draw energy from him. It's not just his seed that's entered me but also his soul.

I never thought this would happen to me. I hate how weak my desire for this man has made me. Now I understand why Emily Dickinson and Christina Rossetti, my favorite poets, poured their hearts and souls onto the page. While reading their poems as a teenager, I never thought I'd ever allow myself to fall so sick with love. Gripped by their visceral poetry, I promised myself never to let anyone control my inner world like that.

Fast-forward twenty years and here I am, lost in Dylan's mysterious wilderness.

Twenty-Nine

DYLAN'S SNORING. A TURNOFF normally, but not with him. I could probably even tolerate incontinence where he's involved.

I want to grow old with him.

As that pipe dream percolates, I toss and turn. Endless thoughts are keeping me awake.

Now that I've adopted a new name, I need to create a whole new profile. Change my hair. Maybe wear fake glasses and hats.

Dylan's comment that money goes fast reminds me that I need to invest. That was Erik's world, not mine. I recall all those dull friends of his talking about their portfolios at all those boring dinners.

Art is probably my best way forward, but then that will connect me to people I might have dealt with in the past. The art world can be small.

Or I could do the sensible thing and buy myself that lawyer I researched and return to my old life.

I rise and pad over to the balcony, where the moon stamps a silvery pathway along the sea. In the distance, bouzouki echoes along with the muffled sounds of laughter and revelry. They certainly love the night here.

I totally get that. There's something romantic about the night. I prefer it. One can hide in the dim light of night. All our flaws are less pronounced. Airbrushed.

Dylan's heavy breathing confirms he's out cold. The safe is still open, and without thinking about it, I remove the egg.

It's a solid piece, I find, as I lift the elliptical ornament out of the velvet box. The gold scroll digs into the pads of my fingers as I carefully handle the precious egg.

I'm in possession of something rare and considered lost—or so Dylan says. He's avoided talking about it, but I did get that much from him.

The panic attack on the yacht enters my thoughts. He had plenty of chances to kill me. A push is all it would have taken. But am I imagining that? I mean, he did grab me. But for what? To help me or something more sinister?

Erik used to accuse me of being paranoid. He suggested I take medication for it, even though I didn't dream up the black eyes he gave me.

In any case, Dylan could have run away by now. Instead, we're here together, and I'm in his arms while he strokes my hair and tells me how nice I feel.

Adrenaline's charging through me suddenly. I could run off with the egg, but my legs turn to concrete. My heart's in the driver's seat, insisting I remain put.

Clutching the egg with two hands, I place it on the small table by the window to take advantage of the light beaming in from the pool area. The egg sits up on its three golden legs, and the opaline enamel glistens in the moonlight like an amulet from some supernatural world.

I find a tiny latch, push down on it, and bingo, the egg splits open to reveal a lush blue-satin interior housing a miniature gold jewelry box.

I'm that child again. Wonder has reached fever pitch with such intricate delicacy arousing my senses. I'm reminded of humans at their best, a realization that started in Rome and continues to follow me. All the contemporary art I was brought up on, especially while studying at college, fades into meaninglessness after what I've witnessed, especially as I study this magnificent ornament as a child might her first doll or, more aptly, her first jewelry box.

The box must open, I decide, and needing more light, I go to the bathroom.

I soon discover a keyhole in the jewelry box and search for that key. I run my hands over the silky interior of the egg and find a hidden pocket. The little golden key falls into my fingers.

Using my nails, for the key is tiny, I try to fit it into its designated hole. It drops to the floor, and I get on my knees, crawling on the bathroom floor until I find it. This time, I take out my eyebrow tweezers and move the operation to a small stool with a towel beneath to catch the key. I can't have it falling into a drain.

After a few attempts, with sweat dripping down my shoulder blades, I open the box and remove a small red-velvet pouch.

I pull the drawstring, and dark-pink diamonds sparkle back at me. Against the velvet, they resemble a galaxy of jewels.

As I balance the weighty pouch on my palm, I try to count its contents. There are too many, and my heart starts to pound against my chest. They must be worth a fortune.

My attention returns to the contents of the jewelry box. In search of more surprises, I discover a ruby-encrusted gold heart.

I remove it and place it on my palm, the cool metal soon turning warm against my skin. It's a moment of magic, and I'm bewitched by its beauty.

"What are you doing?" comes from behind me, and I bury the heart in my grasp. That piece of jewelry has my name on it.

Dylan studies the opened egg.

I smile meekly. "Curiosity got the better of me. It's beyond splendid."

He stares at the opened jewelry box, where I have returned the pouch. After picking up the pouch, he opens it, and the anger on his face melts into surprise.

"That's a valuable cache you have there," I say.

He exhales loudly, and I've lost him to the wonder before him.

We leave the bathroom, and he places the pouch back in the jewelry box and closes the egg.

The gold heart digs into my palm. I return to the bathroom and place it in my makeup bag. That's my little gift. A good-luck charm.

After he's locked the safe, Dylan returns to bed and gulps some water. "What time is it?" he asks.

"It's three." I stand by the balcony, and the music from the streets floats in and is strangely comforting. Silence always amplifies my thoughts.

Back to his inscrutable best, Dylan's silence screams volumes at me, and now I'm that mischievous child, punished not by harsh words but by the uncertainty of what's to follow.

Thirty

I CAN'T SAY WHAT excites me more: that I'm off to Paris on a private jet or that Dylan is there by my side.

But it's the latter. I'd travel on a camel if it meant being with him. I don't know what changed his mind about my accompanying him, but our passion feels real.

With a spring in my step and wearing a dress that cost my former monthly wage, I'm so light-footed, even in my new Manolos, that I feel like I could fly. *Who said money can't buy happiness?*

In his cream slacks and loose-fitting white linen shirt flapping in the breeze, Dylan is all smiles too.

We've spent the past two days relaxing, drinking ouzo, and even dancing last night. Our stay at Thira has entered my most-cherished-moments' journal, not that such a diary exists.

We line up to have our documents checked, and Dylan, who seems attuned to my moods, gives me a reassuring smile. I need it. Getting used to the name Melanie Johnson and memorizing my new birth date has unnerved me. I must avoid slipping up. At least Melanie and Mallory sound similar.

Carrying the attaché case, Dylan goes through first.

I wonder why he insisted on taking all the cash, my portion included, but I push that thought aside, as I've already got enough to grapple with while getting a grasp of my new identity.

The man asks me to remove my shades and hat. I do so. He asks me to step in front of a machine that scans my face and body.

It's taking longer than Dylan's screening, and I stand there and wait. Meanwhile, Dylan has moved away. My pulse starts to race, with my fingernails digging into my sticky palms.

Why is this taking so long?

A man returns and says, "Madam, please come this way."

"What? Why? I'm on a flight and my..." I search for Dylan. He's gone. *What the hell?*

I'm not sure what to do. I want to run, but my legs have turned to wood.

I follow the man, who tells me to wait in a room. The room has no windows, and my life flashes before me.

TWO MONTHS LATER

Penelope Pinkman snaps shut her crimson Louis Vuitton bag. The woman is gilded in designer wear. Should everything go to plan, one day, I'll model myself on her.

"Mission accomplished." She smiles. "You're free."

I feel like kissing her. It's been a tough couple of months.

Following my extradition from Greece, I was led into a dark room, interrogated, and arrested. I told them very little, only that I feared for my freedom by returning home and being charged with a murder I did *not* commit. I told them about how Sawyer's hounding me had forced me into a corner.

Once on home soil, I sat in a smelly cell for two days and stewed with anger, my throat red-raw from screaming in frustration.

Maggie from the shelter came to my rescue and bailed me out. What a queen. I can never thank her enough.

Then the sheet of poisonous herbs torn out of my mother's precious book sprang to mind. I found it hard to believe the cops hadn't found it while searching for incriminating evidence. It wasn't exactly hidden.

The proof was right there, with my mother's fingerprints stamped all over it, no doubt.

Sawyer went pale reading the report that confirmed her DNA.

"Your fingerprints are on that sheet too," he said, looking almost hopeful. *Prick.* He was determined to nail me.

"Of course mine would be there," I argued. "I handled the piece of paper. I imagine you read all about my stepfather's sudden death. A serious health freak with no family history of heart problems."

"But why would your mother kill your husband? What was her motive?" he asked.

I shrugged. "She hated how Erik was abusing me. Since I thought Erik died of natural causes, I never drew a connection. And, I might add, snitching on a parent isn't exactly sitting well. But I'm left with little choice."

He stared me down with his cold, penetrating eyes. "I could charge you with wasting police time and preventing the course of justice."

I squared my shoulders. "As I just said, it never occurred to me. Until now. There's no way I'll rot in jail for a crime I did not commit."

Two months later, I'm sitting in my lawyer's plush office with a million-dollar view of the Hudson. "Not even a charge for traveling with a fake passport?"

She tidies a pile of papers. "That took a little more song and dance on my part. I handed them the psychological report. You've been through the wars and were faced with the threat of incarceration despite your innocence. I argued hard, and lucky for us, we had a merciful judge known to favor women in hard-to-prove cases."

"I'm so glad you were able to do this," I say.

Maggie and Jane lent me the money for the lawyer's considerable fee. Now I have to figure out how to repay them. Though, I have an idea.

She rises and straightens her designer sheath. The epitome of style, Penelope Pinkman is what success looks like in the right hands. None of that shopping-mall crap my mother favors. She won't need any of that where she's going. Orange was never her best color.

I'm free at last. And now I can focus on Dylan Hyde. He has my money, and I have something that could ruin him forever.

Thirty-One

Dylan

THE SEA POUNDS AGAINST the rugged cliff face as the howling wind soars through my hair, which is in need of a trim. Biting chill makes my eyes water, and for someone who's spent his adult life chasing the sun, my return to the UK is taking some acclimatizing.

My stay in Cornwall since returning two months ago has given me the distance I need to catch my breath. But there's more trouble in sight since I haven't fulfilled my mission.

Alec Valence has been called away, buying me more time. Given how sought-after the rare Fabergé egg is, I imagine he'll have no problem finding a buyer. As to whether they can pull it apart without damaging the rare antique, that remains to be seen. Whatever vital information he needed, apparently buried somewhere in the egg, is missing.

As he made no mention of the red diamonds, I can only assume Valence is unaware of their existence. That suits me fine, considering the death-defying mission he sent me on.

For now, I'm staying at my mother's cottage. My body can't take further battering, and while I'm not necessarily in danger, I can't ignore how Valence turned from a well-spoken and polite agent into someone more sinister.

"It's been opened," he'd said, holding the egg while scrutinizing me with alarming intensity, leaving me to question whether he was even with MI5.

When I took on the assignment to obtain the metal case, due diligence slipped by the wayside in that I was taken by the promise of cash rather than seeing his shiny badge.

I'm richer than I could have ever imagined. If only the mission had ended there. Much to my chagrin, now I'm in the firing line over the mysterious disappearance of this all-important token.

As I make my way to the cottage, I pick up kindling along the way. Violent overnight wind has left branches scattered all over the cobbled pathway, and there's nothing like a roaring fire at night.

One looks different in their own space. *Could it be the light or something more complicated, like uncomfortable memories?*

Speaking of mixed feelings, my brother, Julian, arrived a day ago for a visit. He rarely leaves London, but for some reason, he's here.

The gate squeaks as I push on it, and I make a mental note to oil it. The damn thing has been keeping me awake, along with nightmares. Killing rarely leaves one alone.

As I approach the side of the house, I place the wood in a box by the door then unlatch the door to my makeshift art studio—a former observatory in the backyard. Despite that short stint at art college quashing my creative drive, my urge to paint has reignited. On my first day of arrival, I pulled out a canvas and paints I'd had stored in boxes at my mother's and haven't stopped painting since.

I decide on a cup of tea before embarking on my latest seascape and head for the kitchen. My mother, who's at the table reading a magazine, peers up and smiles.

She can't stop thanking me for changing her life. Moving to Cornwall has meant the world to her. She was born in Penzance and always dreamt of returning to her birth home, but on a pension and living in a council flat, she found such a move impossible.

"How is it out there?" she asks.

"It's blowing a gale." I smooth back my hair with my hands.

"I imagine it will rain today." She holds up the teapot. "Tea, love?"

I nod.

My brother's on the phone in the other room. "Juls is up, I hear. I'm just going to do some painting." I balance the cup and saucer on my palm and head to my studio.

As I remove the cover from my painting, Julian enters and settles before my easel. Wearing a bespoke bright-red-check jacket, he looks more suited to a London nightspot than this sleepy fishing village.

"You're channeling Turner," he says, studying my painting.

"Maybe." Not in the mood for a catch-up, I keep it brief.

Thick-skinned, Julian ignores my disinterest and walks around the windowed room that looks out onto a veggie garden propagated by our mother, who's become a keen gardener. Though not technically a plant, mold was the only living organism in the crumbling London flat we all called home while I was growing up.

All our lives have changed dramatically since then. None more so than that of my brother, who likes to keep his wealth a secret.

"You haven't told me how you can afford all of this." Julian waves his hand in the air.

"I just ran into a few profitable sales." I keep it vague. There's no way I'm telling him about the contents of the Roman vault, though he does suspect something, I'm sure. My brother has a radar where money and crime are concerned. He's in the thick of it, after all.

"They've yet to find who was behind Dimitri's murder," he says as though reading my thoughts.

On a practice canvas, I test the color I've just mixed.

"You were there," he presses.

"Yep. As no doubt your informants have reported."

"Who was the woman?"

I take a moment to respond. At the thought of Mallory, my temperature rises. "Someone I connected with at an auction."

"In Matera, I know," he says, continuing to pace.

"Is there anything you don't know?" I snap.

Wearing a self-satisfied grin, he ignores that question.

"You did get that painting, I trust." I put down my brush and study him. "How much did it go for again?"

Our arrangement for nearly two decades involved me buying art for my brother's art dealership. In return, he financed my itinerant lifestyle traveling throughout Europe and living in five-star hotels.

What I didn't know, however, until Mallory apprised me of her mission, was that he was pumping out forgeries with my name attached, something I've yet to bring up, mainly out of respect for our mother, because it could turn ugly. Although we're no longer teenagers fighting over anything and everything, the war between us is now more mental than physical.

Julian itching for details of what happened on the yacht doesn't surprise me, however, since Dimitri was part of his inner sanctum.

But does my brother know about my and Alec Valence's mission?

I'm not about to ask. The less he knows, the better.

I should never have left that safe open in Thera. Silly me. Blame it on hot sex.

Mallory wasn't meant to be there either, but I couldn't follow through on Valence's demands to knock her off. Seeing her wide-eyed panic gleaming back at me, I just couldn't do it. The more humane option was arranging a piss-poor passport instead.

Two dark characters coming together make for an explosive connection. That much, I've learnt from this experience.

Murder for self-defense is one thing but not in cold blood.

She also saved my bloody life.

How could I do away with someone who'd risked their own life to save me?

I would have survived. That short training stint in the army served me well. The army is where I met Alec, who went on to become an MI5 agent. But that was a long time ago, and as I discovered one year into my training, at twenty-one, I was not suited to that macho world. How ironic, since I'm now embroiled in some heavy macho shit.

"How can you afford all of this?" Julian repeats.

"None of your fucking business." Using a palette knife, I mix blue with a hint of green.

As far as I know, Julian's ignorant of my mission to return the Fabergé egg unopened, and as a reward, I keep the case contents. Given my relationship with Dimitri as his art buyer, along with my former military training, I was Valence's perfect choice. I'm just surprised he hasn't mentioned the diamonds. But it's far from smooth sailing because if this mysterious object isn't soon found, my head could be on the chopping block.

Julian removes a canvas from a chair and takes a seat while tipping his head to assess one of my finished paintings. "It's not bad. Keep this up and I can sell those."

"Or make forgeries, you mean?"

"Don't flatter yourself. You're not that good."

I place the brush in a jar of solvent and walk off. It's pointless trying to work while he's around.

"Why are you palming off forgeries with my name attached?" I ask as we enter the kitchen.

He picks up his phone and scrolls through it.

"I repeat, why have my name on the provenance?"

He peers up from his glasses. "Must be someone else."

I roll my eyes. "Bollocks. I know that your international smuggling ring involves more than just fake art."

I push past him and head for the living room. It's the time of day for a hit of something stronger than tea.

A close affiliate of my brother from Scotland Yard, someone Julian met at a gay club years ago, is a dirty cop who also happens to be connected to Dimitri's dark world. Julian introduced me to the Russian ten years ago. I knew Dimitri was crooked, but as his art buyer, I managed to keep my hands clean. Until now.

My brother's whole successful-art-dealer front is just a cover for more nefarious activities, I've only recently learnt. In those loud, shiny Italian shoes and ostentatious designer jackets, he conveys the art dealer stereotype well enough.

Shrewd and detached, Julian views people for what they offer and nothing else. It started at sixteen. I suspect our father introduced him to a bunch of lowlifes, but Julian had the cunning and ruthlessness to make it work for him.

Now that I'm richer than ever, I can walk away from him. But how to do so presents a Herculean challenge, since Julian has this claustrophobic tendency to stick close.

As I sip a single malt, I gaze out the window, determined to make my last night here a restful one, despite Julian's presence.

Thirty-Two

Ariane Thornley, art collector and a member of London's elite, is all smiles and kisses. She looks even younger now than when I last saw her some years ago. The miracles of modern science.

"It's been too long," she says. "And look at you. You're even more handsome than ever. It's not fair."

I smile. "Blame it on a strict moisturizing regime."

Her brow tries to pull a frown. "Really?"

"No. Just kidding." I smile. "So, you're selling up?" I take a glass of champagne from the waiter's tray.

She nods. "I've decided to embrace my inner gypsy and travel the world on a liner."

I sip on the excellent champagne. "Won't you miss London?"

"I won't be short of a penny. I can always stay at Lovechildes in Knightsbridge. Caroline's a personal friend of mine."

"You've got an impressive collection, I must say. Even a Turner." I point at the catalog.

"It belonged to Mummy." Her blue eyes shine with warmth. "She purchased it in the forties. For a song, of course."

"Julian wants me to bid for the Renoir. I'm not sure if his budget extends to the Turner."

She scrutinizes me. "That Renoir holds a special place in my heart. I hope it's not going to some unworthy entity."

If only she knew.

"They're hardly living, breathing things, Ariane. And you do realize once you sell them, you no longer have control over which estate owns them."

She sighs. "I know. But they are living things for me. You of all people should know that."

I nod. She's right. Art does have this preternatural pull on me, like I can feel the artist's presence in the work.

Just as I'm about to speak, I see a woman with her back to me. It's her neck, the curve of her waist, and her long slender legs, exposed in a short skirt, that catch my eye.

Ariane touches my arm. "See you in there." She pauses. "I can do you a deal on the Turner."

Diverting my attention from the blonde's backside, I return my attention to Ariane. "Oh?"

"How's ten sound?"

I nod slowly. "You would sell it for so little when you might at least double that?"

She strokes my cheek. "I have a soft spot for you, Dylan. You gave me my first orgasm, so I think I owe you."

My eyebrows rise sharply. Ariane's always been refreshingly open about subjects that would make some recoil, but I'm still gobsmacked. "Oh?"

She laughs. "Now you're blushing. Am I being boorish?"

"No." I smile. "I'm interested in the Turner, though."

"On one proviso," she says.

"What's that?"

"Dinner."

My forehead contracts.

She chuckles. "Don't worry. Nothing untoward. I've closed shop down there." She tips her head downwards. "I'd like to spend some time with you and talk about the fun times we shared. We had fun, didn't we?"

I nod. I did enjoy those times, despite the ups and downs of being an art student with no life plan.

"It was fun," I add. "And I'd love to have dinner. Let's make it a few dinners, whenever you're in town. I always enjoyed our conversations."

"Then it's a deal. I'll red-dot it, shall I?" she asks.

"Please do."

I make my way into the ballroom and am immediately dazzled by the quality of art on show. I stand before the Renoir, a portrait of a woman, that Julian has asked me to bid on.

The room is filled with familiar faces. Over the years, we've moved in the same circles. The true connoisseurs stand out, for they're the ones who can discuss the virtues of a painting for hours. With the event being invite only, Ariane has weeded out new wealth. Elitism notwithstanding, I do understand her need to ensure safe passage for these masterpieces.

I can't help but wonder what my brother has in store for the Renoir I'm about to bid on. The only reason I agreed to be there on his behalf was to see the collection Ariane had kept locked away in a vault all these years.

"She's quite the Peggy Guggenheim," someone says over my shoulder.

I turn and almost drop my drink. Mallory stands before me, wearing a smile that doesn't make it to her eyes. I'm left speechless as indescribable emotion steals my tongue. I expected her to be locked up by now.

"I thought I might run into you," she says, almost in a mocking tone.

Our eyes lock, and her smile fades. I see struggle, anger, and questions.

She's changed. Her hair is longer and more natural. She's even more beautiful.

"Can we go somewhere to talk?" Understandable as it is, I can see I'm in for a grilling.

"Show the way, then." Tapping my arm, Mallory adds, "And don't even think of running off."

I tilt my head. "I wouldn't dream of it."

Her eye roll makes me chuckle, albeit nervously. Yes, I had that coming, plus more. Even my heart stopped for a minute. Now I'm scrambling for excuses. I mean, I can't exactly confess to having her passport made by an amateur on purpose.

When we're outside, I offer her a cigarette, but she declines. "I've been searching for you on the internet."

"Have you really?" she asks, dripping in sarcasm.

"I've got your money. I invested it. It's doing well."

She cocks her head. She's not buying it. I wouldn't either, but the last thing I need is a scene.

Her frosty reception has me searching for words. "When the authorities led you away, I had to run. I couldn't hang around. There was too much to lose."

Her lips form a tight line. "You set me up, didn't you?"

I shake my head. I hope she can't see through me, because it's a lie.

How do I explain that I had to, for her own safety, given there's a price on her head?

She was safer back in the States than she would have been tagging along with me.

Only, now that she's here, danger won't be far away given Valence's determination to find that missing part, putting me in a real bind. Because if I warn her, I'll incriminate myself by admitting that I knew about the key all along.

The ring of a bell cuts through the sudden tension, and I welcome the interruption. "I must go in. I'm bidding for the Renoir."

"Of course you are." Mallory returns one of her cool smiles.

"We will catch up after. Yes?" I follow her in.

"That's why I'm here." Her cool gaze holds mine. "To get what's mine."

"How did you wangle this?" I ask as we step into the crowded ballroom that smells like the Harrods perfume counter. "It's an invite-only event."

"I have my ways." She's so cold I feel a blast of ice.

I return a warm smile, if only to try to melt some of the tension.

She turns away and casts her attention on the painting about to be auctioned.

Despite her less-than-friendly manner, I persist. "Are you bidding for something?"

"Jane asked me to look out for anything under the million mark, but there's nothing that takes my fancy."

"How did the Italian acquisitions go?"

"Made a killing for the gallery," she says, maintaining a note of disinterest. "She wants me to head off to Italy again."

"Oh? And are the FBI in on this one?" I tilt my head.

She pulls a mock smile as though responding to a weak joke.

After that, the bids come in furiously for the Renoir, but I manage to win at twenty million.

"For Elliot?" Mallory keeps looking at me as though I'm in cahoots with Lucifer.

"No." As I've gotten what I came for, I ask, "A drink?"

After another staring contest, she nods. "I'll just step outside and wait in the courtyard. And don't you dare try to run. I've got something so incriminating that your pretty ass won't stand a chance."

I frown and smile at the same time. "It's not that pretty, is it?"

Mallory's lips curve slightly before drawing a straight line. "Trust me. What I've got in my possession will wipe that smirk from your ugly face."

"You remembered to pack your compliments." Though I'm pretending to be unaffected, she's got my total attention. I sense she's talking about this mysterious missing item Valence is sweating over, but I don't understand how it could incriminate me. "I'll be there. Promise."

"Just like you promised to take me to Paris on a private jet?" She snickers. "You're full of shit. If you didn't have something of mine, I would have reported you two months ago, and right now, that head that you so admire would need a visit to a plastic surgeon."

A vein in my temple starts to throb. Here comes more drama. It seems to follow me.

Changing tacks, I take her hand, the warmth of which contradicts her coldness. "I'm glad to see you."

That's strangely true, which only sends me hurtling towards a wall again, because what am I to tell her?

"I'll be there, waiting." She points at the courtyard. "As I just said, don't even think of fucking off."

I wear a thin smile. "I'll see you in a minute, then."

And off she glides, looking even more desirable than ever. I take a deep breath. What is it about Mallory that makes my pulse race: the danger that follows her or my libido waking up after a two-month hiatus?

Whatever the case, I'm about to find out. If that involves a little rough-and-tumble in the bedroom, well, then, all the better.

Or all the worse?

I seem to lose my mind around her. That much, I do know.

Thirty-Three

Mallory

DYLAN MEETS ME IN the courtyard as promised, and off we go in silence to the main road and hail a cab.

Cold sweat makes me shiver as I sit next to him. At least the spacious seating in the taxi offers distance between us. With heightened anxiety levels affecting my ability to think straight, I do my best to look ahead and not at him. Because any minute, I might just lose it.

For the past couple of months, I've fantasized about scratching his eyes out. Even killing him. But I've had enough dealings with the law to last me a lifetime, and I still love the slippery douche. Talk about self-sabotage.

How can I still be attracted to him after all that he's done to me?

But as I sit there, his cologne wafts over, and smoldering desire and seething hatred jostle for space.

I leave him to direct the driver. It's better that we take this discussion somewhere alone, because I feel like I'll erupt any minute.

Stealing the odd glance, Dylan remains quiet. I imagine he's cooking up all kinds of bullshit excuses for leaving me in Greece.

The cab drops us in an alleyway in Soho, which happens to be close to my hotel.

Once we're inside the bar, Dylan asks, "What will it be?"

"Your ugly head on a platter," I say.

He laughs. "I can see we're in for a fun evening."

I squeeze my lips together because he's back to swinging his dick. "A gin and tonic. Make it a double."

Dylan strolls to the bar. Even his gait is sexy. I want to make him ugly somehow and to remain on point and not waver like some hormone-drunk teenager dying to get laid.

It wasn't hard to find him. I just searched for the latest season of private auctions and discovered Ariane Thornley's stellar event, which came with an invite-only and no-riffraff caveat, which made me smile. I had to prove that I wasn't representing some tacky New York arthouse servicing tech billionaires, not an easy feat. Jane even suggested I let it go, but I was too invested in finding Dylan. After a little digging, I pumped a fist upon discovering Artly had a Rothschild on its books.

So here I am, about to share a drink with a man who's stolen everything from me, reason included. Just smelling him is turning me into a puddle of want. But I stifle that bodily response and instead stare daggers at him casually walking back with our drinks.

After he sets down the glasses and gets comfortable, I say, "You do realize I'm not letting you out of my sight until I get that money?" I tap my glass with my new nails—little weapons at the ends of my fingers. I had them attached before leaving New York for London.

"Indubitably." His very kissable mouth curls slowly at one end.

If he wasn't so fucking gorgeous, I would describe him as on the sly side. I reflect on our intimate moments and those long conversations we shared about life and art. There's a good guy in there, I sense.

Or is he the best actor the world has seen?

He had plenty of opportunities to kill me, something I've thought about a lot.

Why didn't he?

There's the night on the ship, which I dismissed as a panic attack and not my first.

Was it that?

He saved me from those men in Positano. If Dylan wanted me gone, he wouldn't have saved me.

Or was he scared I'd talk?

I want to scream, it's all so darn confusing. I need answers.

After a long, tense silence, Dylan pulls a tight smile. "I take it you weren't convicted?"

Looking downward, I play with the coaster. "No." I study his face for signs of disappointment, given that my being locked away would serve him well.

"Not even for traveling with a fake passport?" He frowns, looking surprised.

"Isn't that what we were talking about?" I ask. "I bought one of the best lawyers in New York."

"And the whole poisoning-husband thing?"

I take a moment. "That was my mother."

"Huh?" Dylan's eyebrows rise.

I remain quiet.

"How?" he presses.

I huff. He clearly won't leave this alone, so I give him what I gave that smelly cop. "She killed husband number two the same way. It's not such a stretch to imagine her knocking off my husband."

"She knew he was hurting you?" Dylan asks. It's the most animated he's been. His cool demeanor has switched to shock.

"Uh-huh."

Silence follows as he continues to search my face for further explanation.

"Why are you looking at me like that?" I ask.

"You're not at all upset? You're as cool as a cucumber."

"I've had a good teacher, Mr. Inscrutable."

His frown fades. "It's the English way, isn't it?"

"I've heard that excuse one time too often." Okay, enough of this chitchat shit.

A surge of emotion finally surfaces. "You blindsided me." My throat thickens from a growing sob. "I was blinded by your fucking lies." I suck back the tears. There's no way he's going to see my vulnerability. I refuse to empower him.

My hand tightens into a fist. I'd love to punch him in that handsome face. He looks even better. Asshole.

"Maybe you're blinded by your own lies, Mallory." He traps me in a staring competition.

I turn my attention to the Tiffany lamps dotted about the dimly lit bar. "I'm innocent. Always have been. I'm not blinded by any lies. I've been honest all along."

His head draws back. "Oh? Like pretending to be an art buyer when all along you were spying on me?"

I roll my eyes. My mouth trembles as I gulp down my drink. I'm lost for a response.

He rises. "Another?"

I should storm out but not until I make my final winning shot. My checkmate moment. Taking a deep breath, I nod.

While at the bar, I notice a couple of women giving him the eye, and he returns a smile.

That makes me even angrier. I hate how easily he's taking this. No apology, nothing, whereas I'm having to take breaths just to douse this roaring firestorm within. I'm dying to yell at him.

He returns with our drinks, and I glare at him. If I can't use words, I can at least hate him with my eyes.

"What?" He smiles. He's loving this. Dylan loves riling me. He even admitted once that seeing me provoked made him hard.

Is he hard now?

I push that useless thought aside. Maybe I can take my anger out on him with rough sex and bite his dick. That thought brings a grin to my face.

"Why the smirk suddenly?" he asks.

"I'm just wondering whether to blow you or kick you in the balls."

He laughs. "Oh, there's no contest there. You've got the nicest lips I've ever experienced."

Reverting to business, I say, "I'm here to get what's mine."

"So you've said." He swallows a mouthful of beer.

"I also have something interesting to show you. I brought it along as insurance."

"Oh?" He tilts his head. "Insurance?"

"You owe me at least ten million euros from the last count. And then there are those rare diamonds. I think I deserve a cut of those, too, don't you? After all, without me, you wouldn't be here."

He wipes his mouth with a napkin. "I mentioned the money earlier."

"And the rare diamonds?" I ask. "Had you played Mr. Nice, I would have been happy with the money. But you had no intention of ever splitting it with me. It was just one big ruse."

For the first time all night, his manner turns deadly serious. "I did what I had to do to protect you. There are some pretty heavy actors involved in this story."

"So you *did* set me up, then." I gulp back tears. "It was a fucking shit show in Greece. I was handcuffed, left in a windowless room without water for hours, and sent back home like a common criminal, where I was locked up for two days." My voice cracks as suppressed anger bursts at the seams like a gut trapped in a corset about to snap.

I point at him. "You arranged it, you son of a bitch." Rage has finally made a show. "To get rid of me."

He looks around at patrons who are staring at our table. "Keep your voice down." He huffs audibly. I can see I'm finally challenging him.

"It's not what you think. And I agree, we do have serious business to discuss but *not* here."

"Then let's go back to my dingy hotel, shall we?" I go to rise. "Which doesn't mean I'm going to let you fuck me."

He smiles apologetically at an older couple at the table close by.

I almost laugh. He's so anal. I couldn't give a shit what people think. Not anymore. I'm a free woman. A rich one at that.

At least, I will be after tonight.

Thirty-Four

Dylan

WE'VE JUST WALKED THROUGH the door to her hotel room when Mallory turns around and slaps me with such force that the sting vibrates through my jaw.

I touch my cheek. "I guess I had that coming."

"That's for all the shit you put me through and for fucking with my head." Her voice trembles.

I take her in my arms, and her body softens into mine before she pushes me away. "Don't!"

I open my hands in defense. "Sorry. I just thought..."

"What?" Her eyes are wide and angry.

After taking a few steps away, I pull out my phone, open an app, and show her an investment account I set up. It wasn't technically for Mallory, but she needn't know that. And she did earn it. The diamonds are another story, but I'm not about to stoke the fire, given the wild look in her eyes.

"There it is," I say. "I can have it transferred by morning."

She stares at the ten-million-pound balance and then walks over to the bar fridge. "That means I can afford to raid this."

I grin. "Good to see old habits die hard."

She pauses and, wearing a frown, studies me, ignoring my weak attempt at banter. "Am I still in danger?"

"Not from me." I settle down onto the couch that smells of disinfectant.

"Then why do I get this sense I'm being followed? And this was too easy. I thought you'd at least try to ignore me."

I shake my head. "You like to see the worst in people, don't you?"

"Easy to do when you've been screwed. And you fucking screwed me."

"Well..." I smile. "You seemed to enjoy it."

She throws a pillow at me. "I hate you."

My head draws back. "That's a little harsh."

She sighs, sounding frustrated.

I get it. She wants to tear my eyes out. Understandable. But I'm not going to tell her everything either. She'll get her cash, and then, well, hopefully, I can convince her to leave.

"What are you drinking?" she asks, sounding resigned to at least being civil toward me.

"Just water."

I am curious about her so-called insurance. That puzzles me. I'm wondering if that's the missing token that's got Valence threatening to knock me off.

I've got my own trump card—attraction. Mallory's considerable sexual appetite and her sudden disdain towards me is like that of a junky pretending they don't need drugs.

She passes me a bottle of water. "Are you on a health kick?"

Welcoming the change of subject, I cross my legs. "Nope."

Mallory stares at me. "You do look different."

"More gray hair." I touch my temples.

"Not that. You look healthier."

I gulp back some water. "Must be the sea air. I've been staying with my mother in a quaint seaside village."

"Oh?" She returns a mystified frown. "That's not very you."

"You only know the art dealer side of me."

She traps my gaze and nods slowly. "Yep, you're a man of many guises."

Her blue eyes almost burn a hole in my face. "You missed your calling in Hollywood, you know." She continues to walk about the room, putting me on edge, like I'm suddenly in a courtroom and being interrogated by a cynical barrister. "And by the way, this isn't some nice catch-up between old friends. I've spent the past two months sticking pins into your effigy."

I flinch. "So that's what's been keeping me awake at night, and here I was thinking it was those dreaded thorny bushes along my favorite coast walk."

Rolling her eyes, she's clearly not up to jesting.

I open out my hands. "I never set out to hurt you. Trust me."

"I did that once, and look what happened." She fiddles with the sleeve of her shirt. "You were talking about your new home."

Jarring as her sudden shift to civility is, I welcome it.

"Just that it suits me, being away from the rat race. I feel like I'm finally finding myself."

"And what have you discovered about yourself?" As a derisive grin forms, Mallory tips her head.

"I've found my love of painting again."

She stands by the window looking out onto a back alley. "You mentioned that you were once a budding artist. I just assumed it was your way of trying to get into my panties."

I smile. "You're the last person I'd expect to impress with such trivialities as the fleeting aspirations of an art student."

"I'm only human. And talent is an aphrodisiac."

"As they say." I exhale. "I never said I was talented."

"No." Her eyes settle on mine again, and I'm reading tiredness, like her anger is weighing her down and all she wants to do is sit, drink, and chat. That, I can do. Gladly.

"Why did you drop out, again?"

"The minimalist movement bludgeoned out of me my desire to paint."

She pours another mini bottle of gin into a glass. "Art school can be a little brutal. College degrees are only as good as the people who teach them."

"Tell me about it." I sigh. "My college tutors were either hung up on Lucian Freud or falling over themselves for some inane installation artist-cum-social-media junkie."

Her laughter puts me at ease. At last. She can be very intense. In this case, with good cause. I'm almost at ease, but I expect something to come flying at me at any moment. Mallory's mood changes can be unpredictable.

She stands across the room and stares me down again like she's trying to solve a puzzle. That's the old Mallory—bullshit radar on high alert while debating whether to seduce me.

I might be reading it all wrong, but I know that my libido has reached a fever pitch. Tension with this woman will do that to me. She's the only one. Normally, I walk away from combative types, but the more complicated Mallory gets, the more she fuels my desire for her.

That was never meant to happen. Even these past months, I've tried pushing aside what happened between us—the good, the bad, and the ugly bits—but I kept seeing her smiling face, and it warmed me.

She's got something I need. Or at least, I sense she does, so I need to play this carefully. Valence's threats are real.

"I'm meant to hate you." She sighs like she's fighting some natural impulse for a chat about old times.

"It was an adventure, wasn't it? Intense to say the least." I smile tightly. "But I think we're rather alike in some ways."

"How's that exactly?" She tilts her head.

"Our love of art and..." I pause, searching for the right words. "We have chemistry."

Her lips curl slowly. "So who are you charming these days?"

"You're the last woman I fucked. Or... made love to."

Mallory's eyebrows gather. "You're just saying that."

I sniff. "You're very suspicious, aren't you?"

"Around you, I am. Justifiably, I might add." She finishes her drink in one gulp. "I'm in possession of something disturbing. I shouldn't even have you here, let alone getting off on this ego-tickling act of yours."

"From memory, you always enjoyed the odd bit of tickling," I say, keeping up the smutty innuendo, one of Mallory's favorite pastimes.

Distracted by a sudden rush of lust, especially after noticing she's not wearing a bra, I backtrack to her previous statement. "What do you mean you have something disturbing?"

She rises, walks over to her handbag, and removes a golden heart.

I sit up. *Bingo.*

She rubs the heart, and it snaps apart.

"Oh, it opens."

"It sure does." She holds up a tiny flash memory card and places it in the portal of the laptop on the coffee table. "Take a look."

I watch a scene play out. It's a little dark, and whoever's filming is shaking, but it still manages to capture some hair-raising and damaging footage.

Footage that can put someone in jail forever, and the players in it are close to home.

Too close to home.

My earlier meal's refluxing as I squirm.

Mallory grins. She seems to take delight in my sudden look of horror. "I thought it would shock you."

I reflect on my meeting with Valence upon my return from Thera, after I handed him the Fabergé egg.

Holding the rare heirloom, he'd asked, "What am I to do with this?"

That threw me. "It's one of the missing Fabergé eggs. You could almost name your price."

"I want to know what happened to the gold heart."

Taken by surprise by his gruffness, I searched for the well-spoken MI5 operative stunt he pulled when originally contracting me for this role.

"I never opened it," I appealed.

A half-truth since Mallory opened it.

I then asked him, "Is that why we were chased halfway around Italy by a bunch of murderous thugs? For a gold heart?"

I was surprised he hadn't mentioned the diamonds. I'd grown rather attached to those glittering jewels, especially since learning that red diamonds are so rare they're worth around five million dollars a carat.

"The heart belonged to my great-grandmother."

"And all the death-defying acts I endured were for some family keepsake?"

"It's more than that." He kept fidgeting with the egg and running his finger over the blue-silk interior as though searching for some secret compartment.

"How did Dimitri get ahold of this gold heart?"

"He fucking stole it, the cunt. You did me a favor, wiping him."

His dark gangster-like tone made me flinch.

I thought back to when he first approached me, giving me an assignment like I was a part of some spy network, which of course I wasn't. "Why me?" I'd asked him at the time.

"You know Dimitri. You'll be well compensated. There's cash. Lots of it."

That got my attention.

"All you need to do is get the key and go to Rome. The address of the vault will follow. Sophia, whom we both know, will procure the case from the vault. The cash in the case is yours, and the rest is mine."

"What's in there other than cash?"

"There's a Fabergé egg," he said.

That piqued my interest. "Oh?"

"I want the egg and what's inside it."

"Being?" I had to ask.

"That doesn't concern you," he replied. "I'm told there's around five million in cash. That's a nice payday."

Fast-forward, and while clutching the egg, he said, "You fucked up by involving that American blonde. You were told to wipe her out. You didn't follow orders."

"Whose orders? MI5's or yours? I assumed this was some government job relating to an arms-dealing syndicate headed by Dimitri, not some sentimental token passed down from your grandmother."

"Great-grandmother. You've been watching too many crime shows." He smirked. "Not completely inaccurate, however, given Dimitri's involvement, along with that of your brother and that dirty cop he keeps close, in illegal weapons."

"So was this really an MI5 assignment?" I asked, reflecting on that first meeting at a London government office that required security clearance to enter.

"The less you know, the better."

"This missing family keepsake involved bloodshed and nearly cost us our lives," I reminded him.

"Stan was after the key too. He knew about the vault."

"He wanted the heart too?" I asked.

"There's a pile of cash, and as you put it, that egg can name its own price. How much did you make again?"

I took my time. He hadn't answered my question about Stan and the heart, and therefore, I lied about the sum. "Five mil."

"Nice payday, wouldn't you say?"

"So Stan kills Dimitri for the key. But why try to kill me?" I asked. "Did he know something more?"

He shrugged. "You were just at the wrong place at the wrong time, I'd say. But he was a dirty arsehole too. So there's no tears there."

I thought it best not to mention that Mallory did the deed. The less detail about her, the better.

"We're following Mallory Storm in New York," he said as though reading my thoughts. "That heart, or heads will roll. For now, I'm off to see if it's buried somewhere in this." He pointed at the gilded ornament.

"You're not going to destroy it, are you? It's a rare piece."

"I know someone in Paris who'll take it off my hands for a tidy sum. I'll be back."

As he rose to leave, he added, "I'll give you a month. If the heart's not in my possession after that, then…"

"Then what?" My spine stiffened.

His mouth turned up at one end. "I'm sure you can guess." And off he went.

A month has expired. He's pushing harder, and I'm finally staring at his precious gold heart. I also now understand why Valence's eager to grab ahold of it.

The footage is dynamite. A few familiar heads will roll for sure.

But what does that mean for Alec Valence, and why go to such lengths?

Thirty-Five

THE CAFÉ I'M SITTING in has a postcard view of Westminster. Outside, the city's bustling crowds are either busy snapping photos, glued to their phones, or simply going about their lives. London seems busier every time I visit.

Brendan McIlroy arrives five minutes later. He's fatter than I recall and wears the flushed features of a heavy drinker.

High up in Scotland Yard, McIlroy comes from that era when homosexuality was frowned upon, especially for a cop. Society could almost stomach a politician, given that most came from public school educations, where pederasty was as common as morning prayer, but not from the butch and conservative constabulary.

I wait until the server has delivered our tea before starting what will be an interesting conversation. He reaches into his pocket, removes a small container of artificial sweetener, and pops a pill into his cup.

"Diabetes," he says. "Who hasn't got it?"

"Me," I say soberly.

He sniffs. "You're still young. Wait until you reach your mid-fifties. That's when the fun begins. Pills for this and that. Even for fucking." A hoarse laugh more like a grunt follows.

He studies me. "I imagine this isn't some kind of friendly catch-up."

He got that right. I never liked the creep. And now, with what I'm in possession of, it seems my gut instincts about him were spot on.

I remove my phone from my inner pocket and make sure the volume is down, considering we're in public. The footage he's about to watch sounds like a scene from a violent crime show.

Passing it to him, I say, "Check this out."

He presses the arrow, and I watch the color drain from his face. The memory card that Mallory discovered shows a man with a bag over his head. My brother is in one corner watching and looking cool, calm, and collected as though he's a spectator at a card game. The man brandishing the gun is Brendan McIlroy.

The cop-cum-murderer passes the phone to me, and his saggy eyelids rise slowly as we lock eyes. "Where did you get this?"

"That doesn't matter."

His earlier smirk has been replaced by a cold hard stare. "So that was you?"

"What are you referring to?" I ask.

"Dimitri and Stan. The bodies have been found, you realize."

"That was nothing to do with me." I remain cool despite the knot in my gut.

"You were there, I'm told, with a leggy American, Mallory Storm, a suspected black widow who's just been exonerated for the murder of her husband."

"She didn't murder him."

He sniffs at me as a father might a child's naivety. "That's what they all say. The courts are filled with those kinds of cases. Hard to prove most of the time, especially when there are mushrooms involved. And these days, it's all about the battered woman. It's the cause célèbre, as the toffs call it."

My annoyance grows at this digression into Mallory's past. It's like he just rubbed salt onto a wound, however, because there's no doubt that Mallory possesses a dark edge. I recall how stone-cold she was about her mother's recent conviction.

I can't take my hands off her, though.

What does that make me?

Certainly not the murderer she thinks I am.

I can't believe she thought I was the man who fired one of those shots into that hooded victim's skull. A second shot. The first was fired by McIlroy, and then Julian followed suit like it was some kind of ritual killing.

The sight of the footage triggered my on-off reflux, whereas this demonic cop might have been watching some innocuous home video, judging by his unruffled manner. Mallory thinks Julian's me, a matter that needs addressing.

She planned to use that footage to blackmail me into giving her the cash. I think she believes everyone's got a touch of malevolence.

Growing up with a mother who committed the unthinkable—murdering her father, stepfather, and now her husband—Mallory has experienced her fair share of hell. It's no wonder she wears that prickly attitude on her sleeve. But then, I also caught her slipping cash into beggars' cups, even when she was down to her last euro.

"What must you think of Julian?" he says.

"Why would you care?"

His mouth rises at one end. "We go back."

That was his way of saying they play in the same dark corners.

It's like I've been thrown into one of those strategic war games. I need to consider which way this should go. My conundrum lies with Julian's involvement because if Valence gets this footage, my brother's head will roll.

Resent him as I might, especially since learning he's been palming off forgeries in my name, Julian's still my brother. I need more answers before deciding on my next move. That's why I convened this meeting with a man who triggers my inner misanthrope.

He sits back, crossing his hands over his paunch. "You've done me a favor, you realize. Dimitri was getting too big for his bolshie boots."

That inference to Dimitri's communist upbringing draws my first smile since meeting with the cop. "He made no secret of his love for capitalism, though."

"Oh, the oligarchs are crazy about it. Putin's war, however, means many are swapping their lavish, central-heated Mayfair mansions for some Siberian shack."

Switching back to the matter of incriminating footage, I ask, "Who's the guy with the hood?"

"Some scumbag whom society will appreciate gone."

"So this was a kind of vigilante act?"

"You've met him, I think. A fallen comrade of Dimitri's."

"Okay. Fallen? In what sense? And why is Julian firing that shot?"

"Ivan had done a dirty, the fucking pillock. First, he cheats on Dimitri's only daughter, Natasha, with one of her best friends, and then, to worm his way out of his father-in-law's ire threatens to uncover a matter that would impact not only Dimitri but also Julian."

"And you, let's not forget."

His silence is as good as a yes.

"Okay, so you knock him off as a directive from Dimitri, yes?"

McIlroy remains blank. "Where did you get this, and how much do you want?"

"I need to know why Julian's firing a bullet into the hooded man's head."

"All you need to know is that Ivan was a dirty cunt. He won't be missed."

I wonder why this tape is so important to Valence.

Is it to bring down McIlroy?

How do I find that out without revealing my source?

But then, McIlroy could offer protection, which means I keep the diamonds. Even if Valence has yet to mention their existence, I can't be sure of what's around the corner.

Call it greed, but I've grown rather attached to those rare jewels, more for what they can do. I can walk away from this scene, particularly from my brother's art dealership, which, as I'm discovering, is a front for more nefarious dealings.

"Tell me what you know." I'm growing impatient with his coy act. "This will help me decide what comes next. And by the way, if anything happens to me, this footage will go straight to the media."

He exhales. "Ivan was a dirty bastard who drank too much and talked too much to anyone who'd listen and for the right price."

"What are we talking about here?"

"It was a personal matter, mate. Let's just say that Ivan ripped us off, and he was also spreading vicious rumors about Julian."

"But it's about more than just fake art." I huff. "Enough skirting around the fucking edges, *mate*."

We're not fucking mates. I hate that term anyway.

"Dimitri would have sold his mother if he knew there was a profit to be made."

"But you were doing business with him," I press.

He shrugs. "As you said, there was art involved."

"And more." I look around, lean in, and with anger building, I whisper, "Fucking tell me, or this goes live."

"And you would do that to your brother?"

I stare him hard in the eyes. Time stretches.

"There was a shipment of guns that was never delivered, and then he goes and threatens to blab. The fuckwit. Looking for extra dough, he blackmails us. That's it in a nutshell. Ivan was a dirty cunt."

"So you keep saying." I exhale. "Arms dealing, then?"

He gives me a faint nod.

"I would have thought there's a back room in Scotland Yard filled with weapons waiting to be discharged for the right price."

"Maybe once." His long, cool stare tells me that this man has been a rotten cop from the word go. "So where do we go from here?"

"If I reveal my source, I want him gone."

His bloodshot eyes grip mine. "You want him hit, you mean?"

I return a blank stare.

Is that what I mean?

I can't say, but I need to sleep at night again.

"We need a name, you realize," he says at last.

We both rise, and he gestures. "After you."

When we're on the crowded street, I say, "Lay off Mallory Storm."

His mouth turns down into mock sadness. "Oh, you're in love." For a heavy cop, he likes to play the jester.

He reverts to tough cop. "Don't drag this out, Hyde."

As I watch him lumber off, questions come flooding in about my brother. I always knew Julian moved in dark circles but never would have thought him capable of murder.

Thirty-Six

Mallory

"WHY ARE WE HERE?" I ask as we step into a bar where not one woman is in sight. "Am I even allowed to be here?"

Dylan chuckles as he places his hand on my back. "I'm sure you can handle it."

It's been three days since I first laid eyes on him again, and my resolve to get my money has been fulfilled. The transfer went through with little fuss. Too easy. It's like he's paid me off and now I can disappear.

Not so fast, though. The diamonds still shimmer away in my thoughts, and Dylan's sidestepping that issue again. No surprise there. The man's an enigma. That part hasn't changed, but then my libido isn't complaining, despite my suspicions and inability to trust him.

I have to believe that my fake passport failed the test and that he didn't set me up. My body decided to believe that side of the story. Besides, hate is exhausting, and scowling is bad for wrinkles.

I'm putty in his caressing hands. Dylan knows how to pleasure me, and he always says the nicest things. I'm also filthy-stinking rich, and that's making me smile for the first time in months.

After showing him that vile recording, despite me promising myself not to fuck him, we ended up in bed. Yes, we slept together, and yes, that was weak of me.

I meant to push him away, and for a moment, I did. I got him all hot and bothered and pranced around in sexy lingerie I'd worn on purpose to provoke him. It was nice seeing him get all aroused and hungry as I fed him crumbs between heaping him with abuse. That even got him hotter. Dylan likes me tongue-lashing him. I even proposed I bring a whip next time.

He winced and said, "I don't like pain."

Memories of the injuries and bruising he sustained in Rome came flooding back. "Sorry if that triggered something."

He shrugged it off.

"But really," I persisted. "Have you spoken to someone? You copped a battering in Italy."

"Painting, tea and scones with my sweet mother, and going for long coastal walks is all the therapy I need."

After that, I fell on his lap, and who can resist this man? His dreamy kisses alone beat therapy any day.

I'm about to ask why we're in this male-only bar when my eyes widen. "Holy crap. Your double's over there."

He smiles and, cocking his head, leads me over to his look-alike, who's chatting up some guy.

Noticing us, the guy turns. "What are you doing here?" He looks at Dylan while giving me a passing glance.

Dylan turns to me. "This is my brother, Julian." He then turns to his brother. "This is Mallory."

I can't believe how alike they look. It's almost difficult to tell them apart, only Julian's far more reserved, if not cold.

"There's a scar." Dylan points at Julian's temple.

Julian smirks despite his eyes showing little.

Dylan turns to me. "Now you've met my brother, can we go?"

"Please. I'm not getting a very welcoming vibe here," I whisper. *Talk about an icy reception.*

As we're about to leave, Julian takes Dylan's arm and asks, "What have you decided?"

"Don't worry. Flesh and blood come first, no matter how fucking rotten."

They lock eyes, and one can cut the tension between them with a knife.

"Let's go." Dylan takes my hand.

His warm palm has a nice touch after that frosty little scenario.

"Call me," Julian tells Dylan just as we're leaving.

Once we're back on Oxford Street, dodging the masses, I stop and ask, "I don't get why you wouldn't tell me you had a twin."

"We haven't exactly been sharing family tidbits, have we?"

"I told you about my marriage," I appeal.

"The edited version." His eyes grip mine.

"I've told you all you need to know. The rest makes for dull reading. I don't wish to bore you."

He sniffs. "You'd never do that, Mallory."

He grabs me by the waist, swings me around to face him, and a passionate kiss follows. I melt into his arms. No more fighting at my end. Not when someone kisses like that.

I break away first, smoothing my hair. "What was that for?"

"I couldn't resist. It's nice to have you here."

I stare him in the eyes. "I'm not sure whether to believe you, but I'll let my ego soak in the sun for a while."

"The body doesn't lie, Mallory." Wearing an earnest half smile, he places his hand around my waist, which feels not only nice but protective. I get that he's attracted, and so am I. Like at stratospheric levels. *But can I trust him?* Oh boy, I want to.

As we move along, he says, "So now you know I'm not the man in the video. I can't believe that all this time, you thought that was me."

"Why wouldn't I?" I ask. "You're still a mystery to me. I saw how organized you were in Italy, cleaning the mess in Polignano while my knees trembled. Then there was your Mr. Cool act while being chased on that hairy drive along the Amalfi. Not to mention the fight scene in Rome wrestling a pair of bears. I'm convinced you're part of some spy network."

He laughs. "Good to see you've brought your Hollywood view on life along."

I roll my eyes at his subterfuge because he's not exactly denying my speculation.

He leads me along. "Come. It's cold. Let's get back."

"So Julian also knew Dimitri?" I ask.

He nods. "He introduced us years ago."

"Could he have arranged for Stan to pull a gun on you?"

"I imagine it was McIlroy, the first shooter in the video. He must have known Dimitri had that footage on a flash drive. He also probably got wind of the key."

"But why try to murder you?" I ask.

"Maybe they thought I knew too much."

"Who's they? Your brother and this McIlroy? Or Stan?"

He shrugs. "If I had the answer to that, I might finally manage a good night's sleep."

I stop walking again. "Why does your brother need you?"

"I'm his art buyer, remember?"

"Art that he has forged and sold off with your name attached."

He rakes his fingers through his hair three times. "He's promised to cease that."

"Oh? But why do it in the first place?"

"It's his way of controlling me, I think."

I stop walking again. "But why would he do that?"

"My brother's always resented the fact that doors opened easier for me than him when we were growing up."

"So it's a way of getting back at you, then?"

He leads me along, picking up the pace. "Let's leave the psychoanalyzing for another time, shall we?"

Huddling close to him, I'm keen to get out of the cold wind too.

It's not until we're back in my upgraded room, smelling of roses and not bleach for a change, that the conversation about his brother resumes. I pour us a drink, and we settle on the sofa.

"Tell me about your relationship with Julian. He's nasty. I can see that. And he's also ugly."

"Oh?" Dylan wears a bemused grin. "He's my double. Even you noticed that."

"Yes, but he's not you, is he? He's bad. Like really bad, and you're... well, you've got some good in you, I sense."

"Some?" He tips his head, wearing a cheeky grin that makes me want to either slap him or fuck him.

I push that thought aside and ask, "Aren't twins meant to be close?"

"Not always. Julian came out an hour before me, and he thought that gave him the right to boss me around. I'm more like my mother, and Julian's like our dad."

"You told me you don't know your father."

He looks confused. "Oh, we spoke about that?"

"We talked about a lot of things."

He traces my waist with his finger. "I remember only the nice bits."

There he goes, teasing me again, making my cheeks fire up.

He rises and walks over to the window, which looks out on Big Ben.

I join him and gaze at Westminster Bridge, packed with pedestrians rushing along, pushed by the wind. Below it, the Thames resembles a sheet of shimmering satin refracting golden flickering streetlamps.

"What are you going to do about that footage? You've got a lot of leverage there, you realize."

"Don't I know it," he says quietly, almost under his breath.

"I take it he's loaded."

"Julian's a billionaire."

"Then you have to make sure you're in his will."

Dylan turns sharply to face me. "That has never crossed my mind."

I shrug. "It should. Members of organized crime rarely make it to old age. And I take it he's not about to marry and arrange an Indian surrogate to birth a pair of made-to-order babies."

He laughs. "My brother's not one for traipsing in the shoes of convention."

I shake my head with a dry chuckle. "And I thought my family history was fucked up."

"If you look hard enough, you'll find most families have some skeleton rattling away in the cupboard."

"Enough talk about Julian," I say with a flirty smile. "I'll be back in a minute."

Five minutes later, I return in a lacy negligee, dance over to him, kneel, and unzip his slacks.

"Mm, what have we here?" I lick my lips.

His head drops back, and he groans.

Five minutes or so later, I'm wiping my lips.

He takes a moment to talk, but his eyes have that sated lusty look I've come to crave.

"You seem to enjoy that."

"It beats collagen shots," I say. "Great for the skin."

He strokes my half-naked breast. "And yours is very soft."

After a few moments of staring into my eyes, he adds, "Does this mean I'm forgiven?"

"No. It means that I want you to fuck me until I scream for you to stop."

He laughs as he follows me to the bed.

Sex has never been so much fun, despite the secrets. I still don't trust him, but while we're hanging close, I guess I can factor in a bit of playtime. After all, I earned it.

Thirty-Seven

Dylan

IT'S SUNDAY, AND WE'VE slept in. That suits me, even if my body's sore. Mallory's gymnastic lovemaking had me tangled in all kinds of positions. I think we were making up for lost time.

She stretches her arms. "That's the best sleep I've had in months."

I cuddle her. "Me too."

My phone pings, and I stretch my arm out for my satchel, which is by the bed. After running my hands over my face, I take a deep breath before reading the text.

Valence wants to meet me in an hour.

"Bad news?" Mallory sits up and stretches her arms.

"I have to go." I climb out of bed, have a quick shower, and dress.

"You still haven't told me what happened to the Fabergé egg, and about the diamonds."

As much as I'd prefer to hold off on details, I accept that I owe her some explanation, a story of some kind.

While that's percolating away, it occurs to me that Mallory might be in danger, as it won't take Valence long to discover she's in London. He might torture her, the thought of which panics me.

Whatever she means to me, I can't have her being interrogated, diamonds or not. Although the possibility of Mallory being harmed is my main concern, I also wish to keep the contents of that vault hidden. The least Valence knows—or even McIlroy, for that matter—the better.

"Let's discuss this later, shall we?" I suggest.

Holding a towel, Mallory says, "I was hoping you could show me around London. Maybe we can visit the Tate?"

Welcoming the change of subject, I nod slowly. "How about we catch up later this afternoon and take a spin around the gallery?"

Her face brightens. "That gives me time to do some shopping. There's a pair of shoes that have caught my attention."

"You've still got a thing for those uncomfortable stilettos, I see."

"You don't seem to mind having them around your ears."

I laugh. "They come in handy as weapons, I suppose."

"Speaking of weapons, are you still wielding one?"

"No." I give her a goodbye kiss.

As I leave the hotel, I decide it might be a good idea to carry a gun.

Valence is sitting in Hyde Park, reading a newspaper.

I take a sip of water from a fountain. That coffee I gulped down earlier is not sitting well, a combination of caffeine on an empty stomach and nerves.

I join him on the bench. "No trench coat, I see."

He's wearing shades, so I can't read his eyes. "What can you tell me?"

"I take it you had some success selling the egg in Paris?"

"It was substantially lucrative. But that's not why I called you. You know what I want." He seems twitchy, looking over his shoulder, putting me more on edge.

"Nothing's changed since our last meeting."

"That's not true. My sources tell me you were spotted with McIlroy at his hangout."

I remain cool. "So?"

"What were you showing him?"

"Some family pictures." I echo his curtness.

"Bullshit. You know something."

I shake my head slowly. "Brendan set up the meeting. He's heard about Dimitri, and he wanted answers."

"And?"

"Well, I kept it brief. I just showed him the picture of the artwork Dimitri had instructed me to buy."

"Why would that interest him?"

I take a deep breath. "Because he wanted to know why I was on the yacht." I pause. "Tell me, are you still working for the service?"

"Mallory Storm's in London." Ignoring my question, he goes straight for the jugular.

"And?"

"She's my next target. If I don't get what I want, then she'll be wishing it's her sitting in the prison cell and not her mother." He rises.

My veins tighten. "What's to stop me from going to MI5?"

He shakes his head, and his mouth curls for the first time. "What's to stop me from having you arrested for all those forgeries getting around? There's also a lipstick found in a bathroom next to where Dimitri was murdered."

Checkmate.

I walk away lost in thought. *Can they bring Mallory in based on her lipstick?* They can at least question her. Even that's a problem.

Whichever way, the possibility of Valence killing us, whether he gets the footage or not, has become my main concern.

The quick spin around the Tate isn't easy with someone like Mallory, who keeps pulling me back to absorb the gallery's extraordinary collection. She gushes over the pre-Raphaelites, which puts a smile on my face, the first for the day.

"Oh. My. God." She stands before Waterhouse's famous *Lady of Shalott* and is close to tears.

The Tate was my weekly indulgence back in art college, situated close to the gallery, around the corner. I've forgotten how moving the work is. As a young man, I developed a crush on the redheaded pre-Raphaelite model who appeared in most of the famous paintings.

"She's like the Nicole Kidman of the art-modeling world," Mallory comments as we discuss the ubiquitous model.

I nod. "That's a fair comparison. I guess certain models back then got starring roles and are now immortalized."

Her eyes brim with excitement. It's like I'm staring at the teenage version of her. That sweet moment is short-lived as a sense of dread stalks me like some shadowy figure breathing down my neck.

How do I deal with Valence? Tomorrow is only hours away.

"You seem very distracted." Mallory sounds disappointed. "Is it because of that meeting?"

"It's about the footage."

"Are you going to tell me who you met?"

"The less you know for now, the better."

She rolls her eyes. "That's not an answer. Why don't you just give it to whoever wants it and move on?" She says it as though I'm returning a book.

Were it not for Julian, I might do that then run and hide somewhere. I owe McIlroy nothing. He's as rotten as all the characters in this underworld Julian dragged me into.

"There's more to it," she says, narrowing her eyes.

We leave the red room. "I need to be somewhere. We can catch up for dinner later, yes?"

"I didn't say earlier, but I sensed someone following me before arriving," she says.

I think about Valence's threat. "Then be sure to hang out in public places."

"Now you're worrying me." Mallory looks over her shoulder.

"How about a visit to Cornwall? We can stay at my mother's cottage, which is where I've been for the past month."

"To hide?" She frowns. "From whom?"

Just as I'm searching for an explanation, I notice her brow smooth and her eyes spark with interest. "You want to introduce me to your mother?"

I've thrown her and me, for that matter, a curve-ball, given that my mother would love to see me settled down with someone.

"We'll talk later. Okay?" I give her a hug, and her body softens into mine.

After I leave Mallory, I head over to Julian's Mayfair home. Julian's watching football on a large screen in his living room, which is filled with nothing but male artifacts ranging from a decent replica of Da Vinci's *David* to paintings of male nudes. It's a mishmash of styles and clutter. When it comes to taste, he missed out. It seems money doesn't buy it, as they say.

Clutching a remote, he turns down the sound. "Now to what do I owe this pleasure?"

"Has McIlroy discussed the footage?"

He balances a cup and saucer in his hand. "Yep."

I can't believe how nonplussed he looks, considering the footage shows him shooting someone in the head. "I've got Alec Valence breathing down my back."

He shrugs. "He's a fucking pillock. Don't worry. I'm sure it will get sorted."

Getting nowhere and with Julian's sickly cologne adding to my nausea, I leave. Severely disturbed, I sit in the park, lost in thought, before visiting a bar for a drink.

If Valence gets that footage, McIlroy will have my head on a platter. *Would Julian protect me were the situation reversed?*

I need to figure out how to deal with Valence and McIlroy. The best outcome is to have McIlroy do the heavy lifting since killing is something he's good at.

Thirty-Eight

Mallory

We've been on the road now for a few hours. Staring out the window, I'm in awe of the pretty English countryside as lush rolling green hills, stone-clad villages, winding lanes, and fields dotted with sheep and ancient oaks flash past us.

Apart from looking in his rearview mirror a bit too often for my liking, Dylan's otherwise relaxed. That says little, though, given that he's back to his elusive best.

Inviting me to stay at his mother's is a nice touch, though I do wonder if it's a trick. Or whether he might lose me somewhere in the middle of nowhere. *Who knows with this man?*

Still, I wouldn't miss this for the world, despite lingering trust issues. I can face life, dangerous and mysterious as it might be, when I have Dylan holding me tight at night.

Putting aside secrets and possible lies, I focus on the fact that he's addictively affectionate and a hot lover who's made my heart shine for the first time ever.

I can't shake off vulnerability, though, like I might snap at any minute, just like I did back in Thera. I cried so hard, not just from the shock of being held there but from frustration too. I despised myself for missing a man who'd turned traitor. That's why I'm trying to suppress my heart from getting too involved.

But then, mystery stokes my libido as much as his exquisite tongue-kisses. I also love how he always tells me how nice I look.

I've never had those compliments before, except from my dad, who always had a nice thing to say. But then, he also had my back. Can't say if Dylan has mine.

I'm still alive despite the horror of being dragged away at Thera. But then, had the situation been reversed, I would have run, too, given the money and jewels. Just thinking about it almost exonerates Dylan.

Or am I finding any excuse for allowing myself to fall into his buff arms?

When I asked why he wasn't searched, Dylan explained he'd booked a private jet to avoid just that. He seems to have an answer for most things, and when he doesn't, he either goes silent or changes the topic.

I touch his leg. "This is so nice. I was dreading returning home."

Dylan glances at me. "You haven't told me what happened with your mother and how she came to be convicted. I didn't see anything in the media about it."

My body tenses at the mention of that shit show. "Let's not talk about that. It will only depress me." I turn to him. "You looked me up?"

He nods. "I was curious. And I wanted to get the money to you some-how."

I sigh. "I find that hard to believe. You looked rather pale a week ago when I first turned up."

He forces a smile. "I was feeling a little off."

I roll my eyes, but not in the mood for a debate, I switch subjects. "Tell me about your art-college days. Did you find yourself there?"

"Find myself?" He chuckles. "Quite the opposite. Although I'd been accepted on the merits of my drawing skills, conceptual art sweeping the art scene left me cold. I wanted to learn to paint like the masters, an ambition that was treated with a patronizing pat on the shoulders like I was aiming for the moon."

I smile at his dry tone. I would have loved to introduce Dylan to my late grandfather, who shared a similar view when it came to the masters and how their extraordinary artistic contribution made contemporary art pale in significance.

"College degrees tend to focus on what will best serve us in current markets. It's more about making a living than self-exploration."

"True." He looks into the rearview mirror again.

I follow suit, and my heart races, a residual response from the dramatic car chase in Italy. "Are we being followed?"

He shakes his head, and my shoulders relax.

"It's just that you keep looking in the mirror."

Dylan smiles. "It's a habit, I guess."

"Was Julian always bad?" I ask.

He takes a moment to respond. Dylan hates questions, as do I, but we're in the thick of something here, which means I have a right to question him going forward, wherever that happens to be. I have no real plans, only to get what's owed to me.

Ten million pounds sits in my new foreign account, set up by some friend of Dylan's. Even that makes me wonder, but it's mine, legit. And that's good, seeing as I've been spending like a drunken sailor.

"Julian showed some troubling signs from a young age," Dylan says at last. "At times, he acted a little creepy towards my friends, and that, by today's standards, might have gotten him sued."

"Seriously? Like what, for instance?"

"Well, there was one incident involving a local boy—someone we played with as kids—but he was paid off, I believe."

"Like sexual assault? How old was the boy?" I ask.

"Young. Anyway, my brother, by his own admission, doesn't like women much either."

"I've noticed. He gave me the evil eye," I say.

Dylan sniffs. "Yes, sorry about that. He's always treated my girlfriends with disdain."

"Am I your girlfriend?" A smile warms my face.

He shrugs. "You're a girl and a friend, so sure."

I slap his arm. "You know what I mean. So how does Julian end up being tied to that crooked cop?"

"He met Brendan McIlroy at some gay bar frequented by politicians and powerful men. They're thick as thieves."

"So what's Julian got over you?"

"Nothing. Only that we've had this working relationship for twenty years or so. I've only since learnt of his involvement in fraudulent art. Thanks to you, largely."

I turn to him, "How did you get Into this business?"

"Possessing a good eye for art along with a decent grasp of art history, I moved easily among art lovers and collectors. Julian, whose social skills are somewhat lacking, decided to employ me as his buyer. He took me to Christie's one night and introduced me to Dimitri, who wanted to furnish his homes with quality art. From there, the Russian took a liking to me, and I soon became his art buyer."

"And then Julian arranges forgeries to sell to uninformed buyers. I'd have his balls on a platter by now."

He laughs. "You're made of tougher stuff than me."

"Oh, I don't know. I've seen you pull a mean face," I retort.

"Let's just enjoy the coast, shall we?" Dylan tilts his handsome head, and I leave it there and cast my attention out the window.

We've just hit the winding coast road, which, much to my relief, is at sea level. A boat sailing peacefully on the wide expanse of blue-gray water stills my mind, and I forget about all that's passed. For now.

We finally arrive at his mother's charming postcard cottage, where she's at the door, welcoming us in. After kissing Dylan, she greets me with a warm hug.

"It's lovely to meet you," she says before turning to Dylan with a bright smile. "She's so pretty."

"That's nice of you to say." I'm almost blushing and feel unusually shy.

His mother looks from Dylan to me and back. I can see she's a little nervous. "I trust you had a good journey?"

"It was lovely. Especially the coastal drive," I respond as Dylan picks up my bags.

"We'll just go and unpack," he says.

"I changed the sheets, and your room's nice and clean," she says.

Dylan leans in and kisses her cheek. "Thanks."

It's lovely to see how close and caring he is toward his mother, who despite showing glimpses of a pretty face, especially with those large blue eyes that she's passed on to Dylan, also shows signs of life's struggles.

"While you're settling in, I'll make some tea." She turns to me. "Do you drink tea?"

I smile at how sweet she is. If only I had a mother like that. "I do now. And sure, that would be lovely."

"Do you eat steak and kidney?" She looks concerned.

"It's an acquired taste, Mum. Maybe a shepherd's pie?" Dylan suggests.

"Of course. I have one already cooked up." She strokes his cheek. "Dylan loves his shepherd's pie, don't you, love?"

It's so touching. She's such a caring person, despite that worried, almost needy expression in her eyes. Like most good mothers, she wants the best for her son. I respect that and even feel a bit of envy.

Our bedroom is decorated in florals—from wallpaper to curtains and duvet cover—in that fluffy 1980s style. It's not my thing, but it's so fresh and clean and has a marvelous window seat with a view into a flourishing garden and a weeping willow. I suddenly entertain the thought of sitting at the window and reading Daphne du Maurier's *Rebecca*. The setting for Mandalay, I'm told, is in a village not so far from here.

As I unpack my gear, I say, "Your mom's lovely. Like a mother should be."

Dylan's eyebrows rise. "Oh? And how should a mother be?"

"Caring and genuine."

He holds my eyes. "Your mother isn't?"

"She can get a bit over-the-top and gushing, but that's just for show."

"That's American, isn't it?" Dylan unzips his overnight bag.

I roll my eyes. "More like a Hollywood stereotype."

"I'm sorry. I didn't mean to take the piss."

"Take the piss?" I shake my head and laugh. "What a strange saying."

"Welcome to England. We're rather proud of our nonsensical sayings."

We hug, and he gently pushes me onto the springy bed.

"Is this okay here?" I ask, drawing away from his arms.

He chuckles. "I'm a forty-two-year-old man. Although you *are* the first woman I've brought here."

"Am I just?" I switch from demure to sultry and slowly unbutton my blouse. If this is what it takes to keep this man close, then I might as well have fun doing so.

"Perhaps just keep your screaming down a little." His eyes wear that smoldering glint that makes my toes curl.

"I don't scream." I giggle as he struggles to unclasp my bra.

"Oh, you do, and I'm fine with that, normally. But not here."

I surrender into his arms as his lips crush mine.

Thirty-Nine

Dylan

THE FOLLOWING DAY, JULIAN arrives unannounced. "Oh, you're here together, I see." He casts his attention directly at me while ignoring Mallory.

"My, twice in a month," I say. "Soon we'll be seeing you in padded waistcoats, a Shetland pullover, and a tweed cap."

Julian grimaces at that rural stereotype. Wearing a leery-green jacket over a polka-dot shirt, he's far too London for any of that.

He sets me aside. "I thought I'd drop in to go over your discussion with Brendan."

While my brother's talking to me, Mallory decides to take a bike ride into the village. I think it's an excuse to stay away from Julian. Though she's no shrinking violet when it comes to combat, it's out of respect for my mother, I sense.

When we're alone in the living room, Julian stands by a shelf and picks up a picture of us as teenagers. "You always wore that jumper," he says.

The jumper was a rare gift from our father, and I wore it to death.

"Was it because it reminded you of him?" he asks.

"Back then, it might have. It wouldn't now, though. Can't stand the sight of him." I study him. "Do you know where he is?"

He puts the picture down and falls into the armchair. "We talk. I send him money."

"You're serious?"

He sniffs at my surprise. "Yeah, I am. He's my father."

"Someone who was never around and when he was caused nothing but trouble."

He opens his hands. "So he liked to steal every now and then. Everyone does."

"I don't." I shift in the springy armchair. It's time I buy my mother some comfortable new furniture.

"This is coming from someone who's just scored a ton of cash and rare diamonds. All stolen goods."

My chest tightens at the mention of the diamonds, which are no longer a secret, it would seem. "So why are you here?"

He stretches out his legs, revealing his shiny burgundy Oxfords. "Brendan's getting edgy over Alec. And then there's the diamonds. He wants to retire, and I wouldn't mind winding things back a little."

I notice no mention of how many diamonds, and to my thinking, giving these worms, my brother included, six carats won't hurt my bank account too much.

"That doesn't sound like you. What will you do if you're not wheeling and dealing?"

He smirks. "Oh, I've got plans." He tips his head and studies me. "So, are you in love?"

I hate the way he brandishes the word "love" like it's some kind of illness. "That's none of your business."

Even though that question remains hard to answer, the less Julian knows about this unusual situation with Mallory, the better.

Yes, I am stringing Mallory along, mainly because she knows too much. That's the easy explanation. On a deeper level, however, she's always in my thoughts. I worry about her safety. She gets on with my mother, which counts for a lot in my book.

Dare I say I'm craving some kind of domestic harmony?

That's something I've never truly experienced, and going on Mallory's disrupted upbringing, I sense she hasn't either.

I also want to stand still for a change. Money helps, and that cat-and-mouse game in Italy exhausted me, as does knowing that it's not over yet.

How this all ends remains a deep puzzle, like one of those complex mathematical equations that a bunch of masterminds keep tweaking to arrive at some final answer. Only in this case, the conclusion can mean something deadly for both me and Mallory.

"Love weakens us," Julian says, brushing lint off his jacket. His tone, although cool, offers something more.

"Oh, please tell me. You've been hurt? I'd like to think that the person I spent nine months incubating with feels something."

He rises and walks to the window. A few minutes go by before he speaks. "I feel. I'm just not into hugging strangers."

"I'm not much of a hugger myself. But really, tell me who broke your heart?"

"You did."

My neck cracks. "What?"

A hint of emotion reflects from his eyes. I've hit a nerve, it seems.

"You were the star at school, with all the friends, whereas I was the one they picked on. Remember?"

"I helped. I did all your exams," I say.

He nods, staring at his fingers. "And then you left."

"I left for art school. It was my interest in art that set up this empire of yours."

This is the first time he's opened up about school and his dyslexia.

"And you repay me by forging art and palming it off with my name attached."

He winces at my raised voice. "They were none the wiser, and the originals are still here. Originals that one day, should you outlive me, will be yours."

On that rather sobering note, Mallory walks in. She heard, of course, judging by her throwing me a knowing look.

"How was your ride?"

She removes the jacket that my mother lent her. "It was nice but too many hills." She falls into an armchair and drinks from a bottle of water.

Julian goes to leave. "I'm off for a coffee." He turns to me. "Let's get that business sorted when I return. I'm leaving early."

After he's gone, I take a deep breath and rub my neck to release the sudden tension. I give Mallory the bare bones of our conversation, including the part about the diamonds. "What do you think I should do?"

"I suggest you give him the footage, and if he keeps on about the diamonds, then six pieces should suffice."

I puff slowly. "I suppose that's the best way forward."

"And all of what's his will be yours."

"That's neither here nor there. I don't think about such things."

"You should. The artwork in his possession would be worth a fortune."

Just as I'm about to respond, my mother enters. "Who's for scones and tea?"

Mallory and I nod in unison.

It's five in the afternoon, and after I've shown Mallory my art—rather reluctantly, I might add—she decides on a walk to the village to pick up some female products.

I offer to drive, but she shakes her head. "No need. It's not that far, as I discovered during my bike ride, and I need to exercise those scones and cream off."

I draw her close to me and whisper, "I can think of better ways to work off some pounds."

She pulls away and rolls her eyes. "You're worse than me."

I laugh. Coming here has been the best medicine, even after my brother's unexpected visit. But then, I shouldn't be surprised. They're sweating on that footage.

Forty

IT'S SEVEN O'CLOCK, AND Mallory hasn't returned. My mother's wringing her hands, saying what I'm thinking. "Where is she, and why hasn't she returned?"

I've just come back from driving through the village looking for her, including a visit to the only pub. Mallory hasn't answered my calls or texts either.

"You should call the police," my mother says.

I look over at Julian, and his head gives a subtle shake at the mention of the law. In this case, I agree since I can only assume that Valence is behind her disappearance.

I signal Julian to follow me outside, and turning to my mother, I say, "Don't worry. She's probably having a drink somewhere."

"Oh? But there's only one pub." Her brow creases with worry.

When we're outside, I light a cigarette. "It's fucking Alec Valence for sure."

"Let me call Brendan."

I don't stop him and walk off.

Julian holds up his hand. "Wait." He runs inside, returns, and hands me a pistol. "This might come in handy."

I take it. My Beretta is packed away.

"You know how to use one, I take it," he says.

"Twelve months in the military, remember?"

"Oh yeah." As I'm about to leave, he tugs on my sleeve. "Where are the diamonds and footage?"

I shrug him off and walk on. It's dark and moonless. This time, I walk to the cliffs, where there are plenty of spots to hide someone. It's a long shot, and I haven't heard from Valence. Yet.

An hour later, I return with nothing but scratches and the odd bruise after clambering through rough scrub. As I'm about to enter the house, my phone vibrates in my pocket. I don't recognize the number and take the call. "Yes."

"It's me." Mallory sounds overwrought.

"Where are you?"

"I'm in London."

"What? How?"

"I was dragged back here."

"Are you okay?"

"They haven't hurt me. But..."

There's a pause, then a new voice jumps on. "If you don't want to see her hurt, we want the footage. No more fucking around."

I don't recognize the voice. "Where's Valence?"

"The footage. Now."

"You better not harm her," I say. "And I'm hours away."

"I want the thumb drive."

"What's to stop me from copying it?" I ask.

"You won't be able to copy it."

Now I know why I couldn't make a copy.

There's another pause. "Where is it?" a male voice asks.

"I have it. I'm coming now. Where are you?"

"I'll send instructions when you're in London."

"I won't get there until early morning."

"Fine. We're not going anywhere."

"You better not harm her."

"She'll be fine as long as we get what we want. And there's a deadline. Literally." His sinister grunt makes my skin crawl.

"How do I know you won't kill us after that?"

The phone cuts out.

I hurry inside. Julian's on his phone, and my mother's in the kitchen, sipping tea. Her face is filled with concern. "Anything?"

I shake my head. "I'm going to have to leave for London, like, now." Before she can respond, I'm in the bedroom to gather my gear.

Julian enters. "I'll come with you. I've done all I have to here."

I study his face, which shows nothing, as usual. "Why did you come again?"

He jiggles his keys. "I'll drive."

I'm too tired to argue. At least this way, we can share the long drive back.

After four hours of driving, we're on the M1, around thirty minutes from London. Julian's snoozing. We swapped after he nearly fell asleep at the wheel. As his heavy breathing fills the air, a war rages in my stomach. At least my overactive nervous system is doing more to keep me awake than those acid-producing coffees.

It's not until we take a turn-off to London that I spot a black SUV weaving up to my rear and driving suspiciously close. Too close.

Its rumbling engine grows louder behind me, sending a flood of adrenaline through my veins as I slam down the accelerator. Julian's BMW fires up with ease.

He's jolted awake. "Hey."

"We're being chased," I say.

He looks behind him.

Without a moment to lose, I veer sharply into another lane, narrowly missing a car as I swerve to avoid a collision.

"Fuck, Dylan. Watch it!" Julian yells over squealing tires as a burn of rubber fills the air.

I'm weaving in and out as a menacing growl at my rear pushes me along. A truck sounds its horn as I cut him off, and he ends up having to change lanes. His carriage veers from side to side and knocks into a car, sending it tumbling.

Gripping the steering wheel, I take a quick peek in the rear mirror, praying no one's been killed.

"Take this exit," Julian says, his voice high-pitched.

I cut off another car. As I slide sharply between two cars to change lanes without warning, an SUV knocks a car out of its way. The car goes for a roll, setting off a chain reaction from other oncoming vehicles.

I groan. "It's fucking carnage."

I slam down the accelerator and push the vehicle to its limit as everything in my periphery blurs. Peering down at the speedometer, I'm pleased to learn that the deft vehicle is up to the challenge as it climbs to 150 Ks with ease. The SUV struggles to keep up.

We duck down a tiny street and send bins flying. The SUV is close behind again as it sideswipes a line of cars.

My heart thuds against my chest. I haven't got time to freak out. Everything's in sharp focus.

A flashing light comes on the dashboard.

"Fuck! We're out of petrol." I've got one eye on the rearview mirror and another on the gauge.

"Watch out!" Julian yells as I'm about to crash into a brick wall. The car splutters to a halt. "We have to get out and make a run for it."

"You told me that a full tank would do this," I grumble as Julian reaches into his inner lapel pocket for his gun and phone.

The SUV has slowed down. They've seen us.

I jump out of the car, and we run for our lives. I have to scale a wall and find myself in someone's backyard. It's about survival, and I have no idea where Julian's gotten to.

They're after me, I soon discover. The pair have also jumped the wall.

I trample on someone's garden. Tomatoes squish under my shoes as I make my way to a side gate and slip and slide as I wipe the sludge off my shoes.

It's locked, just my luck, so more clambering over fences.

Lights come on in the house, and I hear voices. I'm not hanging around to apologize, so I jump over the fence and make my way up the street.

Footsteps speed up, and before my next breath, a bullet fires just past my head.

Puffing and panting, I hold on to my stomach to ease a sidesplitting stitch. My heart's thumping so loudly it reverberates in my ear.

I come to a labyrinth of alleyways. With no time to choose, I head for one. Behind me, endless footsteps echo off the cobblestones, accentuated by piercing blasts of gunfire as bullets narrowly fly past. Ignoring the muscle burn, I race into an unlit alleyway.

Like large, looming shadows, the pair are heading my way.

I squat in hiding, trying to quiet my panting. Fear and tension elevate the sound of my breathing. As they pass me, I turn from side to side and see that I've lost them.

What happened to Julian?

I can't think straight. It's all about getting out alive to save Mallory.

Why follow me? Why try to kill me?

They're either really bad shots, or they've been sent to shake me up. Whichever way, I'm not hanging around to find out.

Sneaking off, I make my way out and find a main road. Just my luck—they're there waiting.

It's my phone. They're tracking me, but I can't risk losing contact with Mallory. If I lose the phone, I lose contact.

My only option is to keep running. My straining muscles threaten to snap any minute, but adrenaline fires me on as gunfire crackles through the air, and a bullet flies past, too close for comfort.

I jump over a fence, sending dogs barking, and lights come on.

A lady stands at the doorway. "Who's there?"

I loudly whisper, "Call the police. I'm in danger."

A gun fires, and she screams then shuts the door.

Crouching behind the fence, I shield myself as bullets whiz past. Saturated in sweat, I inhale the sickening stench of burnt metal and sulfur, a terrifying reminder that I'm close to extinction.

My breath hitches as I grip my pistol and squeeze the trigger, returning fire. It's a game of cat and mouse with me firing as good as I'm getting.

A bullet pierces my arm, and an agonizing shock wave ripples through every nerve. Blood pours down my sleeve and drips onto my pistol.

No more bullets. I'm sunk. Just as I'm about to hold up my arms and surrender, sirens roar down the street, and flickering lights blind me. I'm like a creature caught in headlights, wide-eyed, battered, and bruised.

Their timing's impeccable. I've never been so glad to see cops in my life.

A pair of constables are giving chase as one of my assailants jumps out of a bush and makes a run for it. An ambulance appears, and in the next minute, I'm strapped down and ferried off. At least I'm still alive. Getting to Mallory is all I can think about as a needle pierces my skin. That's the last thing I remember.

Forty-One

THE SOUND OF BEEPING monitors and antiseptic smells filter through as I force my lids open. Bleary-eyed and heavy-headed, I struggle to focus. In the distance, I hear footsteps and murmuring, and the machines around me seem more alive than me.

A shot of pain up my arm reminds me that what happened wasn't a nightmare. As I try to sit up, a stinging ache shoots down to my wrist. At least it's my left arm and not my right.

As I gain focus, I notice a policeman at the door.

"Hey, can I speak to someone? How long have I been here?" Mallory enters my thoughts, and fire bites my belly as I go to rise. "I need to go."

Holding up his hand, the young guard shakes his head. "Wait."

I press a button for assistance, and a few minutes later, a nurse appears, walks casually to the window, and opens the blind, allowing a beam of sunlight into my room, making me squint.

She comes to my bedside, her floral fragrance mixing with an acrid scent of medicine.

"How are you feeling?" She helps me sit up while adjusting the pillows against my shoulders.

I look around. "Where are my things? My phone?"

She stops me from moving. "Not so quickly. Police wish to question you. They're waiting for a doctor's clearance. He should be here soon now that you've woken."

"How long have I been out?" My heart pounds against my rib cage at the thought of Mallory being harmed.

"You've been asleep for around eight hours or so."

"What time is it?" I ask.

"It's four o'clock."

"Can I at least have my phone?"

A doctor arrives, and she steps aside to give him space as he takes my pulse while studying the various monitors.

"Can I make a call?" I ask again.

The man says something to the nurse and then looks at me. "Let's wait for the police, and then we'll take it from there. Okay?" His mouth curves slightly, and he walks off before I can respond.

Why am I feeling like the bad guy here? I sigh, and the nurse smiles.

"I'll arrange a sandwich. You must be hungry." She points at a glass of juice. "Drink some liquids. Can I get you a tea?"

I nod. "Tea would be great." I'm resigned to being stuck there for now.

What am I to say to the cops, though?

Will I give them everything? I'm tempted to.

But can they keep us safe?

More importantly, can they track down Mallory?

Two police arrive with clipboards. The nurse nods, and they enter.

Just as the men hover over me, Brendan McIlroy strolls in. He shows his badge to the pair, who look young enough to be rookies.

"I'll take it from here," he commands.

As they share a glance, I catch a hint of disappointment. A wounded man caught in an overnight gunfight beats boring paperwork, I imagine.

After they lumber off, I regard McIlroy, who, with those baggy eyelids, looks like he hasn't slept in years.

"So, a bit of drama." He points at my bandaged upper arm.

"You could say that." I scan his face. "Where's Julian?"

"I spoke to him earlier."

"What happened to him?"

"He found a cab at the right time."

"At the right time?" My frown hurts my head. "In the middle of some fucking-nowhere sleepy suburb?"

He shrugs. "Luck, I suppose."

"And he left me out there to die." I shake my head.

"When it comes to the rough and tumble of the streets, Julian's no patch on you. You know that. You were the one taking on the street kids."

"You're just fucking lucky he's in that video because by now, that thick neck of yours would be in a noose."

He grins. "Nothing good will come of your agent contact getting that footage."

"Alec Valence, you mean? You know him, I bet, so don't play coy."

His silence confirms that speculation.

"I've got to get out of here, and you're going to help me. They've taken Mallory, and I need my phone, which has been confiscated for some reason."

"I can clear it so it's in your hand before I leave." He shifts on the spot. "Give me the footage, and all this goes away."

"And what about Valence? He'll wipe us out."

"He'll wipe you out whether he gets the footage or not. He's a double fucking agent. That's why he's in hiding. You didn't know that, did you? You just agreed to head to Italy and get your hands dirty dealing with some pretty heavy people."

"Dimitri was a close affiliate of yours and Julian's from memory."

"I'll take care of Valence."

"That being the case, why haven't you already?" I ask. "That's the only thing that has stopped me from handing the footage over to you. Julian knows that."

His phone pings, and after removing it from his pocket, he reads a message. "I've got to go." He gives me a long, hard stare. "Where's the footage?"

"It's not on me. Otherwise, you'd have it, I imagine."

"Where is it, Dylan? I can't risk Valence getting to you before I do."

"It's not here. As I said. It's locked away somewhere no one can find it. I need to know that Mallory's safe. She was abducted, for Christ's sake. Julian knows. I'm sure he told you. All that fucking carnage on the M1."

"Someone died."

Shaking my head, I feel like punching a wall out of sheer frustration. "That wasn't my fault."

He shrugs as though we're talking about a minor infringement. "That can go away."

I pull a deep frown. "When did you become God?" I'm frustrated at how powerful this dodgy policeman is.

"Is that a rhetorical question?" He smirks, rolling in his filth like a true pig.

"Listen, the best course of action is that you hand over the thumb drive."

My heart pounds again as catastrophic thoughts crawl over me like the creepy aftermath of walking into a web.

"Why the hell would Valence send his bovver boys when he's holding Mallory, knowing full well I was on my way to negotiate?"

"Get me that footage and you'll see Mallory in one piece."

The stench of a rat intensifies by the second. "Why do I get this feeling you know where she is?"

"The doctor said you'll be good to go in the morning. All I need from you now is information on where you've hidden that footage, and let's not forget the diamonds."

I shake my head. "Answer my question. How will you be able to find Mallory?"

"I've got my sources." His cold smile makes me want to lunge at his throat and strangle answers out of him. "You'll be released in the morning. For now, we'll have bodyguards posted here for your protection. I'm sure it won't take much to find that Russian scumbag."

"You seem to be able to find everyone in this city," I say, unsatisfied with this arrangement. "How is it you can't find him?"

"I didn't say that. I've got intel on his daughter's school, so it won't take much. We just haven't been trying that hard. Not until now."

"How can you be confident about Mallory being released?"

"Julian will swing by in the morning to pick you up. And then we can resolve the prickly situation surrounding your American girlfriend, and before you know it, you'll have your leggy yank keeping your feet warm again."

I watch him walk off, and it all starts to add up. No doubt he's behind the kidnap. My brother must have told them where to find us. No one in this town can be trusted. Least of all my own flesh and blood.

Forty-Two

GNAWING PAIN THROBS IN my arm as I wrestle free from the tangle of wires and tubes of hospital contraptions. I'm not hanging around for the morning. Something in this whole story does not sit right.

A trail of blood trickles down my arm as I deal with sharp stabbing pain, but with adrenaline pumping through me, the pain soon numbs.

It's now or never, since the guard's snoozing.

The sterile corridors are dead quiet. The only sound is the machines percussing through the silence in symphony with the odd snoring as I tiptoe on in my socks.

My clothes are in my hand, as are my shoes. At least I managed to get my phone earlier.

I had no messages, which I found rather weird, considering I failed to make that appointment with Mallory's captors, which confirms McIlroy had something to do with her abduction, a nice little twist that, had his acting skills been honed, I might still be none the wiser about.

Why else would Valence send his men to pursue me?

A male nurse is coming. He's wearing earplugs. That seems a bit irresponsible for someone who should be listening out for patients, but who am I to complain?

He can see me, I remind myself, so I hide in a darkened room with a sleeping patient. The stench of illness wreaks havoc on my unsettled stomach, I've never handled painkillers well.

Ear against the door, I can feel my heart competing with the rhythm of the heart monitor. Mine is racing faster. Funny about that.

I wait for his steps to fade away to sneak over to the bathroom, where I remove the gown. Stinging pain makes me fumble as I try to unknot the ties. I end up ripping the fabric off.

The door creaks open, and I jump into a cubicle. Standing there half-naked, I'm careful not to move as the sound of urine splashing against metal echoes off the walls. I wait until the person leaves then change into my clothes before sneaking out.

I opt for the stairs to avoid detection, and eventually, I make it out into the night. It's early morning. Dark. No one around.

Much to my relief, a vacant taxi swings by. Thanks to a quiet weeknight in London, it's only ten minutes until I arrive at Julian's house. The lights are out, but I'm sure he's in. Julian favors his home over others.

I head to his door and knock but get no response. Then I call his phone, but he doesn't answer, so I keep knocking.

This time, I send a message threatening to break a window.

Within a minute, he's at the door, grumbling under his breath.

Ignoring his whining, I push him into a corner. "You told McIlroy where to find Mallory, you fucking snake."

"You're talking bollocks. I was there with you, nearly dying with you in the car."

"Yeah, well, that must have been Valence's crew. That's why I know McIlroy arranged Mallory's abduction, because Valence wouldn't have had us chased, would he?"

I head into his living room. He turns on a lamp, and I pour myself a generous shot of single malt.

I sit down, wincing from pain. "This is how this is going to go. I want Mallory here. Or else Valence gets the footage. Got that?"

Dressed in a purple paisley robe, he picks up a remote, turns up the heat, then reaches for his phone, but I stop him. "No. I can't trust you."

Julian opens his hands. "I'm just calling Brendan."

"I can't believe you did this to me. Your own fucking family. Fucking pillock."

He rolls his eyes. "You're the one who's been playing stubborn here."

Placing my sore arm on the armchair rest, I wince as I adjust my position. "I need some painkillers."

He rises. "Just a minute."

"Wait." I get up. "I'm coming with you. I can't trust you. You'd rather see me dead than have that footage made public. I know that. I know you."

Our eyes lock like they did when we were kids. Only this is a matter of life and death and not some underhanded trick to obtain a better deal with sweets or football cards.

"It's all Brendan's doing."

I puff. "I can imagine."

He passes me a packet of painkillers, and I swallow a couple with a mouthful of water. We return to the living room and sit in wait.

He yawns. "I'm not keen on sitting here staring at your ugly face."

I sniff. "The same face as yours." I sip the liquor despite it mixing badly with tablets. At this point, I'm sticking my middle finger up at death.

"I want Mallory returned. Safely. Once she's here, then we can negotiate. Footage and diamonds. Yes?"

He nods. "I need my phone, then, don't I?"

I pass it to him. "Call him now."

I peer up at the antique clock. It's midday. We're waiting for McIlroy, and I can't do anything until he arrives. Namely, arrange to get the thumb drive from a London bank vault, which was where I was heading before being ambushed.

In strides Valence.

"How the hell did you get in?" I ask.

"For a billionaire, your brother needs to get a better security system."

"Can you walk through walls as well?" I go to rise when he pulls out a revolver.

"Sit."

I sigh. Here we go again.

Julian enters and, seeing Valence, stops abruptly. "How did you get in?"

Valence pulls out a Swiss Army knife. "One of the perks of working for the agency. You learn all kinds of useful life skills."

"Like breaking and entering." My dry response attracts a grin from my former client.

Former client? Maybe not so much that, but if stress is the killer they say it is, the man's responsible for shortening my life by years.

"I suppose you're not here to discuss the latest Man U coaching debacle," Julian says.

"I hate football. A societal scourge that numbs brains," Valence says.

"The thumb drive's not here, Alec," I say soberly.

A bulky character appears at the window. He shakes his head as his eyes meet mine, telling me he's on my side, whatever side that is given that both sides in this fight are equally rotten.

I try to avert my gaze in time, but eagle-eyed Valence, who has his back to the window, notices and turns.

I flick my head for Julian to get out.

"Where is it?" Valence scowls.

"It's in London," I say. "Just not on me."

"I'll make that call to rough up your mother, will I?"

Just as I'm about to comment, someone speaks from behind. "Not if you want to see your pretty daughter again."

Valence does a sharp turn, and there's McIlroy with a gun in his hand and a pair of minders shadowing him like guard dogs.

"What was her name again? Natasha?" McIlroy smirks. "Such a sweet young thing. And you should have seen how willing she was to cooperate after I told her you were in danger."

I sit back and ask, "Tea, anyone?"

"Shut the fuck up," McIlroy says, seriously pissed off at me, it would seem.

He turns to Valence. "Drop the fucking gun." Just as he says that, one of his henchmen pokes a weapon into the former agent's back.

Valence elbows the man in the guts. The gun fires into a painting. It's an ugly piece, which is inconsequential, but everything turns surreal, and trivialities muscle in while I'm deciding how to get out of this in one piece.

"Before you kill me," I yell as Valence rolls on the ground in a tussle with one of McIlroy's heavies, "you all need to know that I've left instructions to send the footage on to the media should I be killed!"

Whether they hear that, I can't say, because it's descended into a full-on brawl as two other bulky figures enter the fray. I'm not sure where they came from, but they're Valence's men.

Everyone tumbles around. Shots are fired.

One man's down, blood pouring on the floor as I duck behind the sofa.

McIlroy, meanwhile, isn't there, which is interesting. I suppose he's smart enough to stay away from friendly fire, or is that enemy fire? I have no idea who's on whose side at this point.

Valence exerts some impressive force as he punches and kicks his way out of the skirmish. He wipes his nose, puffing when Julian appears out of nowhere wielding a gun, and boom. My ears ring as Valence crashes to the ground.

He's shot at close range to the heart.

I rise from behind the couch and kneel down to check his carotid artery. He's dead.

Two men are laid out cold. One's dead, lying in a puddle of blood.

The other prone man comes through and, reaching out, wraps his hand around Julian's ankle and brings my brother down.

Now I'm drawn into the brawl, and before the Hulk can claim my brother's life, I kick him in the groin and stomp on his arm. The gun goes sliding across the floor, and McIlroy arrives just in time.

He picks it up and shoots Julian's would-be killer in the head.

What a bloodbath. I'm not sure what the gentry living next door must be thinking—probably reaching for their top-shelf sherry—but I'm close to throwing up.

Forty-Three

Mallory

BRUISED AND BATTERED, DYLAN strides in as though Mr. Cool has been on a holiday and not caught up in some bloody combat.

If someone had told me I'd become that damsel in distress being saved by a sexy well-spoken Brit, I would have thought they'd ingested enough Ayahuasca to feed an entire retreat of world-weary execs.

Maybe that's something I should consider doing after the two days I've just had.

"Did they hurt you?" He looks around the repurposed barn, which would be a rather cool place to hang out for a week or two. Without being bound to a chair, of course.

I shake my head. "They even bought me Starbucks coffee and food from McDonald's. I sensed we were close to civilization. Where else does one find a McDonald's?"

"Everywhere," he says, brushing back his hair, which is peppered with more grays than I recall.

My heart's smiling at that concerned glimmer in his tired eyes.

At the mention of my abductors' consideration where my nourishment was concerned, Dylan shakes his head in disbelief. Whether that's him being judgmental over my questionable fidelity to franchised American food is anyone's guess.

But all that matters is that he's here and he's the one saving me. Well, kind of. The henchmen left and reassured me that someone would return to free me. A part of me was expecting the Hollywood version of being freed—someone bursting through the door with guns blazing. But hey, I'm alive, and I'm relieved to see Dylan alive.

He gazes at the wide-screen TV and turns it off. "At least you were kept entertained, I see."

"They kept my hands loosely bound so I could operate a remote. I binged on *Breaking Bad*."

He cracks into a half smile. "A nice, light diversion."

I roll my eyes and chuckle at his droll reply.

He produces a Swiss Army knife from his jacket and cuts the cable ties from my wrists. I stand up, and my legs are shaky after being seated for so long. He holds me up and presses his warm body against mine.

"You're injured," I say, noticing him wince.

"I was shot."

Tears burn my eyes as I stare into his face. I can see he's been through the wars. Yet again.

Our eyes meet, and I cuddle him carefully. "Thank you for saving me."

"You're welcome."

We share a long gaze, and tears erupt.

I never thought I was in danger, but the shock of being dragged from the village after I left the supermarket remains raw. Sitting in the car with a nasty pair, I was bound for five hours, unsure if I would ever make it out alive.

Dylan keeps holding me. "You're sure they didn't harm you?"

He's so sweet. All my suspicions about his true intentions have suddenly evaporated, especially after hearing how the footage has found a home and that he's paid off the bad guys. I suppose he means Julian too.

We leave, and as we're walking to his car, I look around at a field of sheep. "I could hear them, you know?"

"Who. The thugs?" He opens the car door for me.

"No, the sheep. I sensed I was in the country somewhere."

"They blindfolded you?" he asks.

"No, but it was dark."

"We're in the Cotswold," he says as we drive away.

I've become a tourist again and stare in wonder at the quaint honey-bricked manors surrounded by vibrant greenery and rocky brooks.

"It's all so idyllic. I'm half expecting Miss Marple to appear on her bike."

Dylan smiles as he turns onto a main road. "You won't find inquisitive pensioners with a penchant for murder mysteries. This place is mainly inhabited by wealthy weekenders and bed-and-breakfasts."

As we drive in silence, despite the pretty surroundings, I have this sudden longing for the States. "I miss home, you know?" I say at last.

"You're thinking of returning soon?"

I nod. "Would you miss me?"

He pulls up at an old pub. "A spot of lunch?"

I smile. Dylan's sidestepping the big questions again, but I leave it for now because I'm starving.

He opens the door, and as I step onto the cobbled sidewalk, he leans in and says, "Yes."

That puts a smile on my face.

I know what this man means to me. When I arrived a month ago, I thought I would tear him to shreds. Instead, now all I want to do is hold him close to my heart.

It helps that he's sharing everything with me—diamonds, money, and a little of himself, or so he says. The money, I have. Diamonds are yet to be placed in my hand, and as for Dylan, well, he's here, and that means more than anything if I'm being honest.

Forty-Four

Dylan

MALLORY'S APARTMENT, A REPURPOSED former warehouse, boasts a perfect view of the Brooklyn Bridge, the angle of which is as familiar to me as the Eiffel Tower, thanks to Hollywood.

The heart and soul of commerce, New York's a photogenic city. Seeing the Statue of Liberty live for the first time sent tingles through me. History means everything to me, and being in that sleepless, crowded city has stirred all kinds of emotion.

I've already conjured up scenes from a roaring twenties party featuring an elegantly spoken F. Scott Fitzgerald, Bukowski loitering in some seedy bar for the fallen, and Burroughs shooting an apple off his beleaguered wife's head.

Industrialization and modern progress are evident with each step I take, from the razzle-dazzle of Broadway lit up like a stage of soft-shoe shufflers to the beatnik enclave of Greenwich Village, where I spot the odd Dylanesque figure ambling along, in my imagination at least, reciting Ginsberg. Then there's the languid Art Deco elegance of Fifth Avenue and bustling Wall Street, where stern bespoke moneymen stride with purpose, phones glued to their ears.

I collapse onto the sofa. After a day of soaking in more contemporary art, visiting seemingly endless Brooklyn galleries and studios, I'm ready for a stiff drink.

Mallory's whipping up a meal in the kitchen, which is an extension of the open-plan room with an island bench as a divider, where hanging lights gleam down on a stainless-steel surface.

"Are you sure you don't need me to help?" I ask again.

"Nope. All good," she says against a backdrop of breezy jazz and street noise.

I take a gulp of whiskey, and five minutes later, I get up and walk over to the large dining table, where I see a copy of *Time*. A vintage one, going by the picture of Clinton on the cover.

"You really don't have to cook again," I say, flicking through the magazine to a photo of a smiling Bill Clinton, a reminder of a less-complicated, pre-social media world when our lives were less exposed.

"I like doing it. I never thought I would, but it's nice having someone to cook for and share a meal with."

I go over and hug her.

"Your heart's racing." She unfolds from my arms.

"It always does when you're near."

Mallory rolls her eyes at my borderline-cliché response and giggles. "You say the cutest things."

She uses her Southern accent, as she often does when I'm heading somewhere deeper, as though she's not sure how to navigate my affection. That makes two of us because I'm not sure what this is, but a week after she left, I booked a flight to New York.

The instigator, my mother, saw how down I looked and, convinced Mallory was my soulmate, suggested I visit her in her habitat. I'm not sure whether that's true about us being soulmates, but I know I missed her.

I still don't know much about her. She knows more about me, especially now that I've buried a few skeletons.

Though, she doesn't need to know that this whole mission has left me soaking in blood, including that do-or-die episode in Italy, resulting in the pair of thugs lying in a burnt-out car somewhere on the outskirts of Rome—a scene that I relive almost nightly.

Mallory clears the table of newspapers, books, and numerous objects. As a clean freak, a title Mallory bestowed upon me back in Italy, I'm somewhat challenged and find myself unconsciously moving things into neat piles. Even when we shared hotel rooms, I picked up her clothes despite her admonishments.

She pops a wok of a colorful stir-fry onto the table. I rise to help, but she shakes her head. "No need. I've got this."

I marvel at my plate, containing a feast of colorful vegetables with thin slices of beef. "This is rather a banquet. I'm not sure I can eat it all."

"Leave what you can't eat. I won't mind," she says. "I rarely eat at this table. Isn't that strange?" She chuckles. "I'm generally on the couch, balancing a plate on my lap in front of the television or my laptop."

"That was me, too, when I wasn't eating out. But since I've been in Cornwell, my mother insists we eat at the table."

"She's a lovely woman." Mallory takes a forkful of food.

"She's crazy about you too," I add.

I'm dying to ask about her husband and whether they, too, shared meals. That thought leads me to his poisoning and her now-convicted mother. It's all too curious, with questions banking up, just like the food spilling over my plate.

For now, I focus on acquainting myself with Mallory in her own world since I've only just arrived, and so far, we haven't done a lot of talking. Mallory is proving irresistible the more I get to know what makes her spark.

I chew on a forkful of beef with rice. "It's delicious."

"Thanks. It's one of a few new dishes I've taught myself."

Sitting across from me, Mallory moves a vase of wilting flowers. I make a mental note to buy a fresh bunch, given I bought those upon my arrival a week ago.

"When I was married, we mainly lived on takeout."

"I suppose your mother would turn up and cook occasionally." The hot peppers in the stir-fry are burning my gut. I hope I remembered to pack my antacids. But the meal's so flavorsome I can't stop eating, despite its predictable damage.

She chews her food and says, "My mother never came here."

That leaves me slightly perplexed. I know her husband died in this apartment. *Or did he?*

"She was never invited?" I prod.

"She visited once when we first bought the apartment. But she hated it. She hates New York." She giggles. "She's very Florida. You know, freshly renovated with all the latest mod cons."

"This apartment would be Buckingham Palace compared to her prison cell."

Going by Mallory's straight face, I sense I've touched a sore spot at the mention of her mother's incarceration.

"Did you move in here after you married?" I ask, careful not to trigger something. After that last comment, Mallory gulped down half a glass of wine.

She nods. "Erik hated it. Said it reminded him of a trendy café or an artist's studio. That's why I loved it. I managed to convince him, though."

"For someone who liked control, that was some compromise on his part, I would imagine."

She puts down her fork and wipes her lips with a napkin. "We were just married at that stage. He hadn't started pushing me around. I think he was hoping to bend me to his will, so he gave me this one win."

"Did he visit your mother in Florida?"

She shakes her head. Her eyebrows gather. "Why all this interest in Erik all of a sudden?"

I sip water to dilute the spice burning my esophagus. "Just curious. I know so little about your life. You seem to know more about mine."

"You've heard most of the juicy bits—a battered wife who fell hard for an art dealer she was meant to be casing." She pulls a face and forces a chuckle.

"Did he hate your work? Is that why he started to hurt you?"

She shook her head. "Oh God no. It was before that. He'd come home from work, drink, and then get nasty."

"I'm sorry."

"No need." Her face brightens. Mallory's sharp mood switch is jarring in many ways. "Anyway, enough of that. How long are you staying?"

I play with my food. My stomach's on fire. Whether it's from the hot peppers or the startling fact that suddenly nothing makes sense, I can't say.

"You don't like it?" Mallory points at my half-full plate.

"I love it, but my guts are not so impressed. It's just a little too spicy, I'm afraid."

"Oh, I forgot about your on-off reflux."

"It's all good. I've got my meds here, I hope." I chuckle.

"I'll be sure to whip up something a little plainer," she says.

I shake my head. "You don't have to do a thing. Just whip out that sexy lace teddy, and I'm happy to live off hot dogs for a month."

"Hot dogs? How phallic of you." She laughs.

I hold up my palms. "Hey, that's your dirty mind. Hot dogs and New York are synonymous from what I've observed."

She sips her wine. "So, how long are you staying?"

"I'm not sure. I've got no real plans. That's the beauty of being rich, wouldn't you say?" I tilt my head.

"Oh yeah. I like it. I'm already shopping around for a Malibu mansion."

"Are you serious?" I frown at the thought of Hollywood types talking over each other and people falling into the swimming pool, half-dead on drugs. As that cliché reel runs through my head, she nods.

"Sure. Why not? An escape from the cold."

I wanted to see Mallory in her own world. And I really did miss her, so perhaps that means us trying a relationship of sorts.

Messiness, I can do. That's why servants exist, but there are layers covering this woman's soul. The only time I get a glimpse is when we're surrounded by beauty or making love while gazing into each other's eyes.

Although I desire her like mad, I'm not sure what to make of Mallory. She was kind to my mother, and that counts for a lot in my book. Perhaps I'm overthinking it.

"I'd live in a hovel if it meant us being together," she says.

I laugh. "You say the nicest things."

After dinner, we jump into a cab and head for Central Park. Despite having visited that large green swath of manicured nature before, I'm craving a hit of open space.

When we're walking along the attractive elm-laden avenue, Mallory asks, "You haven't told me about what happened to the diamonds. Did you give them to McIlroy or Julian?"

"Julian's got six diamonds. As arranged. I left it up to him to work it out with McIlroy. I think the cop was happy to get ahold of that footage."

She sighs. "What a drama."

We walk in silence.

"So why did you come?" Her eyes anchor mine.

I dodge a skater. "To see you, of course. And to get away."

"Get away from your brother?"

I nod. "And everything. I'm glad I did. I love it here."

"I love you being here," she says with a smile, and I take her hand and kiss it as we walk on.

"You've never told me what happened after that bloodbath at Julian's home," she says.

I take a deep breath. "McIlroy called in his cleaners, and all was done away with quietly, and life was back to some semblance of normality. For them, maybe. Not me."

Mallory gives me a sympathetic smile. "Are you sure you don't need to see someone?"

I shake my head. "I'll paint it out of my system."

"I still don't understand how you were mixed up with this Valence character. You haven't explained that to me."

"It's a long story. A bit convoluted in the same way as your mother's story, I suppose." I hold that trump card. Mallory doesn't need to know about my mission to get that key.

Could I have done this better?

Valence should have told me about the incriminating footage in the first place and not colored it so that it was an easy assignment promising to land me a few million euros. It landed me much more than that, including a lifetime of nightmares.

"They haven't asked about the cash in the vault?"

"Nope. For now, they seem happy with thirty million dollars or so worth of diamonds."

"Will six diamonds satisfy them?"

"It will have to." I shrug. "It's come at a cost, but here we are, rolling in money." I face her and take her into my arms. "I missed you these past few weeks."

She gazes into my eyes, and a sad smile touches her beautiful face. "I missed you too."

For a moment, I toyed with the idea of drawing a line and moving on with my life away from Mallory, but at night, my body craved her in my bed. Not just for sex but also for her warmth.

We're both tainted and share a story that's best left for us alone.

"There are a ton of billionaires in LA, all looking for quality art," she says.

"You want to set up a dealership in LA?" I ask.

She looks excited. "Why not?"

"Right now, I think I'll just drift for a while. I can afford to. We can afford to."

"So there is a we?" She tilts her head. The sun streaks through the branches, illuminating her blond hair like she's under a spotlight on stage.

"Let's see where this goes." I kiss her cheek.

With a lingering gaze, she nods slowly, and her smile grows.

I place my arm around her waist, and we grab an ice cream before heading for another look at the *Alice in Wonderland* sculpture.

Forty-Five

BALLOONING BREASTS, WOMEN PARADING by with full faces of makeup, tanned and buff males tossing balls or yelling on their phones—that's my first impression of Malibu. Surreal as it is, take away the circus, and the coastline's a stunner.

We're splashing along the shallows. Mallory sucks on a straw while clutching a plastic container of dark-red juice, something everyone does around there.

"Do you like the house?" she asks.

"It needs renovating. Are you sure the foundations are safe?" I think about the wooden house and how the upstairs balcony seemed a little shaky. *Or was that me?*

"I had a builder look it over. It needs reinforcing, for sure. It should be good to go in six months."

I reflect on the two-story house with a perfect ocean view. "It's an idyllic location."

"Could you live there?" She continues to scrutinize me.

"I'm not sure if I could live here all year around but for a month or two."

"Oh?" Her eyebrows merge. "You're not so into it, then?"

"I like the natural beauty of the place. Maybe not so much the humans, however." A couple of girls walk past just as I'm saying that. "There must be a plastic surgeon on every corner."

She rolls her eyes. "Oh, stop it."

I shrug. Yes, I know I packed my cynicism.

"Why don't we go down to the main street? I could use a spot of lunch," she suggests.

Ten minutes later, we're strolling the main drag.

"I'm thinking of setting up an art dealership here." Mallory peers into a shop for rent.

"It's not already flooded with dealers?"

"Maybe. But I'd like to do it anyway." Mallory pauses at an empty shop for let.

We've been in Malibu for three weeks, coming straight from New York, which I prefer. However, the sun is shining, warming my bare arms, and it's nice to amble along and have some free time to get to know Mallory even if questions continue to surface like weeds through cracked pavement.

"Let's have a drink," she says, pointing at a trendy bar with ocean views. "It must be that hour."

"That's the best suggestion you've made all afternoon." I chuckle.

She stops walking. "You're really not enjoying this?"

"It might take some getting used to." Noticing Mallory's mood dampen, I take her hand. "The company is great, and the sunsets are spectacular."

Her face brightens. Mallory's constantly looking for validation, I'm discovering. We enter a bar that overlooks the sea, and a waiter directs us to a table before taking our order.

Mallory crosses her legs and settles in. "What are your plans? Will you continue to buy art?"

"To be honest, I haven't given it much thought. I do like painting, though."

"Then set up a studio in the new house, and I can arrange an exhibition."

I raise my palms. "Slow down. I'm still just exploring."

"Why not? Your work's good."

We've never really discussed my art before. At art school, like most creatives, I chased approval. But that need for validation has long faded, which is liberating in many ways because now I can roll with wherever my mood takes me, thanks to a healthy bank balance.

I give her a quizzing look. "You like my work?"

She nods. "It's rather formal in that representational way, but sure, you've got skill."

"I'm not into painting abstracts. Is that what you mean?"

"Good art sells. Whether it's a painting of a horse or little dabs of paint strategically applied to a blank canvas. People like art. And you paint in oils, which is always a plus."

"Let me just enjoy not thinking about money for a change."

She sips her drink and nods. "Sure. But it's good to have a plan."

"My only plan right now is to stay alive and take you back to our hotel room and fuck you senseless."

Mallory laughs. Our interest in art is matched by a robust appetite for each other's bodies, which hasn't abated. If anything, it's intensified.

I can live with that.

The following day, after what had been a big day visiting private galleries in LA, we're back at our hotel in Malibu, enjoying a purplish-red sunset that has me reaching for my phone camera. I'm off to London in the morning.

"So what's your plan?" Mallory asks.

There's that question again. A blank-paged diary suits me well. One of the many joys of having money is not having to think too far ahead.

"For now, it's back to Cornwall. I need to arrange help for my mother." I rub my neck.

Mallory plays with her drink. Dressed in a bikini, she suits that pool setting and this place in general.

I see questions in her eyes, and I expect her to delve deeper into a discussion about our relationship, but she shifts her focus and stares out to sea. That glimmer of intensity is soon chased away by a sunny smile as she touches my hand. "You're a good son. You're so nice."

"Oh?" I mirror her grin. "You didn't say that last night. What was it you called me again, wicked and debauched?"

Nothing makes Mallory laugh more than smutty banter. "We had fun, though, didn't we?"

"We did. Only, look, I'm not always going to be that man." I run my hands down my face. "Even now, I feel like I need an energy drink just to get through."

"Are you saying that I'm wearing you out?"

I shake my head. "I'm not doing anything I don't want."

"No." She runs her hand along my thigh. "You certainly aren't. I don't need sex all the time, by the way. I like being around you."

"Well, I'm glad we cleared that up." I stretch my arms and adjust my position on the lounge.

"You've got the women around here giving you the eye, I've noticed. As soon as you open that sexy British mouth of yours, they're virtually reaching for your fly."

I laugh. "You're a horny bunch, that's for sure. I don't know what's in the water over here."

She giggles then goes serious again. "I'll miss you. I wish you didn't have to go so soon."

We lock eyes, and I catch a familiar "lost-girl" glint, which she shakes off within a blink, hiding her vulnerability. I prefer seeing her fragile side. My favorite version of Mallory is when she's discussing Vermeer's preternatural ability in mastering light or telling me about her life growing up with her art-restorer grandfather.

"You might not return," she says, her voice wavering and her eyes wide and searching. "I'm sensing you don't like it here."

"It's growing on me." I give her a reassuring smile. "I just need to sort out my mother's care arrangements."

"I can't believe how good you are to your mom." She shakes her head like that's something rare. "She's so nice."

"She pushed me to come and visit you. She's very hopeful where you're concerned."

"Oh?" Her face tilts. "She had to coax you into visiting me?"

"Not really." I rub my prickly jaw, which needs a shave. I won't tell her how after all the bloodshed back home, I was ready to walk away. Only a long chat with my mother made me realize how much I missed Mallory.

"In what way is she hopeful?" She smiles shyly.

"You know..." I play with my drink. I can't even mention the "marriage" word without breaking into a sweat. But then, here I am. We've been inseparable for a month, and I'm the most relaxed I've been in a long time. "You know mothers and their expectations."

A dark cloud enters the conversation, and I pull an apologetic smile.

She looks down at her hands. "Don't worry. Just because I ended up with a mother from hell doesn't mean every mother's like that. And Adeline is such a lovely woman. Warm and inviting, and easy to be around."

Our eyes lock, and I sense that Malibu might be my new home for a while. I take her hand. "I like being with you."

Scanning my face, she nods slowly. "I'm still scarred from Greece."

"The passport didn't hold up. It was just plain bad luck." I shrug. That's one of a few lies I'll take to my grave.

Wearing one of her scrutinizing stares, Mallory sighs. "I guess I have to believe that."

I return a tight smile, reminding myself that when it comes to secrets, Mallory's got her stash hidden somewhere. And while we pull each other apart learning about our quirks, some things are best left unspoken.

Whether I can live with myself while going forward with this fascinating woman remains to be seen. For now, it's all about indulgence. We've earned our little moment in the sun. And while Mallory's crafting some plan, I'm indulging my natural inner drifter. Life's too short. The beauty of money means living life on my own terms by making space for those little surprises. Plans stifle spontaneity.

She stretches. "I think I might try out that hot tub. Interested?" Wearing a flirtatious smirk, she turns and sashays off.

Yep, it's all about sex, pleasure, and art. I can do that as I follow along and pinch her ass.

Forty-Six

WHILE CORNWALL IS COLD, Malibu is sweltering, and instead of a dark-green and at-times-gray sea, the rippling turquoise Pacific entices me in for a dip. I welcome the sunshine after two rainy weeks in the UK.

My mother insisted on remaining in her cottage even though I offered to upgrade her living arrangements to one of those well-equipped retirement villages. So I did the next best thing and arranged a care package to ensure she was looked after with nurses on call twenty-four-seven.

Being back home brought its stresses. Not to mention that my brother wants me to buy art again. In his dreams. Late at night, the ghosts came back to haunt me too. At least in the US, with Mallory cuddling me, I sleep well. Even if, according to her, I sometimes cry out in my sleep. She suggested I see a therapist.

I asked, "Are you thinking of seeing one?"

"Don't believe in them. And I don't cry out in bed."

Not one to miss a chance to turn a serious topic into something lighter, I said, "Oh, but you do."

Slapping my arm as she's known to do when I hit below the belt, she giggled.

That's why I'm here. Mallory doesn't know it, but she's become my therapy. We're partners in crime. A dark secret shared means less weight to bear alone, a conclusion I arrived at while away in the UK.

I'm still unsure about Mallory's motives. She's got this thing about sharing our money, and then there's those secret phone calls she takes from her mother. I don't eavesdrop, but I can tell something's up by how she walks into another room and lowers her voice.

So now, here I am back in Malibu. The natural beauty of the place is enough to keep me going, I believe. I'll just have to learn to airbrush out some of the crowds.

The US is a healthier option for me, unlike the UK, especially London, where I was constantly looking over my shoulder and my burning-gut issues returned. Even with Mallory's propensity for spicy cooking, I haven't popped one antacid.

Mallory's body wraps around mine in bed, and I enjoy the floral scent of her hair. Seeing her long legs stretched out on the sofa while she reads *Art Review Monthly* works wonders for my moods too. Her vast knowledge of art history never ceases to astound me. There's not one period of art, obscure though it might be, that she doesn't know about. I even suggested she consider lecturing. That took her aback. Looking all emotional, she kissed my cheek.

"What's that for?" I had to ask.

"For believing in me." Her eyes went glassy, and I held her tight. Whether I've become a kind of replacement father, I can't say, but I like feeling needed.

Now that's a revelation. Once upon a time, I would have considered being needed as stifling.

Sure, Mallory has her shallow moments, but I guess we all do. And one can't spend their entire time being profound and earnest. That would be a tad exhausting, I think.

We return to the gigantic glass box that Mallory calls home and enter through the side door that takes us through to the back, where a glistening infinity swimming pool spills onto the horizon.

Stepping over a ton of boxes, I ask, "Do you want me to help you unpack?"

She shrugs. "Sure."

"Have you moved out of New York?"

"No, I'm keeping it for now. Though I'm not sure if I like being there anymore. I've got time to figure that out."

I go into the kitchen to make coffee, and Mallory joins me. "Can I tempt you?" I hold up the pot.

"Oh, you can always tempt me." She gives me a flirtatious smile.

Mallory continues her hasty switch of topic whenever I mention her mother. She simply brushes it off, muttering something vague like I already know everything.

I suppose having a serial killer for a mum would challenge the sanity of even the toughest mind, and Mallory's reluctance to dwell on such an uncomfortable subject makes sense. Especially to someone like me, who prefers to read a book than to poke around in disturbing waters. I leave that to my subconscious and those haunting nightmares. Maybe Mallory's right—a shrink could be useful.

While sipping on coffee, I push that thought aside. For now, I'll do what I do best, focus on nicer things, like Mallory in those tiny shorts and setting up my paints for a series of those inspiring ever-changing sunsets.

The light in the modern two-story house is fantastic for painting. And the large open-plan room, looking out to the pool area, boasts a fabulous view of the ocean and sky. It's a relaxing place to be for sure, despite the lack of ornament.

"Are you going to decorate?" I sit on the sofa in the large room flooded with natural light, where the only furniture, other than a coffee table, is an almost-empty bookshelf housing a handful of airport novels.

"I'm just getting on my feet, but I do plan to shop for some pretty collectibles soon. Interested?"

I smile. "Sure." I peer up at a nondescript pale-blue Rothkoesque paint- ing on the wall. "Did that come with this place?"

Aware of my dislike of minimalist art, Mallory smiles at my derisive tone. "No. I went to an exhibition just after you left for England a month ago. I got drunk on bad champagne and bought it. It's from a local artist. Do you like it?"

I study the painting with a stripe of white cutting through the center to suggest a horizon. "At least it's oil, I suppose."

She laughs. "That's what I thought. The Turner you picked up at that auction where I'd planned to claw your eyes out will sit nicely there." She points at an empty white wall.

I frown. "With this bright light? Really? You of all people should know that's a good way to destroy a work worth preserving."

"We'll stick to local modern art, then, shall we?" She tilts her head.

I regard her. "Claw my eyes out?"

She laughs. "I knew you wouldn't let that comment slide."

"From memory, by night's end, you were clawing my back." I grin. "Delightfully so."

Mallory pulls a face and pokes her tongue out. "Yeah, yeah, Mr. Irresistible."

I laugh. "You're not so bad yourself."

She joins me on the couch, and I kiss her.

Changing the subject, as I'm not in the mood to relive our past, I add, "There's plenty of time to shop around."

As someone who's lived out of a suitcase for two decades, I find this sudden idea of collecting possessions to be novel. Nevertheless, as my back sinks into the white leather sofa, I make a mental note to convince Mallory to replace it with a bottle-green Chesterfield instead.

Stretching my arms, I rise and walk out onto the pool area. The patio is paved in sandstone with potted palms and decking furniture dotted about. Everything in its place like it's been dressed up for a *House Beautiful* spread.

Mallory joins me. "So do you think you can call this home?"

It takes me a moment to respond. "Maybe. I mean, it might need a coat of color here and there. I'm not really into this whole white thing. I'm only just learning how to open the cupboards in the kitchen."

Mallory laughs then goes serious, wearing that "Where are we going?" face again. "We're in love, aren't we?"

After a moment, I nod.

"You strike me as uncertain."

I face her square on. "I can't stay away. But on a deeper level, you're like a stranger to me."

She keeps staring at me while searching for a response. "I'm that to me most of the time."

I have to smile. "What was it that the Oracle of Delphi said? 'Know thyself.'"

She rolls her eyes. "If a shrink said that to me after I'd paid a shitload of money, I'd be pretty pissed."

I chuckle. "They just sit there and listen most of the time. That pithy albeit unsatisfying response is about right. Most of life's complexities are often simpler than we make them."

"Why do I sense that you don't believe me when I tell you I love you? Am I that shallow?" She tilts her pretty face, which always attracts me, no matter what time of day.

"You have your moments." I steady my shoulders in readiness for a tirade and add, "I think I'm only starting to get to know you is what I mean to say. We've known each other for a year, and most of that time, we've either fucked or talked about art."

"What else is there?" she asks, brushing a stray strand from her eyes.

I walk over to the glass table where I left my cigarettes and light up.

Mallory joins me and runs her hands through my hair, massaging my scalp.

"Ah." I lean back. "That's something I missed."

"Why don't I organize a welcome party? Would you like that?" she asks.

"I didn't realize you knew that many people."

"There are the neighbors, and it's not that difficult to round up guests around here. Everyone loves a shindig."

I laugh. "A shindig? Sounds very Malibu circa sixties. Beach Boys and all."

We sit in silence as a bird perches on the ledge of the sandstone wall, my favorite feature.

"I'd like to cash in my share of the diamonds," she says.

"About that." I exhale. "I had to give Julian's detective mate six diamonds."

"Oh?" Her brow creases.

My moment of calm is usurped by the memory of meeting that greedy greaseball, McIlroy, at a dungeon-like East End bar where a bunch of drifters clutching pints with gnarly fingers resembled extras in a Guy Ritchie film.

With that cockney mumble, he muttered, "I'm planning on retiring to Majorca. It's a bit pricier than I expected. Then I recall how Dimitri bragged about those red diamonds and having a nice heavy little bag full of them. Silly cunt, loved to talk about his big dick." He grinned. "The way I see it is that six diamonds don't exactly add up to a heavy little bag, now, do they?"

"What do you want?" I asked, dying to get out of that claustrophobic dive.

"I think another six should do me nicely. That leaves you with enough to set yourself up in America. They love us Brits over there. Shouldn't take you long to hook up with some horny rich widow." Subtle as a sledgehammer, as usual, he arched an eyebrow.

I return my attention to Mallory and explain, "It was either give him six diamonds or have him dredge up Polignano and plant enough incriminating evidence to see you locked up."

"He can't do that, though. Can he?"

"He can do what he likes. He's a dirty cop."

"So how many are left?" she asks.

"Around eighteen, from memory."

Her frown melts into a big smile, and she wraps her slender arms around me. "That sounds just fine to me. On one condition."

"Oh?"

"That you marry me, and we make this all official."

I rake my fingers through my hair. "Let's just see how this month rides out."

"I'd like us to be together. Don't you want that?" She sounds disappointed.

"I think I do. I just don't know if I can live here full time."

"We can have one of those marriages that are open-ended."

"Like polyamory?" I don't like the sound of that. I'm done with complications.

"No way. I'd hate you being with someone else."

I take her in my arms. "I'm not that keen on you fucking someone else either."

A line forms between her smooth brow. "But you once said you don't do jealousy."

I shrug. "I'd never been in love before."

Her face brightens into a sunny smile. "So you do love me, then."

I massage her feet as she places them on my lap. "I do."

"Why sound so worried?" She tilts her head.

"Because I sense you're hiding something from me."

She groans. "Must we? Haven't we been through this?"

"You asked."

We lock eyes, and she returns a sultry smile. "No more about our past. Can we just draw a line?"

I nod slowly, running my hand up her smooth calf to her thigh and beyond. "Let's just see where this takes us."

She opens her thighs a little. "I know where I want this to take me now."

I laugh. Yes, we're in lust, all right. The love bit? Well, who knows what this is, but I wouldn't want to be anywhere else right this minute.

Forty-Seven

People fill the large open-plan living room, spilling onto the swimming pool area.

Mallory's in her element, hugging and kissing newcomers while chatting effusively as though they're long-lost friends.

"This is such a lovely home," a woman comments as she winks at me.

How does one respond to a wink?

I smile back. The champagne's top-shelf, and catering have created sculptural hors d'oeuvres that look barely edible despite being delicious.

Screeching pop divas playing in the background add to the loudness in the room, amplified by a lack of soft furnishing. I toy with finding Mallory's playlist for more subtle background music, although pop divas suit the vibe.

When it comes to getting everything to mix and match, Mallory has done well. As I watch her chatting to all the strangers, I again question whether this is me. There's a complicated yes buried somewhere. Contradiction, after all, is my middle name.

A man who might be my age saunters over. "You're new to town, I hear," he says. "Larry's the name." He holds out his hand, and I take it.

"Pleased to meet you. I'm Dylan." I wince slightly at his firm "mine are bigger than yours" handshake.

"We've heard about you." He smiles.

"Oh? Nothing bad, I hope."

"Only good things."

I smile. "I'm boring most of the time."

"Aren't we all?" He grins. "But hey, I've also heard you've got a great eye for art and that you paint. Now that's something to admire, wouldn't you say?"

"I suppose. I just don't like waving a banner about."

"One has to promote oneself, somehow."

"Yes, it's the ones that scream the loudest that are often heard. Which leaves us introverts out in the cold, I guess," I say.

"You're an introvert?" He frowns, studying my face.

"At times, sure. I'm one of those weirdos that's comfortable in his own space."

"Nothing wrong with that." He pauses as he looks around. "Mallory on the other hand is an extrovert from what I've seen and heard. I like her. She's a mover and a shaker. That will get you far in this town."

"Yes, she's got pluck." I smile.

"I love you Brits and your cute little sayings," a woman says upon overhearing my last comment.

I smile at her, and she wraps her arm around Larry, who says, "This is my wife, Jerry."

I nod and then chat for a few minutes about art and the weather before moving on and chatting about this and that with the rest of the guests.

It's after midnight, everyone's left, and I'm still wide awake as Mallory potters around, getting ready for bed.

Making a note to buy myself a book or two to read, I go to the shelf and select a Lee Child novel. As I flick it open, a sheet falls out. I unfold the photocopied note, and it reads, *"Poisonous herbs."*

There are all manner of herbs from belladonna to foxglove, which, interestingly, is underlined.

As I stare at the faded photocopied sheet, which shows where it was ripped from the original document, I imagine this sheet came from Mallory's mother.

Why hold on to it?

I enter the bedroom to find Mallory prancing about in lacy lingerie. I avert my attention to the large window, where the night sky is in full view.

"What's that you're holding?" she asks.

"This fell out of a novel on your shelf."

I show her, and her brow flinches ever so slightly. She removes it from my hand. "Oh, my mother must have put it there."

"But I was there when you bought the book. And wouldn't the police have the original, since she's been convicted?"

Turning away from me, she screws up the paper and tosses it into the bin. "Maybe it was in my suitcase. I don't know how it got there."

She walks off into the bathroom and, minutes later, returns and slides into bed.

"You still haven't answered my question," I press.

"The cops had the original she ripped straight out of the book. I handed it to them."

"Right. But why keep a copy?"

"Oh, Dylan, I don't know." She sounds annoyed, like I'm peppering her with unnecessary questions.

I can't just leave it there, however. "How's your mother's appeal going?"

"I don't know, and I'm not interested," she says. "Can we not talk about this, please?"

I go to the bathroom and brush my teeth, but when I return and join her in bed, I lie on my back and stare at the ceiling.

Mallory goes to hold me, but I remain inert.

"Why are you being like this?" she asks.

"I'm not being like anything. But I am wondering if I should get my food tasted."

"Oh, Dylan." Her mouth falls open. "What are you saying?"

"Just that I don't understand why you're still in possession of it. And you've never really explained how your mother, who never visited New York, came to poison your husband."

"She did visit us on a few occasions. And now that I think about it, she was there the night before he died."

"Really? This is the woman you admitted to detesting. I recall you saying how you'd prefer to spend your time with some brainless nobody rather than her."

"I was drunk when I said that."

"But you hate her."

"Wouldn't you if your mom had killed your father?"

"Hypothetically speaking, yes," I return.

Mallory sighs heavily. "She killed Erik in the same way she poisoned my stepfather."

"Why keep that sheet?" I ask again.

Mallory screams, "Why are you dredging this shit up? We've been doing good. Haven't we?"

Tears stream down her cheeks, then she sits on the edge of the bed and buries her head.

Protective instincts kicking in, I take her into my arms and rock her gently. "It's okay. Let's drop it. Sorry. I can see it's a difficult subject."

Sniffling, she nods. Looking up at me, her eyes are wide and drowning in tears. Mallory reminds me of a young girl whose world is suddenly turned upside down. I imagine that was her, seeing her father dead on the floor, and my heart goes out to her.

An uncomfortable feeling remains, however. When I made that comment about having my food tasted, I wasn't being funny after this sudden need of hers for us to marry and to merge our wealth.

As she remains in my arms, I stroke her head, despite an ill feeling in my gut calling for some pharmaceutical intervention.

Forty-Eight

IT'S BEEN THREE WEEKS since my return to England. Two days after the party, I left Malibu, only to arrive home tugging excess baggage of the heavy, conflicted-emotions kind. I stayed in London for a week and spent most of my time smoking cigarettes in Hyde Park or barhopping. At this rate, I've got more chance of dying from lung or liver cancer than from poisoning by a woman who's turned my world upside down.

Mallory begged me to stay, even though sudden periods of tense silence descended into disagreements over silly things.

Not one for emotional gymnastics and favoring a more measured approach to life, I had to go, despite Mallory suggesting couple's therapy. Now if anything will make me run, it would be the idea of sharing personal feelings with a stranger in a bright office with a bunch of framed certificates on the wall. I'd prefer to sit in a dark bar and spill my secrets to some unwashed lost soul.

I packed my bags and explained to Mallory that I wanted to check on my mother and to ensure the care arrangement was satisfactory, which wasn't that necessary, as I've been receiving regular reports and attending Zoom meetings with the care providers visiting her on a regular basis.

Now I'm in Cornwall with my mother, who's sitting at the table and looking worried. "Did you have a fight?"

I shake my head.

"Then why are you here and not there?" she asks.

I tell her everything. It feels good to share the crap that's been taking up all my brain space.

Her eyebrows rise at the mention of Mallory's mother being a serial killer. "Poor Mallory. Having to live with a bad mother and then a wife-bashing husband." Wearing a sad smile, my mother is folding tea towels.

"She told you about her marriage?" I ask.

"We spoke. She was very open with me. Told me all about her life growing up and that she was close to her father and how her mother drank too much and caused all kinds of trouble."

I nod. "And what about the chart of poisons?"

She shrugs. "To be honest, darling, it doesn't matter who poisoned that monster husband. The law's never on the woman's side, whichever way it went."

The bitter note in my mother's voice brings back memories of our itinerant criminal father arriving unannounced, drinking everything he could find in the cupboard, and then committing the unspeakable to our mother. Julian and I were too young to understand, even though I sensed something dark. He would waltz in, toss a few coins in our tiny hands, and tell us to buzz off.

We usually arrived back to find our mother crying. The next time he arrived, when I was a little older and had learned to fight, he was the one who left with a black eye.

Returning to the subject of Mallory's domestic dramas, I say, "I'm surprised she shared that with you. Mallory doesn't like talking about her life growing up. Only about her time with her grandfather."

"Yes, she spoke at length about her grandpa. He sounded like a lovely man." She sighs. "She's learned to suffer in silence, love. We all do in the end."

My heart suddenly shrivels at how I treated Mallory. I think it was my way of trying to force the truth out of her when I should have just let sleeping dogs lie.

"Sounds to me like Mallory's mother did her daughter a favor. Mallory's got every right to feel nothing for either her mother or the dead husband, despite a blood connection. It's never so black-and-white, love. Who are we to say what's right or wrong? Killing someone in cold blood is wrong. But killing an enemy threatening us harm, well, that's a little different, wouldn't you say?"

My mother's eyes reflect that same steely resolve I recall her having when I was a lad. She never let my father's violence turn her bitter. I think of the killing I committed—the first and hopefully last time in Rome. It never leaves you. That's the problem.

Nevertheless, my mother has made a cogent point: the lines of morality start to blur when it's evil that's murdered.

Whether that exonerates the vigilante remains morally patchy. In this case, the mother killing her son-in-law to protect her daughter from further harm makes sense.

Does that help her atone for killing Mallory's father?

Not in her daughter's eyes, going by how Mallory bristles at the very mention of her mother, which now makes me wonder whether that's guilt or hate. It's an ethical minefield for sure.

My mother turns serious. "I love you being here, son, but Mallory's good for you. No one should be alone in their old age."

"But you have been." I rub my neck. "I mean, I'm always here if not physically then via phone and Zoom, of course, but you're still here alone for the most part."

She taps my hand. "You're an angel. A gift. I would never expect you to stay with me. What I meant to say was it's nice to find a partner one shares things in common with. Someone you can trust and spend your life with."

I can't disagree about my compatibility with Mallory. It's just the trust part that's rather murky. I've still got my secrets thanks to that Roman mission, where I was left to think on my feet. My sense of morality intervened where Mallory was concerned, though. And if I'm being totally honest, I think I'd already fallen in love with her. The first night we made love was meant to be my way of quietening her down, but the only thing it did was make me desire her in a way I'd never desired a woman before. That came as a big surprise for someone who thought himself incapable of a monogamous relationship or who'd never even cared for one. I'd convinced myself that being a lone wolf would be my life choice—until I met Mallory.

But what's trapped in her heart is getting in the way of us making this work. When I catch glimpses of her soul, I fall harder. I see a good spirit there, someone who shares my values, but then she'll do something to close herself off again. No one wants to share their vulnerability—I get that—but I would have thought that by now she could allow me in.

If I was as untrustworthy as she sometimes suspects, she would be dead by now. That thought alone still haunts me, as do those hard-edged directives, fired at me by Valence, to do away with her.

My mother's forgiving outlook, nevertheless, offers a fresh perspective on the complexity of Mallory's domestic issues. Complex because I can't decide who the bad guy is here—the violent dead husband, the alcoholic serial-killer mother, or Mallory for admitting to her relief at having two of her least favorite people removed from her life.

Where to next? I can't say.

Mallory puts my indecisive nature down to being a Libra. She's a Gemini and swears that's why we're compatible. I know we are. I don't need the stars to tell me.

But am I in danger?

Does she want me for what I can give her financially, or is she for real when she speaks of this profound love she feels for me?

Going on body language, I believe her passion. Then there are those quiet, affectionate glances she sneaks my way when she sees me pat a dog or hold the door for an elderly person. Genuine moments, simple yet profoundly meaningful, give us a glimpse of the goodness in someone.

I kiss my mother's cheek. "I think I'll go for a walk up to the cliffs."

She smiles. "Take care, sweetheart. Some of the rocks, I'm told, are eroding. Don't stand too close."

I'm that boy again. But instead of standing too close to the edge of a cliff, I was warned against slippery characters offering lollies.

"Back soon." Just as I'm leaving, a text with a photo arrives from Mallory.

She's sent a few texts, but apart from relaying that I arrived safely, I've kept my distance. I do miss her, though, especially those simple little moments like sharing coffee and nonsensical babble in the mornings. Or in the evenings, pointing at the sunset's spectacular bleed of color.

I miss our conversations about esoteric art movements like the Futurists and their unquestionable contribution to modern art, or staring in wonder at golden beams of sunlight in forests, producing a kaleidoscope of greens On a recent night at the cinema, Mallory chose *Lawrence of Arabia*. We held hands while engrossed in the spectacular scenery of the Sahara Desert. I was as content as I think I've ever been.

How can I not miss that?

I'm starting to regret finding that sheet of poison. There's a lot to be said for blissful ignorance.

I click on the photo and imagine it being Mallory in a lacy negligee. I must say, I am rather fond of her sexy texts.

The growing smile on my face soon fades, and my jaw drops.

My mother enters the hallway. "What's wrong, Dylan, love? You look pale."

I pass the phone to her, and she takes a moment to process the photo. "Oh, is that what I think it is?"

In shock, I nod slowly.

Forty-Nine

Mallory

A COMMENT SAWYER MADE, "Everyone's capable of murder, Ms. Storm," comes to mind. He made it sound accusatory as he tried to break me during that dark period in New York. I didn't break.

And now I'm richer than I could ever have imagined, with my share of the diamonds sitting in an LA vault. I'm meant to be over the moon, but I'm empty.

Running to the bathroom for the second time, I barely make it.

I'm with child, something I'm still trying to process. Initially, there was a jolt of electricity on discovering my pregnancy. Almost joy. But then, I thought about being a single mother, and my mood came tumbling down. Money will help, but the thought of bringing up a child alone sucks big-time, especially when the father isn't returning my calls.

I can almost imagine the look of horror on his face after he received the photo of the pregnancy stick.

Rubbing my stomach, which is flat, mainly from a lack of food, I lie on my bed, eyes wide and staring at the ceiling. Insomnia's a bitch. Or at least, a bad conscience is.

Is that what I'm suffering from?

Or am I just missing Dylan's strong arms pulling me hard against him, making me feel not just his arousal but also his affection?

I miss everything about him. The twinkle he gets in his eyes when we banter. Even the bad bits. His cynicism. His indecision. His need for order. His unwillingness to eat raw fish, and so on.

I keep ringing him, but there's no response. Just deathly silence.

Rolling over for the umpteenth time, I stare out into the night and wonder if I should buy a pre-war mansion and decorate it with antiques and collectibles in tune with Dylan's tastes.

Would that draw him back into my life? Some pretty antiques?

The thought is almost laughable, but I'm too down to even crack a smile.

Or should I just tell him everything?

After all, that's why he left so suddenly, citing the need for some space. He said we'd gotten too close too soon or some bullshit story.

I almost begged him to stay.

Wouldn't it have been easier to tell him the truth?

That idea ties me in knots.

Time is a healer, they say. But try convincing someone who considers delayed gratification to be torture. If I see something delicious, I want it now.

I reach for my drawer and rummage about for the container of sleeping tablets, a habit that started the day my husband died only to stop the night I slept with Dylan. I didn't even need to take one after that disturbing yacht incident. But then I had Dylan close and soothing my anguish with a gentle hug.

Is that what unconditional love looks like?

How is it I'm thirty-five and haven't got a clue about those deeper things?

Perhaps Dylan was right when he accused me of being shallow after one of our rare disagreements. I can't even recall what it was about, but the makeup sex was almost worth it.

Shallow or not, I am a voluptuary, as Dylan put it, making that condition sound sexy and desirable, especially uttered in that deep sexy voice. I looked it up: a person whose world revolves around pleasure. Okay, I'll take that.

What's the opposite?

Asceticism. Severe self-discipline. No, thanks.

Where's the voluptuary when I need her most?

She's nowhere to be found at this moment. All I have are these ceaseless thoughts, spinning like a carousel of messy fragmented memories. Snapshots of my life, jagged like shards of a broken mirror that draw blood every time I look back.

But the worst of it? That spine-chilling, hateful glare from my mother's half-dead eyes—that's what cuts the deepest.

She got what she deserved, and in return, I freed myself and womankind from a wife-basher. As she lay dying in the hospital, I sat by her bedside, regarding her sagging features, which, denied her regular Botox shots, had fallen victim to gravity's cruel pull.

The flying daggers from her eyes followed me back to LA, keeping me awake, like she'd poisoned me with that venomous glare. She wore the same seething hatred when, at seventeen, I kissed up to my stepfather for an increase in my credit card allowance. I would just laugh it off. Besides, unbuttoning my blouse so that my stepfather could perv on my firm tits wasn't anything different from her marrying him just for his money.

She confronted me one day. "Do your top up. I know what you're doing."

Yes, I was bad. Maybe I still am. But I learned from the best, my mother. And as she lay there wanting to rip my eyes out, all I could do was humor her with a "There, there, there, don't exert yourself" comment.

"You're evil," she spat. "You know I didn't do it, because you did it." She was so weak her yells were more like angry whispers.

I leaned in and said, "You shouldn't have had that book of herbs lying about. If you hadn't killed my dad and then stepdad, you wouldn't be here now, would you?"

"You're an evil bitch. I always knew that. You took sides with your father and ganged up against me."

"That's because you were awful to him. He never hit you. You just made that up. Then you pushed him down the stairs. I'll never forgive you for that."

Tears burned in my eyes as I relived that dark, horrific night. Despite the howling wind, I still heard her drunken tirade at the top of the stairs. When I saw my beloved father's crumpled, inert body below, my world went from technicolor to gray.

Okay, so I didn't see her do it. But guilt was written all over her face. Not shock or disbelief but relief was written all over her cruel eyes.

From then on, my soul started to rot. I went from a happy-go-lucky child to something else. A stranger had taken possession of my spirit. I rarely smiled after that.

"Your father was a useless, spineless man." She looked away from me. Her voice was weak and so quiet, I had to strain to hear.

"I was broke. I wanted the house. I knew I could do better. I admit that as I admit to poisoning Mike." She paused for a breath. "But I didn't poison Erik. But *you* know that. We're more alike than you think."

There it was at last: she admitted it. She killed my sweet, darling father. This cold-hearted woman I called Mother had to be stopped somehow.

Erik needed to go. He would never have agreed to a divorce, and I recall him saying one night, "There's only one way you'll leave, and that's in a coffin."

So I did what I had to do. My mother had made it easy for me by leaving that book lying around, and seeing how my stepfather's death had been put down to natural causes despite my mother's rare stint in the kitchen, I pulled a leaf out of her book—literally. Then my sister-in-law stuck her ugly nose into it and demanded an autopsy, and the rest is history, as they say.

Is evil passed down in DNA?

Is it evil to seek revenge?

Is it evil to protect oneself from a life of abuse and no longer jump at shadows?

Nothing would have protected me from Erik. He would have come after me for sure. I'd seen it all too often at the women's shelter, where the woman ends up dead in the end. The abuser always prevails in this system.

"I'll see you in hell, daught... er" were my mother's last words.

Wasn't revenge meant to clear wounds?

After visiting my mother, I didn't feel any of that. If anything, my steps were heavy. I went straight to the airport and caught a plane back to LA. I made this final trip to her hospital bed because I didn't want the authorities to believe I was that heartless daughter she would rant on about.

It wasn't her last breath, but I imagined it was close. Her pancreatic cancer was inoperable.

Two days after I returned to LA, I got a call, and my mother was gone. My eyes remained dry. My heart, well, that was another matter. It was already broken in pieces.

It's eight o'clock, and the sun's slowly descending on the horizon.

I sip water, missing my daily hit of alcohol.

I'm keeping this baby, so if Dylan wishes to ignore me, then so be it. I refuse to cry. I refuse to be unhappy. Sad hormones affect the fetus, I've read.

A knock comes at the door, which makes me start.

I pad to the door, ready to tell Bill, a randy septuagenarian neighbor who's been trying to get into my pants, to stop pestering me.

When I open the door, gray turns to color. Dylan stands before me, his lips curling into a slow, shyish grin.

Speechless, I drop my jaw and look at him as though he's an apparition.

"Well, aren't you going to invite me in?" He tilts his head, and I crack a smile, making my face muscles ache.

I step out of the way to allow him to pass. "I'd almost given up on you. You haven't returned my messages."

"I know, and I'm sorry." He sets down his case, which much to my delight is of the larger size and not his normal carry-on. "I just needed time to process things." He looks as nervous as I feel, although my inner child is breaking into dance.

"Come in, and I'll make you a nice drink."

He follows me into the living room and points at the sky. "Nice sunset."

I move a few take-out cartons off the table and clear the couch of magazines, books, and whatnot.

Small talk, I can do. "Isn't it just?"

We do very little talking from then on. He takes me into his arms, and we almost stumble into the bedroom and make love. His lips crush mine with as much love and passion as affection.

That night, I'm lying in his arms. "Are you staying?"

"I am now."

"Oh? What changed your mind?" I ask tentatively.

"We're to be parents, aren't we?"

I've been waiting for him to bring up my condition. "Is that the only reason?"

He shakes his head. "I missed you." He stares into my eyes, and I'm warm all over.

We remain in silence, holding each other as I bathe in his tenderness, his caressing fingers making my skin tingle.

"My mother died," I say suddenly.

"I'm sorry," he says.

"Don't be. I'm not."

He pulls away and scans my deadpan face. He's looking for some sign of emotion, I assume.

"For what it's worth," he says after a long pause, "I understand. I get why you did it."

I frown. "Which version? That I snitched on my mother or that I framed her?"

"Either way."

Is he forgiving me?

Should I tell him the whole truth and nothing but the truth?

A part of me wants to, but he's given me a get-out-of-jail-free card. Terrible metaphor, I know.

Should I let it go?

While he says he doesn't care, won't he always see me as someone capable of murder?

I've already proved that by killing Stan, but that was to protect Dylan. It's not the same. It's not premeditated. It's instinctive and protective, and I would do it again and again if it meant we could be together.

"But wouldn't you want to know?" I ask again.

He shrugs. "I thought about it long and hard and did what humans do when deliberating over ethical conundrums. I put myself in your shoes."

"Oh?" I'm loving this man even more, if that's at all possible.

"Well," I say. "Is there more?"

"Just that I would have poisoned my father had I caught him attacking my mother. As it was, I kicked him in the bollocks when I was a lad and never saw him again after that. But I would have done worse had I caught him hurting our mother. If someone harmed you or my mother or our child, I wouldn't think twice about knocking them off."

Without warning, tears blur my vision.

"You would?" I ask, sounding breathless.

We've both killed, so on the face of it, my incredulity is somewhat naive, but I can't stop the wave of relief.

"Let's just leave the past behind, shall we? Why bring up what's been a harrowing chapter? I can't imagine how it felt carrying the burden of your mother doing what she'd done, and at least this way, she got what was coming to her."

I'm frowning so much my head hurts.

"What changed your mind?" I ask after a long, tense pause.

"I spoke to my mother, and she threw a whole new light on what we consider right and wrong and how there's this gray area too often overlooked."

"She's a wise old soul." I smile sadly. "You told her about me? I mean..."

How do I say it?

I can't even utter those words admitting that I killed my husband.

He shrugs. "I needed someone to talk to. I was in knots over this whole situation. And I'm glad I did. She helped me understand what it's like to be living in fear. Women do suffer in silence, and I hate that. I want to protect my daughter from anything like that. I would kill for her too."

"And if it's a son?" I ask.

"Then I will tell him from the moment he utters 'Da-da' that hitting women is a crime punishable by death."

My shoulders slump. Tension I've been carrying all these years untangles, and uncontrollable sobs intensify like I've burst an artery of emotion.

After I settle down, having saturated Dylan's shoulder with my tears, I remove myself from his arms and clean my face with tissues. "Did you tell your mother she's about to be a grandmother?"

"She's over the moon, of course. She pushed me out the door and told me to jump on a plane. That I should be here with you, helping you."

I'm smiling and crying at the same time. "Oh my God. She did?" I pause to think about his mother pushing him to see me. "Would you have come anyway?"

He wraps an arm around my shoulder. "I was scrolling on my phone looking for flights when she came into my room asking, 'Why are you still here?'"

I laugh at him mimicking his mother's cockney accent.

Dylan takes my hand and plays with my fingers.

"I know it's your choice, but I have to say I was immensely relieved that you'd decided to keep the child with or without me."

"So you really want to stick around?" I ask.

"I do." He sighs. "I don't know what kind of father I'll make. But I am willing to be the best man I can be for mother and child."

"Mother too?"

"Well, yes. I mean, you do want me around, don't you?"

Tears burn in my eyes again. The deluge of emotions that started the moment my mother admitted to killing my dad keeps coming. And while I was convinced she'd pushed my dad down those stairs, an inkling of doubt ate away at me nevertheless.

"You didn't have a great dual-parent experience, and neither did I for that matter. Let's make amends, shall we?" He tilts his head. "I'll be the father my own was incapable of being, and you can be the mother you missed out on."

I hug him so tightly, I never want to let him go. As I'm convulsing in tears, pent-up emotion pours out of me, and I drench Dylan's neck.

I move away and wipe my nose. "Sorry about the body fluids."

His eyes smile back, and I chuckle while sobbing, which is almost physically impossible. But then, lots of things I considered impossible have suddenly become very possible. Like me and this man becoming one and rearing a child. But over and above everything, he accepts me, warts and all. No more lies blinding me.

"Speaking of body fluids"—his eyebrow arches—"why don't we, you know..."

I laugh, welcoming a break from the intensity of the moment.

"You really think we can do this? Become the best parents, loving and nurturing and all those things in between?"

His eyes sparkle. "I think we can do this with flying colors, Mallory."

"We can move if you like. Somewhere of your choosing. Only I'd like to stay in California. The sun suits me."

"It does suit you. I like the lack of clothing."

I slap his arm. "You're so shallow."

He laughs. "You called me deep earlier."

I giggle. "I meant I like it deep."

"I've noticed." He wears one of those deliciously aroused looks.

"We can stay here in Malibu," he says. "It's growing on me, and it's a healthier option and a great place to bring up a baby. I might just have to do some decorating if you're okay with that."

"As long as you're here, I'm happy with anything. Even pictures of Mickey Mouse."

His hiss makes me laugh. "No Pop Art. And nothing over the fifties. You know my tastes."

I crawl down the bed. "I certainly do. And I'm happy to indulge them. All the way."

His "Aah" fuels me along. Nothing like giving pleasure to the love of my life. I plan to give him everything.

I did some bad things. Yes, I poisoned Erik and, killing two birds with one stone, so to speak, managed to frame my mother for it.

The idea hadn't occurred to me until I found that book of herbs in a box lying around. I handled that sheet of poison carefully, ripping it out while wearing gloves. I then photocopied it and followed the instructions. The original page, I left lying around, only the police didn't find it. I couldn't exactly say, "Hey, you missed something."

But when I was locked up, I opened up about that, and well, as I explained to the detective, I couldn't exactly snitch on my mother, now could I?

Her fingerprints were all over it, of course.

I lie in Dylan's arms, breathing him in like I would a forest after the rain. *Would I change anything?*

Never.

Otherwise, I wouldn't be here, looking into those ocean-blue eyes filled with as much complexity as the sea itself.

I stare out the window, and the pearly moon smiles back at me.

THE END

Also by Amora Sway – THE WIFE'S NEW MAID

A Domestic Thriller

Linley thought marrying a millionaire wouldbe her escape from the daily grind—a dream life in a lavish suburban paradise. But four years in, and the clock is running out. If she doesn't conceive soon, her ironclad prenup means her husband can cast her aside, leaving her with very little. Meanwhile, her husband is distracted by the stunning new maid. Linley soon finds herself playing a dangerous game to keep her marriage intact. But when a brutal murder shatters their home, it becomes clear: someone in this house has a deadly secret. And now, no one is safe.

From Melbourne, Australia, Amora Sway is the alter-ego of J. J. Sorel, an award-winning Romance novelist who has written more than twenty books throughout her international career as a writer. Follow her on Face-Book.

jjsorel.com

Printed in Dunstable, United Kingdom